Readers love
MARY CALMES

D1738806

A Matter of Time, Vol. 1 & 2

"…a very readable and entertaining package."

—Book Wenches

But For You

"For all fans of Jory and Sam, this book is a must have!"

—Pants Off Reviews

"…everything I hoped it would be plus two."

—Joyfully Reviewed

Acrobat

"The only complaint I had was that I wanted more."

—Poetry Works

"…a very satisfying story and a new couple to love."

—Scattered Thoughts and Rogue Words

"This is going to be a comfort read for me, one of those stories that I return to when I need a little pick me up."

—Guilty Pleasures

"…a delightful romance. Highly recommended."

—Twlib Reviews

"…a story of courage."

—The Novel Approach

By MARY CALMES

Published by DREAMSPINNER PRESS
http://www.dreamspinnerpress.com

PARTING SHOT

Mary Calmes

Dreamspinner Press

Published by
Dreamspinner Press
5032 Capital Circle SW
Ste 2, PMB# 279
Tallahassee, FL 32305-7886
USA
http://www.dreamspinnerpress.com/

Parting Shot

Cover Art by Reese Dante
http://www.reesedante.com

Cover content is being used for illustrative purposes only
and any person depicted on the cover is a model.

ISBN: 978-1-62380-874-7
Digital ISBN: 978-1-62380-875-4

Printed in the United States of America
First Edition
July 2013

To my wonderful fans who were sure, despite all appearances to the contrary, that Aaron Sutter was a nice guy deep down. This book is for you. Thank you for having faith.

ONE

I NEEDED the job to be over so I could go home.

The realization was sort of amazing, because I love New York. Any reason to visit, to eat in Hell's Kitchen, walk through Central Park, or soak up Times Square at night was good. So, the fact that I couldn't wait to leave told me something important.

And it had everything to do with Aaron Sutter.

I thought I knew all about beautiful men. I'd slept with enough of them. Gym bunnies I screwed in clubs, twinks on their knees in alleys, and guys I took to hotels that charged by the hour. I never bothered if they weren't gorgeous. But not one of them could hold a candle to the millionaire.

Billionaire?

I wasn't sure, hadn't checked into it. He was loaded; that was all I knew. Not that I cared. It made no difference. I was already willing to take care of him, be the guy—his guy—the one he could count on. That he was in the closet too had been my big flashing neon sign that I was finally in the same place with another person. It was scary and amazing at the same time.

Whenever I met a guy someplace besides a bar or a club, they were all about having me meet friends, go for drinks with them, and basically let it be known I was gay. Thing was, I couldn't do that. I was a police detective in Chicago; being out and proud was not an option if I ever wanted to move up. And though I knew one detective who had done it, he hadn't stayed on the force, instead becoming a federal marshal. I kidded myself for a short time and thought that was the way I wanted to go as well, but I liked being a homicide detective, bringing closure to people's lives, finding and punishing those responsible. I really wanted to keep doing what I was doing, and the fact of the matter was, so far, I had not found a guy important enough to pick over the job. The one long-term relationship I'd had, two years of my life, had ended over my not being an out and proud gay man.

The moment I'd met Aaron Sutter, though, a warning bell went off in the back of my head. I knew just from talking to him for a few minutes that the only way to be with him was serious. He was not a quick fuck; he was the guy you made a home with. Strangely, that didn't scare me. My fine-tuned flight reflex never kicked in.

It didn't hurt that he was stunning to look at. With his lean, muscled frame, sharp-angled features, and bright blue eyes, I wanted him instantly. When his turquoise gaze met mine, a throb of desire made my chest tight, and it was hard to remember my name. My whole life, I'd been such a sucker for beauty, but halfway through dinner with mutual friends, I knew the truth. It was more. I would do anything to spend some time with him, any that he would allow.

I liked the way the man talked. The sound of his voice—the resonance, the husky quality of it—decadent and sexy. His laugh was good, deep, not timid or quiet. More importantly, he was funny and sarcastic and quick with the barbs. He was smart, and brains being even hotter than looks, I was a goner.

. "Wake up, Stiel," a voice commanded through my earpiece.

Jerking out of my thoughts, I looked across the room to the entrance of the club.

"Head in the game. Evanston's coming in now."

I was covering the back door, so there was no way out for the mob enforcer once he came in. The two men he killed in Chicago, and the three here in New York, would put a needle in his arm if he didn't roll over on his boss. Everyone thought he would die before he gave up any names, but I knew a coward when I saw one.

Once this was finished, I could get on a plane for home, and when I was in my own place, call Aaron Sutter and ask if I could see him.

I *really* wanted to see him.

AFTER the first time we'd spent the night together, I had to get on a plane the next morning. Skipping the shower before I left was my choice. The idea of carrying him around on my skin all day had been so very needed.

"You don't want to wash up?" he teased, a lazy grin on his face, as he watched me from where he lay sprawled across his California king.

"No," I said, my voice hoarse because just looking at him, at his skin covered in marks I'd put there, at his swollen lips and sleep-tousled hair, made my heart stop. "I wanna smell like you a little longer."

"Oh," he said, obviously caught off guard.

It had been wild when we'd hit the door of his place the night before. The second the lock clicked, we were wrestling off jackets and shirts.

Aaron grabbed lube and condoms off a table by the wall, and pushed them at me before his hands went to his belt. He almost lost his balance when I shoved him forward, but recovered enough to stop from going face-first into the wall.

"Hold still," I growled as I came up behind him, grabbing his hip to make sure he didn't move.

"Yes," he promised, palms flat on the black-stained wood, head leaning against his bicep, his breathing rough and shaky.

I shoved my briefs and jeans to my knees, rolled on the condom, and flipped open the cap on the lube.

"Duncan," he cried, and I liked my name all garbled with yearning.

Shucking his underwear and jeans to his ankles, I reached around and fisted his cock with a lube-slicked hand, slathering my sheathed dick with the other.

"Please," he begged, his voice ragged and low. "I want you in me."

The tremble that ran through him was beautiful to see, the want and trust there a gift. When I slid two fingers into him, I realized how tight he was. "Tell me the last time you bottomed."

"Can't," he hissed. "Never have."

I froze.

"No-no-no," he whimpered, arching his back, thrusting his ass out. "I want it. You have no idea how long I've—but it's not in me to ask. I can't. I won't."

Whoever was with him had to simply know, and mind reading was a tough gig.

"I—Duncan!"

I got it. He was goddamn Aaron Sutter, and scary billionaire pillars of power did not ask anyone to fuck them. Ever. Until now, until me.

But the way he pushed on my fingers, rolled his head on his shoulders, and moaned endlessly—it was too much. "Grab your cock," I ordered.

"Just let me—I need… I want to feel you."

I took him at his word, spread the gorgeous round globes of his ass, and lined up the head of my cock with his pretty pink hole.

"Go slow."

I would do nothing else.

He trusted me, wanted me, and I would make the act tender and gentle. I would do for Aaron Sutter what I would have wanted.

"Duncan… I need you."

I moved like molasses poured in winter, covering him, plastering my chest to his back, my right arm around his neck, my hand on his hip, holding him still as I pressed inside him.

"Duncan!"

"Easy," I soothed him, behind his ear and kissing down the side of his neck. His reaction to each graze of my lips—the slow relaxing, the calm settling in his core—spoke to how much he wanted me there.

A fine sheen of sweat broke out over his shoulders, and he panted softly even as his body clenched tight around mine. I longed to be buried in him, to thrust deep, but slowly sinking inside Aaron, inch by delicious inch, was something I found I craved even more. His body opened, stretching around me, wanting me in just as much as he wanted me out. The war of it, the muscles rippling around me, was almost more than I could bear.

"You feel so good," I growled into his skin, loving the salty taste of his sweat, sucking, licking, and finally nibbling up the side of his throat.

"Don't stop."

I didn't. I slid farther, pushing, breaching, and then I was suddenly there, buried to the hilt, my balls against his ass. He turned his head, and I reached over his shoulder to kiss him, my tongue taking absolute possession—mauling him until I felt the last trace of fight in the man disappear.

"Could you…." He swallowed. "Tighter."

He was so vulnerable, naked in a way that had nothing to do with clothes. I wanted him to know he could wear me, that he had me.

I wrapped him up tight so he could feel my heart beating against his back.

His hands moved from the wall to my hips, and he slowly undulated against me.

"Oh fuck," I said and chuckled into his sweaty hair, rubbing my chin over his shoulder. "I won't last if you keep doing that." Every tingling, electric shiver made him jolt against me, and the muscles in his ass rippled around my shaft.

"Please." The word was barely audible, more a shaky huff of air than a sound. His passion-glazed eyes lifted to me. "Use me."

I couldn't pull out a couple of inches and then plunge back inside him like they did in all the best pornos. I was too swollen with arousal and he was too tight. All I could do was make the strokes as smooth as possible.

"Duncan!" he yelled, and his muscles squeezed tight, wringing a response from me, the sizzling heat simmering in the base of my spine.

I wanted to feel my body fit into his, wanted the give and take, the slow build and the blind rush of nothing but adrenaline and the euphoric high before the crash. I wanted to fuck him so hard only I would ever do. Once would never be enough.

"I need you," he ground out.

I knew he did.

"Don't leave me."

"No," I promised and pushed into him.

He was loud, and I loved it because there was no need to guess what he wanted, and his tears were of no consequence because they were about walls breaking and nothing bad.

I curled over him; my face pressed into the back of his neck, kissing gently, before I took hold of his hips and began the rhythm of thrust and retreat.

"Harder," he moaned.

"Come!" I demanded because I was too close, too engorged inside him, but I needed him sated first.

"I… Duncan…."

I shifted my angle and didn't have to guess if I got the spot I was after. He lost his language; there was only a guttural cry before he splattered over the wall in front of him. My climax was seconds behind his, and as we stood together, aftershocks wracking through us, I realized I was probably holding him too tight.

"Oh," I said softly and tried to ease free.

"No," he stopped me, content within the cocoon of my arms. "Stay."

And I had, all night, but I tried to leave with my pride intact the next morning. Telling the man I wanted to carry the smell of his sweat on me all day, that washing his dried come off my stomach from his second orgasm of the night was not something I wanted to do, was probably too much for the morning after our first date. I would scare him to death.

When he sat up and stared at me, I charged toward the door. I didn't want to hear I was being stupid, and I was sorry I'd said it even as it had come out. I had a tendency to get attached way too fast.

"Duncan."

I stopped and glanced over my shoulder.

"Will you call me when you get back?"

It took everything in me not to turn and bolt to the bed and kiss him until he begged me to stay. He looked so good, so tempting, so much like home, I had to swallow down my heart to not move. "Yeah," I said huskily, "if you want."

He nodded. "Please."

I tried to smile but it didn't come off, more a grimace of pain than anything else, I was sure. "Okay. I'll see ya."

"You don't need my driver to—"

"Nah. I got a cab waiting outside."

"Oh," he exhaled.

I didn't want to say "okay" again, so I opened the door and left.

It felt wrong to leave him. Staying seemed right, but I was too scared to tell him. And even though I had only known him for twelve hours, since dinner the night before, the thought of leaving him was physically painful.

I never stayed. I always ran the next morning. Sometimes I went home with people, but as soon as we were done, I made an excuse to bail. I had to leave. I never wanted to sleep with and hold someone until first Nate, my ex, and now, suddenly, a man I didn't expect.

Sharing a bed with Aaron Sutter was something I couldn't get out of my head. After a week, the desire was getting the better of me. I was dying to see him.

"HERE we go."

Jolted back to the task at hand, I watched as two men walked into the club. The second one was familiar, but I couldn't instantly place him.

"Visual confirmed. Everyone move."

I watched Evanston weave his way through the crowd at the dance club and stop in front of Joaquin Hierra's table.

"Wait—wait, new player, new player! All units hold."

As soon as I saw the third man pushing to get through the throng, I recognized him immediately. Once I did, everything fell into place, and it was a mess.

Goddamn it!

Moving fast, I was behind Joaquin and leaned down to whisper in his ear before I had time to apprise anyone of my intentions.

"This guy with your boy is hot, Boss," I said softly. "He's got a federal marshal right on his ass."

He stiffened, grabbed the lapel of my suit jacket, and held tight as he took in the sight of Evanston and Dr. Kevin Dwyer, the man I thought looked familiar. "You're sure?"

"Yep. Right there behind him, you see?"

Joaquin leaned close, looked around Evanston, and had to see Sam Kage barging his way by people in the teeming club, dressed as he always was at work: in a suit with a top coat over it, badge on his belt, and a holstered gun on the opposite side.

"Can you get me out of here?"

"I'll create a diversion; you go out the back with Benny and Andre."

He fisted his hand in my dress shirt. "Is it Evanston? Is he dirty?"

I had a second to decide if I was going to be the guy. Was I going to be the one wired for sound, or would I pass the baton to someone else?

It had been so simple: I was undercover to wait for Evanston to show up. He was an enforcer for the Delgado cartel and had been sent to Chicago to clean up two loose ends. Unfortunately, Jared Gibson, 15, got caught in the crossfire. I promised his mother, when we figured out how her son died, that I would bring the man to justice. She counted on me.

Riley Evanston had been dispatched by Esau Modella who was in charge of security and enforcement for the crime family. I followed Evanston to New York because it was my priority, to bring him in so he could stand trial. It was my department's chief concern.

In New York, where our fugitive had run to, the police there were following Arjun Ruiz and the drugs he moved into the city. They were out to bust one of the largest drug suppliers in the city of New York. We were after a killer. I understood our goals did not meet, but my captain, Lorena Gaines, had been sure Chicago homicide and New York vice could find common ground. But it was not to be.

Because no interdepartmental cooperation happened in this instance, the feds stepped in to coordinate a task force that would supposedly let us all reach our goals. Since I was already in place shadowing Joaquin, working as his muscle, I stayed, along with others I didn't know. It was strange to think some of the men I had met were undercover, just like I was.

I had been hired by Hierra based on a faked background, and several incarcerated criminals had vouched for me in exchange for new privileges and other concessions. It had been easy to pull off, and even though I was on the fringe working for Hierra—the man himself a pawn on the vast chessboard that was the Delgado crime family—it gave me access to Evanston, who had been sent to collect payment from Joaquin for his sloppy work in Chicago. Why the higher ups had sent Evanston to get the Delgado family money from Joaquin, I didn't know. Evanston moved drugs; his end wasn't murder, so it didn't make much sense. Perhaps he was being tested, groomed to move up—it hardly mattered to me. The important thing was, Evanston was in my sights. I could break cover and bust him. And that seemed like the plan until right that second.

It would take months to get another guy close to Hierra, and I was there, right there, ready to show my loyalty in a huge way, poised to become his most trusted man or simply disappear at the end of the bust.

I could go home, or I could stay and work with vice in New York. If I saved Joaquin from a federal marshal, I was in, and he would want me permanently on the payroll. Because yes, getting close to Joaquin Hierra had netted us Riley Evanston, but if I got in deep with Hierra, we could get access, eventually, to the whole operation, the big fish, the top tier of the Delgado drug cartel. Right now I was low level, but I could be in, just because he thought I was saving him from federal custody. Maybe Sam Kage showing up was not such a bad thing.

And maybe it was the worst.

I had only seconds to decide.

"He's gotta be dirty," I said flatly, staring back at the man with unwavering regard. "He led the feds here."

"How do you know?"

I tipped my head toward Sam and lied. "That's the same fed who took Javier Musa into protective custody. I saw him at the courthouse when they picked him up after he testified against Pascal."

His eyes widened; and he stood and slipped around me. "Tonight," he said, and then he moved away through the crowd.

"Where the hell is he going?" Evanston snarled at me.

I came around the table, Andre squeezed my shoulder as I moved by him, and Benny patted my back as I faced the mob enforcer. "What the fuck are you doing bringing a goddamn federal fugitive into Joaquin's place?"

"What?" he gasped, head swiveling to Kevin Dwyer. "You've got a tail?"

"No," Dwyer scoffed even as Sam yelled *Freeze!* over the driving trance music.

"You stupid fuck," I snarled at Evanston, swinging on him.

The man had a good fifty pounds of muscle on me, and at six four, two twenty, I was not small myself. So when he blocked my throw and drove his fist into my face, I knew it was going to hurt.

It was a fight then, with yelling and screaming, stampeding for the exits, punches flying, and finally guns being drawn.

I wound up on the bottom of a pile, stepped on, kicked, punched, and cut. I had no idea who had the knife, but the diversion created an irresistible opportunity for someone looking to take out a rival. My money was on Pedro, who had never liked me. I was the one who had taken his friend Musa's place in his boss's circle after his buddy went to prison for trafficking in stolen goods. He had never made it a secret he didn't trust me, and even though he did, in fact, have good reason, since I was undercover, he didn't know that.

By the time I was pulled out from under all the other bodies, I was bleeding enough to know I needed stitches.

"This one's gotta go to the hospital before booking," Sam Kage yelled, pulling me to my feet fast, but more gently, I was certain, than anyone would be able to discern.

When he shoved me up against the wall, I groaned.

"Broken?" He asked, leaning in close, talking in my ear as he pinned me there.

"Bruised," I muttered, giving him the lowdown on the state of my ribs. "Just losing blood."

"Hold on," he said so only I could hear.

Like I had a choice.

Ten minutes later, I was in an ambulance, on my back, looking up at Sam Kage.

"Asshole," I barked as the EMT tried to stop the bleeding.

He shrugged his massive shoulders.

"How the fuck does your guy know my guy?" We couldn't do names in front of the tired-looking EMT.

"Before your guy was hired muscle for the family, he worked for my guy."

"Who's really the doctor," I grunted.

"Actually, the doctor *is* the bad guy," Sam mocked me. "I mean, if you're concerned about being precise."

"How the fuck is Salcedo walking around to begin with?" I yelled, using his name before I could stop myself. "I thought he was in federal custody?"

"We had one more leak," Sam informed me. "But we're all good now, obviously."

"What if you lose him again?"

"*My* team is on it," Sam assured me. "*Mine*. You understand?"

I was quiet, the pain getting to me. "Yeah."

He stayed with me, which I didn't expect. As the hours rolled by in the hospital, as I got twenty-seven stitches down my left side over my ribs, as the drugs made me a little loopy, and as a full inventory of cuts, bruises, and a split lip was taken, Sam remained.

"Why are you here?"

"'Cause nobody else is," he said frankly, one eyebrow lifting like I was stupid.

And because he'd made me feel like crap with that answer, I took a shot at him. "So, how does Jory feel about you working with your ex?"

"I'm not working with him, asshole, I'm recapturing him, and Jory's glad he's back in custody."

"And that's all?"

"He knows me, Duncan; he knows who I love and who I don't give a shit about."

I squinted. "Yeah, but you and that Salcedo guy, that was on like *Donkey Kong* in Colombia, huh?"

He was horrified. "What did they give you?"

It had to be something strong, because I was smiling like an idiot and using Nintendo references. My instinct for self-preservation was MIA.

"And no." He shook his head.

"I heard all about it, Kage," I huffed out. "You were with the good doctor for a year while you—"

"For your information—" Sam cut me off, his voice low and dark, making me just a little nervous. Yes, we were friends, but the man was menacing, no way around it. "I screwed the doctor for three months while me and Jory were apart. It never meant shit. If I could take it back, would I? Oh hell yeah, I would, but not why you think."

"Why do I think?"

"I never thought of it like cheating on Jory," he explained. "A year had gone by. He was sleeping around by that time, and so was I. The reason I wish it didn't happen was because of how it made me feel."

"How'd ya feel?"

"Like crap," he barked at me. "You know when you confessed to me that you screw guys at bathhouses and places like that?"

"Thanks for bringing that shit up," I groused.

"Just—do you remember?"

"Yes, I fuckin' remember!" I flared.

"You know how gross you feel when you do it?"

"I do."

"It's was like that," he confessed. "I didn't care any more about Kevin Dwyer than you do about all those guys you fuck and forget, but—"

"Even from the little I know of Jory, I bet he doesn't think it was nothing."

"Because it lasted longer than one night," he grumbled. "Jory fucked a ton of guys while we were apart, but the one he spent any time with—"

"Aaron," I supplied.

"Yeah. Aaron he had feelings for."

"So since Jory cared about Aaron, he figures you cared about the doctor."

"Yeah."

"But you didn't?"

"No," Sam sighed. "I really didn't."

"But you were together how long?"

"Three months."

"So, that's kind of a dick thing you did there."

"Yeah, I know!" he barked at me. "I told you that already."

"Okay, so Jory thinks what?"

"Jory thinks I was as attached to Salcedo as he was to Aaron, because he thinks we have the same kind of heart. In fact, he thinks everyone's heart works just like his."

"They don't," I said sadly.

"No, they don't. But that's why I'm here, to protect him."

It was funny to hear gentle words from such a fierce man.

"I've never loved anyone but him, and that's why I had to get him back. When you're faced with the truth, you have to act on it."

It seemed like he was trying to get me to admit something.

"Did you love your professor?" he asked.

He was talking about my ex, Nathan Qells, the only man I had ever been in a real, grown-up relationship with.

"Did you love him the way I love Jory?"

"Why are you asking me that?"

He shrugged before leaning back in his chair. "Sorry, buddy; you're the one who wanted to go swimming in the deep end."

I studied him a minute. He was right. I had been the one to try and pry out secrets. And I knew why. I was all hopped up on drugs. If I weren't, I would have never had the balls to talk to Sam so openly. "No."

"No what?"

I cleared my throat. "No, I wasn't in love with Nate the same way you love Jory. I chose my job over him. You chose Jory over the job."

"I actually never had to make that decision," he said thoughtfully. "I was fortunate. By the time Jory and I were ready for me to say what we were; I had a captain who got it and a new partner who didn't care who I slept with. Right after that, I became a marshal."

"And now?"

"Now I'm pretty much set. I do my job well and no one screws with me. If they look, they see I have a domestic partner, but why would they even look?"

"Your own little don't ask, don't tell, huh?"

"That's belittling a lot of pain there."

"I ain't belittling anything. I just don't have the luxury you did. I didn't get to go off and work with the DEA for two years and switch from homicide to vice or become a marshal. I like my job. I like catching the bad guy. This is all I know how to do."

"So do it, but don't forget that I've seen how you look at Jory."

My heart almost stopped. "What the fuck are you talking about?"

"Not like that, idiot." He glared at me. "I've seen you look at Jory and how he looks at me, and I know you fuckin' want that. You want a man to come home to. I get it."

I scoffed. "So you think Jory thinks you walk on water, huh?"

"No," he said huskily. "Jory can see every single one of my faults. He just forgives them. And I know how he looks at me. I know I'm loved. Who loves you?"

And it was a question I couldn't answer.

AFTER Sam finally left, they moved me to another room and fixed all the reports with my fake name, Tucker Ross. Soon after, DEA agent, Derrick Chun, and his partner, Agent Maxwell Owens, were brought into my room by Special Agent Conner Wray. He thanked me, shook my hand, and cautioned me to be careful. It was nice that he gave me his card, with his cell number scribbled on the back, and said if I got in trouble, to call. The look he shot the two DEA agents was not kind. Yes, they were all working together, but it was more than obvious Wray thought they might get me killed.

"We won't let you get killed" was the first thing Chun imparted.

It did not inspire confidence.

They left quickly, promised to be in touch, gave me an untraceable cell to hide, which was not great, considering I was in the hospital, and then I was alone to consider the state of my life. It was fucked, was what it was.

Chapter TWO

THE hospital wanted to keep me overnight in case I had a concussion, but I'd had enough of them in my life to know the difference. I wasn't nauseous, nor did I have a splintering headache behind my right eye, but most of all—and this was the clincher—everything was the correct color. My vision wasn't blurred or spotty, so against medical advice, I signed myself out.

I was walking out of my room when I saw Joaquin and the others at the nurses' station.

"Hey," I called to them.

Joaquin levered up off the counter where he was leaning and jogged over to me, Benny and Andre close behind him.

"You all right?" he inquired, looking worried, his gaze met mine, and when he reached me, his hand went on my shoulder. It was funny, but it seemed like he honestly cared.

"Yeah, I'm good."

He didn't look convinced. "So where is your crib, man?"

"Brooklyn," I said as I was programmed to.

He shook his head. "Nah. Now you live in Musa's old place. I had it all cleaned up for ya."

"Oh no, Boss, you don't gotta do that."

"Yeah, he does," Benny assured me.

"Yeah, I do." Joaquin chuckled as Andre slid his arm around my shoulder.

"Come on, man, let's go. We'll go get your shit first."

"You look like ass." Benny scrunched up his face like I smelled.

"I'll be fine."

"How many stitches?" Joaquin wanted to know.

"Only fifteen or so," I lied. "It's not a big deal."

"I said diversion, buddy, not World War Three."

"I think Pedro was the one with the knife."

Joaquin agreed. "Yeah. I think he's been pissed at you since Musa."

"Me moving into his place ain't gonna help," I said frankly.

"I'll take care of Pedro." Benny smiled in that sort of sinister way he had. It was very cat-that-swallowed-the-canary.

"Oh no, I didn't mean—"

"No, no," Joaquin soothed me. "Not like that. Calm down."

"I just don't wanna cause a problem."

"No, man. You fix them, as far as I can tell."

"That shit was federal," Andre reminded me, his voice low, easing me sideways so I had to give him some of my weight. "That prick Evanston brought a guy to us with a marshal on his ass."

I nodded.

"Did you know that Evanston shot some kid in Chicago?"

Yes. "No, I didn't."

"Yeah, he's gettin' life for that shit, or a needle in his arm."

"If he doesn't roll." Benny smirked. "You always gotta figure on that shit with guys like him."

Joaquin shook his head. "That's Modella's problem. I already called him."

"Too bad we didn't get the name of the marshal," I fished. "We could've taken care of that too."

"Oh fuck that," Andre grumbled. "We ain't messin' with no goddamn marshal. He wasn't even there for us; all he wanted was that piece of shit Evanston."

"Nobody needs that kind of heat," Andre chimed in.

I was glad to hear Sam wasn't even on their radar. "Okay." I winced. "Let's go before all my pain meds are gone."

"I got shit for pain," Benny assured me. "Just say the word."

Even though I was cleared to do drugs if necessary to maintain my cover, I didn't think taking anything stronger than Tylenol for stitches was what anyone behind the scenes on the task force had in mind.

THE apartment was small and clean, in an older building that had been restored. It was not far from the theater district, close enough to walk, if a twenty-minute stroll was something you were up for. It was like staying at a hotel, and Joaquin suggested I get either a plant or a cat. Benny suggested I find a woman, instead, and forget anything else. Andre went over the good places to pick up pastries, tapas, or to get a drink.

It was nice that, on his way out, Joaquin squeezed the back of my neck and ordered me into bed. He gave me the keys: one for the security door outside, one to get from the foyer where the mailboxes were into the building, and the last one for the apartment.

"I don't wanna see your face 'til at least Monday."

As it was Thursday night, that gave me a nice three-day weekend. Maybe I could fly back to Chicago and see Aaron Sutter. "Okay," I agreed.

Once they were gone, I called Agent Chun, reported what happened, and then hung up. I promised to talk to him no later than Tuesday. I thought about taking a shower and changing out of my bloodied T-shirt but just couldn't muster the energy. Both my suit jacket and shirt had been sacrificed in the line of duty, first pierced with the knife used to stab me and then shredded by the paramedics. Many articles of clothing had been lost that way over the years. I had to add up what the Chicago PD owed me in dry cleaning and replacement wardrobe one of these days. It had to be in the thousands.

Lying down on the couch, I picked up my own phone from the coffee table and called Aaron.

He answered on the second ring. "Duncan?"

"Yeah. How did you know?"

"I—" He coughed. "—put your number in my phone."

It was nice to hear. "So," I said, my voice low and full of gravel. "How are you?"

"I'm good," he said quickly. "You?"

"I just got stitches." I grinned because, God, he sounded good. "So I'm a little beat to shit, if you wanna know the truth."

"You got—who hurt you?"

"I'm a cop. You know how it is."

He cleared his throat. "I don't, actually."

I grunted. "It happens. I'll live."

"Yeah?"

Why did he sound scared? "Are you all right?"

"I don't want to freak you out."

"Why would you?"

"I, uhm," he hedged, "I'm in New York. I have been for a week."

There had to be more.

"Duncan?"

"Yeah, still here."

"Are you—is that freaking you out?"

"You do business all over the world, yeah?"

"Yes."

"So you probably hafta come to New York a lot, right?"

"I do, yes."

"I guess I'm not getting why you being here would be weird."

"I just"—his voice cracked—"didn't want you to think I was stalking you or something."

"Oh, wouldn't that be something," I mused.

"Something?"

"Yeah, I mean, that'd be cool, right? How many guys could say that Aaron Sutter was following them around? I should be so lucky."

He whimpered.

The sound about shredded what little control I had left. Hurt and tired, with the last of my buzz wearing off, I was damn needy. "You maybe wanna see me?"

Silence.

"Aaron?"

"Yes, please," he murmured. "I would love to see you. Where are you? I'll come get you."

"No. It's not safe. You tell me where you are, and I'll come to you."

"How 'bout this," he said shakily. "You walk one street over from where you are, and I'll be there in a car in ten minutes to get you. Deal?"

"What if I'm not in the city?"

"Fine. However long it takes," he huffed out. "Where are you?"

"Tenth Avenue and 49th Street."

"Oh man, I'm like minutes from you. I'm staying at The Pierre on 5th."

"I don't know that place. Is it fancy?" I teased.

"It is."

Of course it was. "Okay. Will they let me in?"

"You'll be with me."

"True."

"So—are you working?"

"Yeah."

"I see."

"But not until Monday."

"Oh?" His voice rose, and I could hear the reprieve and the happiness.

I made a noise that didn't quite qualify as communication.

"You think you'd want to stay with me a couple days?"

"Yeah. Ya know I was thinking of flying back to Chicago just to see you," I said without even thinking of how scary psycho it sounded. "Awww shit."

Several long moments passed, but I was too panicked to speak. I had no filter because of everything, and now I would pay for it.

"You were thinking of returning to Chicago for just two days?"

"Well, three actually," I corrected him. "But, yeah."

Quick, sharp exhale. "Okay, you win. That's like one of the nicest things anyone's ever said to me."

It was? "It is?" I was baffled. "Shit, who've you been hangin' out with?"

"People who like my money," he said, clipping the words. "I'm leaving now. Can you walk?"

"Yes, I can walk," I grumbled.

He chuckled. "Hurry up, all right?"

The phone went dead, and I realized he had basically ordered me to get my ass in gear. And though I started to ache, I got up anyway to change into some clean clothes.

IT WAS a nice car: some kind of big, fancy black BMW sedan with tinted windows, a shiny paint job that reflected all the city lights, and sparkling chrome. When it rolled up to the curb beside me, I stood there looking at my reflection for a minute before the window rolled down and I was looking at Aaron Sutter.

The luminous aqua eyes, fringed with long gold lashes, stared out at me from the darkness of the car. I nearly swallowed my tongue. "Hi," I said lamely.

The door opened. "Get in."

The driver was suddenly there beside me, holding out a hand for my bag. I passed it to him as I saw the trunk open, and then got in, closing the door behind me. When I turned to Aaron, he gasped.

"Aww, it's not that bad." I grinned, trying to sound normal and not like my heart was about to pound its way out of my chest.

His brows were furrowed, and his eyes glinted in the low light. "It's worse, actually," he assured me, reaching out to put a hand on my cheek.

I leaned into his touch. I couldn't help it.

"Jesus, I so get this now," he said.

"Mmmm?"

"Yeah. The whole comforting-a-policeman thing," he clarified. "No wonder I never had a chance with Jory. This is scary addictive."

"What?"

He shook his head, then told the driver we were ready to go.

As the car pulled away from the curb, I covered his hand with mine and slid it down my cheek before turning it over to kiss his palm. "I'm really happy to see you," I said, watching him, memorizing every reaction as I leaned close, unable to resist the temptation of his ear. Gently, I sucked the soft flesh just past my lips and nibbled slowly around the curve of his lobe.

He shivered hard and tilted his head away, just barely. I followed the sway of his body, moving my mouth to the tender skin behind his ear and then trailing down the side of his neck, kissing and suckling. Using the cord of muscle as my guide, I licked and finally bit, not enough to hurt, just enough so he could feel my teeth.

"Duncan." He jolted, pulling away.

"Shit, I'm—"

"No," he stopped me. "I just don't want to attack you right here in the car. It's sort of tacky, right?"

"Is it?"

He scowled. "Let me get you to my suite. You can take a long, hot bath, I'll order room service, and we can sit out on the terrace and take in the view of Central Park."

"And?"

"And after I take care of you and make sure you're fine—then I'm all yours."

He was used to giving orders; I wasn't used to taking them. "Screw that," I growled, cupping his face in my hands and pulling him close for a kiss.

I didn't even have to press: he opened for me the second our lips sealed together. Sliding inside his wet heat, I rubbed my tongue over his, tasting, reminding him I had done this before. He melted against me, pliant and willing, his moan deep and throaty. He had no idea how much I loved surrender noises, how thick and aching my cock suddenly was, swelling almost painfully inside my jeans.

When he kissed me back, grinding our mouths together, stroking my tongue with his, sucking on my lips, hands fluttering on the side of my neck, I knew he was mine for the taking.

"You taste good," I barely got out, shifting sideways, tugging him over into my lap so he straddled my hips. He tried to untangle himself, but I kissed him, hard and rough, and drained the fight out of him.

"Duncan," he moaned softly when I finally let him breathe, shoving his groin against my abdomen, needing the friction, his hands gripping my chest as he began a slow, driving rhythm. "I missed you... I...." He couldn't finish, his words stilted.

I found that incredibly hot.

"This isn't me," he said.

"What?"

"I never... need."

He was about control. I understood that. He was rich and powerful; Aaron Sutter was not the kind of man who should get off on rubbing his cock against my abs. But he was, and the hunger and the yearning were his undoing. He was coming apart in my arms, and I wanted to see it, to feel it in my hands even more. I made quick work of his belt, and I had the stays of his dress pants open and the zipper down seconds later.

"You're hurt," he said, his voice cracking as he puffed air over my skin, wet and hot.

I slipped his cock from under his briefs, and wrapped my hand around the long, thick length of him, loving the feel of the silky skin, smearing the leaking precome over the flared head, and slowly, sensuously, jerking him off.

He shoved forward into my grip and barked at the driver at the same time. "Park the car!"

When you were worth billions, I guessed, people just knew what you meant. But I was only peripherally aware we had gone in a different direction. I was much too focused on the breathtaking man in my lap, writhing with need, pistoning in and out of my fist.

I lifted my left hand to his lips. "Suck on my fingers. Get 'em real wet."

He understood, opening instantly, taking them deep into his mouth, coating and laving my index and middle fingers until, when I eased them free, they were slick with saliva.

We stopped, and I heard the door open and close, was aware of the sound of the power locks and then the footsteps of dress shoes over concrete.

"Lift up," I ordered, and he rose, leaning forward and curling his back so it grazed the roof of the car instead of bumping it as I put my hand down the back of his trousers.

"I never… I don't… I…."

He was good, proper, and only sinful behind closed doors. He was Aaron fucking Sutter. He didn't shed inhibitions in public; it was unseemly. The idea that he was so far gone all his reticence sailed right out the window, was just about the hottest thing I could think of.

I squeezed his shaft as I pressed my middle finger inside him. He bucked forward, and it hurt me—my ribs, my side—but only sharply for a second and not enough to stop. His head thrown back, the arch of his spine, how he was biting his bottom lip: he was a vision, and I couldn't be bothered with my comfort. All that mattered was him.

I dragged my fingertip over his prostate, and he babbled something incomprehensible as he pushed in and out of my fist. "Is it good?" I prodded, my voice rumbling out of me because watching him was a gift.

His mouth was open and all I heard were gasps as I added a second finger, scissoring, breaching the tight muscles, feeling the give as they loosened and I pressed deep inside the tight, hot channel.

"Duncan, please," he begged me, hands clenched on my shoulders, taking my fingers to the knuckles, rising up and shoving back down, over and over.

"Turn around and I'll shove my tongue up your ass."

His moan was raw and strangled; he had nearly climaxed with just the suggestion.

"You want me to do that? Huh? Aaron? You want me to rim you 'til you scream?"

He shuddered and shot come onto the front of my gray T-shirt, yelling my name as his orgasm rushed through him, freezing all his muscles.

I didn't move. I let the aftershocks roll through him, felt the shiver begin as semen seeped from his slowly softening dick.

His hands relaxed their grip on my shoulders, and he bent down, burrowing into my chest as I eased my fingers from his spasming passage. His sharp inhale, his arms wrapped tight around my neck, and his face in the hollow of my throat changed passion to possession in an instant. I had the overwhelming urge to demand no one ever be allowed to see him like this except me. I wanted to tell him he belonged to me, but it was too fast, and I was afraid it would scare him off.

I didn't want him to run. More importantly, I didn't want him to order me to stay away from him.

"Get your dick out so I can suck it," he directed softly, still twitching, his body overstimulated, overly sensitized, and quivering with the sensation of coming down from the euphoria of his orgasm.

"Just let me hold you, all right?" I said, gathering him in my arms, pressing him tight to my chest, the pain of no consequence, and I kissed his forehead. "Can I be shelter for just a sec?"

He gave me his weight, sort of melting over me, and I sighed deeply. He was vulnerable, and I was there for him. It felt good to not only be wanted, but needed too.

THREE

HE DIDN'T want us to separate to walk into the lobby, but I insisted. He got out first, and minutes later, I followed, having collected my duffel from the trunk and thanked the driver. I wasn't sure if I should tip him, but I had a feeling, from the fact he didn't pick up anyone else but simply drove away, Mr. Sutter had compensated him already.

Inside, Aaron waited, and I joined him in an elevator you had to put a key into before the buttons would light up for the higher floors. Apparently, the suite we were going to was the penthouse.

"Holy shit," I said, awed at the spectacle once I was inside.

The room was huge; you could see the skyline and park from the enormous terrace, and the windows and the city lights…. I was overwhelmed.

"This is gorgeous," I gushed. "Thank you for inviting me."

He seemed like he was in pain.

"What's wrong with you?"

"Why won't you let me touch you?"

I gave out a very undignified snort of laughter. "Are you kidding?" I opened my arms wide for him. "Come touch me. Put your hands all over me."

"I want to suck your cock," he almost yelled at me. "Why won't you let me?"

"You think I'm just gonna come down your throat without showing you a paper that tells you I'm clean? What kind of ruthless prick do you think I am?"

He charged across the room, stopping just inches from me, staring deep into my eyes. "I know all about your many, many conquests. I checked you out backward and forward, just so you're aware, Detective."

"Did you?"

"Yes, I did." He was adamant. "I wanted to learn every dirty little secret you had, and guess what? Besides the being gay thing and the fucking anything with a pulse thing, you don't have any skeletons at all."

But that was a lie, and we both knew it because if he had checked me out like he said, then he knew there was a piece of my life that was hidden away. But we weren't talking about that, not about ancient history, we were talking about now. And there was nothing recent, that was true, nothing new, but there were things he would never know unless I offered them up.

"You might think you're all badass, but in comparison to people I know, you're a damn boy scout."

He was trying to sound all pissed off and tough, but all I saw were his puffy lips, the stubble burn on his cheeks, the flush of sex, and the hickeys on his throat. The blown pupils, slight tremble, and tousled hair were all dead giveaways of sated passion.

"You wanna go to bed?" I asked.

"What?"

"Do you… want me… to take you to bed?"

He nodded as he stared up into my face.

"What happened to feeding me and a hot bath and all that shit?"

His eyes were turbulent. "I'm—I feel sort of off balance."

I grinned. "That's okay. Me too."

He scowled. "How do you just say what you mean?"

"Why not?" I shrugged. "You like me right?"

"I do."

"Same here," I said bluntly. "When I'm with you, I feel really good. I want that."

He shook his head.

"What?"

"You don't believe in games? Just don't play them?"

I shrugged. "Why? This is new, and I haven't screwed it up yet, and you're looking at me like I'm special. Let's go with that."

He studied me.

"What?"

"You don't worry that I'll lose interest without the mystery?"

I met his gaze. "Are you bored?"

"No."

"What do you want?"

"To spend time with you."

"Well there ya go." I chuckled. "So we're on the same page, and you're still into me, at least so far."

"So far," he said, his voice husky.

Everything blurred for a second, and I squinted until my vision cleared.

"Maybe you should lie down."

"Maybe," I agreed.

He was there fast, his arm around me, and I leaned as we walked into the bedroom.

"This suite is like a million dollars a night, huh?"

"Yep," he said, and I could hear the smile in his voice as we crossed from the doorway to the bed, and he dumped me down onto it.

"I take it back." I groaned, letting my arms fall open, my legs too, the California King able to accommodate all of me, even stretched out. "You're trying to kill me."

"No," he sighed, taking a seat beside me as my eyes fluttered shut. "I promise you, that's the very last thing on my mind."

"This might not have been the best idea," I managed to get out. "I think I might pass out on you."

"That's fine. Go right ahead."

And I was going to argue, but the bed felt so good and soft, and I exhaled and assured myself I would rest just for a minute.

SOMETHING smelled amazing. My eyes fluttered open, and I found a bemused Aaron Sutter sitting beside me in a T-shirt and sleep shorts.

"Crap," I groaned.

He did a curious thing then: bent and kissed me.

"How do I deserve that?"

"Because it's raining outside and we're warm in here, and I sat in bed and watched a movie while you slept beside me. It was really nice."

"Man, you are easy to please."

"Not normally," he said gruffly.

I rolled over into his lap, wrapped my arm around his hip, and used him for a pillow as I focused my eyes on the huge flat screen in front of me. "CNN? Really?"

His fingers curled languidly through my hair. "One must stay apprised, Detective."

"At whatever the hell time it is on a Thursday night?"

"Always."

"Why don't you watch *Lord of the Rings* or something?"

He grunted.

"Come on, Viggo's hot."

"You think?"

"You don't?"

"I prefer Sean Bean."

"Yeah?"

The rumbling purr made me clutch him tighter. "Big men do it for me."

It was a good answer. "Nice."

"Are you hungry?"

"Starving, actually."

"Good," he said, twisting his hand in my thick hair. "Eat and then take a shower and lay back down with me."

"How is that any fun for you?"

"No one ever lets me take care of them. If you'd let me—that would be good."

Why would I argue? I lifted up until we were eye to eye and stared. He held my gaze, and there we were, looking at each other for long minutes, seemingly content to do so, until I leaned forward and kissed him.

"What'd you get me to eat?"

He wrapped his arms around my neck and squeezed tight. It was really nice, just to be held, just to be wanted.

The burger he ordered was enormous. It was covered in onion rings, barbecue sauce, and blue cheese, as well as jack. Apparently it was a Sutter original the chef there only made for him. I had coleslaw and sweet-potato fries and a skewer of sautéed mushrooms with a thick chocolate milkshake to wash it down and a pitcher of ice water. Normally, he said, he'd ply me with alcohol, but with a maybe concussion, he wasn't willing to risk it.

After I ate, I needed to be clean, having not showered when I got home from the hospital.

The shower was enormous, and it had a removable head, which made things so much easier. I was sore, so I was careful to wash around the stitches. When I was out and looking at my swollen cheek, red, puffy eye, and the various scrapes and cuts, I realized I must have looked worse when Aaron saw me earlier.

"What are you looking at?" he asked as he walked into the bathroom behind me.

I faced him, leaning back against the counter, the towel around my hips all I was wearing. "I don't get you."

"You're changing the sub—"

"What's with you and the slumming?"

"In what way am I slumming?" he wanted to know, moving closer, his gaze hot as he took me in.

I crossed my arms and legs as I surveyed him, and he slid a hand up my left bicep, his fingers tracing the muscle and veins under my pale skin. "How come you don't have a rich boyfriend?"

He slipped his hand to my shoulder and left it there as the knuckles of his other hand smoothed over my abdomen, up and down. The motion was lulling and erotic at the same time. "That would make sense, wouldn't it?"

"To me it would."

"I'm sure to most people it would," he said, crowding me, putting both hands on my face as he leaned toward me. "Have someone to just call and meet in Paris at a moment's notice."

I murmured some form of yes before his lips sealed over mine.

Even compared to what I'd felt with Nate, my ex—who I thought I'd loved almost desperately—it was *more* with Aaron Sutter. I didn't have that overwhelming feeling he had one foot out the door. I didn't feel like the man in front of me would one day just be gone, which was weird since, by rights, he wasn't even mine.

His tongue pressed for entrance, sliding over the seam of my lips, and I opened for him as he fell forward into me.

I was lost in the feel of him: the heat from his body, his groin grinding against mine through the towel, his hands on my hips, working it open.

My shiver was uncontrollable, and he pulled back, breaking the kiss in response. "I'm not slumming," he panted as he stared into my eyes. The next moment, he succeeded in opening my towel before he dropped to his knees.

My cock strained toward him, and when he touched his tongue there to taste the slit, a deep, guttural moan came up out of me.

"Most people—" He paused to take hold of me and lick a long, wet line from balls to crown, flattening his tongue as he did it before pulling back to continue. "—bore me to tears. I have a hard time caring, even being interested, because I've seen so much, been indulged my whole life, and now can have whatever I want."

My breath got short as he leaned back in and sucked the crown inside his hot mouth. Watching him go at it—lips clamped around my cock, head bobbing with the motion, the suction and the swirl thing he did—I had to stop him after only minutes so I wouldn't come.

His smile was wicked as he lifted his eyes to me. "You don't bore me."

"That's good," I said, my voice strained as I leaned back against the free-standing sink, no cabinets underneath, just the counter it was on.

"It is good," he agreed and then deep throated me in a smooth motion, the man's gag reflex nonexistent.

The way his throat opened around me, his hands clenching my ass, made it impossible for me not to drive deeper. When I hit the back, he sucked, swallowed, and I carded my fingers through his hair and grabbed hold.

I pushed him off me and then yanked him back, fucking his mouth, making him take all of me over and over, as his fingers massaged my ass, spreading my cheeks. It felt so good, and I realized I wanted him inside me more than I wanted to dump into his mouth. Shoving him off, I saw the longing on his face for a second before I hauled him to his feet.

"Duncan—"

"No," I cut him off, turning to face the sink, hands splayed on the cold marble, bracing my legs apart, and letting my head fall forward.

His hands were instantly on my hips, and I felt his mouth between my shoulder blades. "I never bottomed before that night with you," he said, kissing down my spine. "And it was so good riding you, I was... I've never come like that." He pressed more kisses to the small of my back, and then his tongue touched the top of my crease.

Instinctively, I pushed back, and he was on his knees again, hands parting my cheeks as his tongue slid over my puckered hole. He laved my entrance, spearing the tip inside me just for a moment before speaking again. "But Duncan," he said gruffly, "I can't get the idea of fucking you out of my head."

I shivered. "Where's your lube and condoms?"

"There. Right drawer."

"Your hotel bathroom comes stocked with supplies?"

"No. I called ahead and had it put there once you said you'd meet me."

"Me," I choked out, "or any—"

"You," he growled and bit my right cheek. I yelped and laughed, and he rose and smacked the other cheek before yanking open the drawer and snatching the unopened tube and a condom. "I don't...," he began, and I could hear the snap of the cover. "I would never have just anyone with me, in bed, to sleep with. Do you understand that?"

I gripped the edge of counter for balance and looked at him in the mirror. "Yes."

"Are you sure?" he checked, voice muffled by the condom I could see dangling from between his teeth as he slid one lube-slicked finger into my ass.

"Aaron," I whispered, my eyes fluttering shut before my head fell back on my shoulders. "Don't do all the prep and... just get the glove on and fuck me."

"We need to go slow," he rasped, and I heard the tearing of the foil wrapper.

"No."

"I refuse to hurt you," he said, pulling out and pushing back in, deeper, stroking his fingertip over my gland, making me buck against the counter.

"Nobody ever topped except—" I gasped. "—one."

"Your ex, I know," he soothed me. "I know your submission is a gift."

I bent over, wanting him almost painfully. "Please."

"I'll take care of you," he promised before the head of his cock opened me wide. He pressed inside, the lube easing the breach and the stretch, my muscles clenching around him as he shoved deep.

"Jesus, Duncan, you're so tight," he whispered, stroking down my flanks, kissing over my shoulders, leaning with me, giving my body time to adjust to the intrusion.

The pressure inside, the way he filled me, the slight retreat before the rough thrust home, all of it was welcome. I wanted him there.

"I have to move."

"Yeah, do that."

He eased out and slammed back into me.

I moaned his name.

"This fucking condom," he growled. "I hate it."

"Take it off," I snarled back. "You checked me out. I know you're good. Get rid of it."

He was gone and then back, plunging inside me, and I could feel the difference, the drag and catch of skin even as I felt his hands tight on my ass.

"I'm gonna come watching my dick slide in and out of your hole," he said, and his voice was low and full of gravel. "And I'm not gonna pull out and come on your back. I'm coming in your ass. Do you understand?"

I nodded.

"Say yes."

"Yes," I rasped.

And there was no more talking, just him, with his hands on my hips to hold me still as he pounded into me as hard and as fast as he could. I grabbed my dick and pumped, my head lolling back as I came on the counter.

I squeezed him all at once, my muscles clamping tight, and he fucked me through my aftershocks and his orgasm. When silky wet heat filled my channel, I gasped at the long-forgotten sensation.

"Promise I can do it again, whenever I want?"

"Yes. Whenever you want."

"Nobody else," he said with a catch in his voice. "It's not safe."

"That's not the reason." I looked at him over my shoulder.

"No," he agreed, and I saw the shudder. "I don't want you to see anyone else but me."

"Then I won't. And you don't either."

"I promise," he whispered and then collapsed across my back.

Because I could, because I was big and strong, even as hurt as I still was, I held us both up. The gush of fluid when he eased free was a reminder of what I had allowed, and he moved quickly to turn the shower on.

"Come here; let me take care of you."

I was in and out quickly; he was speedy with the mesh sponge and the removable showerhead, and much more careful of my stitches than I was. Once I was in bed, I was given a couple of Tylenol, directed to drink the glass of water, and then I was on my side in the dark, the lights of the city the only illumination in the vast room.

"You can watch TV," I said as he spooned against my back, his groin pressed to my crease, face in my hair, bicep tucked under my cheek, and his hand on my chest. "It won't bother me."

"No, I want to sleep with you, Duncan. I've been waiting."

I grunted as my eyes fluttered closed and he settled around me.

"I have," he insisted.

"I'm glad," I assured him. "Kiss me goodnight."

"Turn your head so I can."

I leaned back and he lifted up. The kiss was sweet, just a brush of lips, but somehow very intimate.

"Go to sleep, baby."

And I did, safe in his arms.

FOUR

I WOKE to the sound of swearing.

"I'll leave already," I called out as I rolled over on my back, groggy with sleep. It was a gray, overcast day, but I had slept in, so it was already good. "Don't be mad."

"Shut up!" he yelled from the bathroom.

I yawned and stretched, and when he came striding out of the bathroom dressed for— I wasn't sure, I couldn't keep from grinning.

He gave me a dismissive wave. "Just don't say anything."

"You look hot," I said, sitting up and scrubbing my eyes with the heels of my hands before taking in the sight of him again. "Where ya goin'?"

He put on the helmet he carried under his arm. "To a charity polo match."

"That sounds like fun," I joked. "So I'll just hang out here 'til you—"

"You wouldn't want to come with me, would you?"

The way he asked, nonchalantly like it didn't matter one way or the other, was completely betrayed by the way he chewed the inside his left cheek. Like I wasn't a police detective, trained to look at the whole person, or as though details were ever lost on me.

"I'd like to," I replied sincerely. "But who would I be?"

"What are you talking about?"

I fixed him with a stare. "I mean, am I your bodyguard, a friend? Who am I?"

He walked to the window, stood there, and crossed his arms.

"I'm not tryin' to be a dick," I said honestly. "I just need to know."

He made a noise of understanding, a hum and a sort of grunt.

"Either way, I can't touch you so—"

"I got it," he cut me off.

We were quiet, and in the silence, the buzz of his cell phone was loud.

He stalked across the room to it and checked the display. Anger flared across his beautiful features as he took the helmet off and tucked it under his arm before answering. "Yes," he said sharply into the phone, and I was surprised that whoever was on the other end was on speaker.

"You can't hide forever, Aaron," the man barked. "And the board is convening in a week to hear the charges."

"All right."

"You're awfully cavalier."

"How would you have me be?"

"I'd prefer that the rumors were true," the man on the other end snarled at Aaron. "That you're a womanizer and not a sodomite."

"Anything else?"

"You will be charged with moral turpitude."

"So you've said."

"You will be removed, and I will be reinstated!"

"Think what you will."

"You should be worried. When you're out, I'll take everything, and you'll be on the street, where men like you belong."

"Men like me," Aaron scoffed. "Whatever. It's not going to happen like that."

"I think you underestimate your own board. Your dalliances undermine the credibility of this company and will no longer reflect poorly on Sutter."

"I assume I'll get a memo of the date and time of this witch hunt?"

"But here's the thing," the man sighed. "This time it's not a witch hunt. This time we have proof."

"Uh-huh."

"Jaden Cobb."

"What about him?"

"He lived with you, and you put him through cooking school after you two broke up."

Aaron sighed. "And you sent someone who scared the crap out of him? You told him things like he'd be responsible for repaying his loan to me with interest or some crap?"

"We did what had to be done."

"That's a yes." He was matter-of-fact.

"Aaron—"

"I wish he'd called me first but… what's done is done."

"You have no idea how much trouble you're in, do you?"

"It's you who's confused. You're playing with fire."

"Aaron—"

His eyes lifted to me. "I'm done hiding from you."

"Son," he began, and you could have knocked me over with a feather. "I—"

"Stop," Aaron ordered him, and I was even more stunned to see he smiled.

I probably looked like a fish out of water, gulping stupidly.

"I'll see you at my trial," he said and hung up.

"That was your father?"

He was delighted with me, with my reaction; it was all over his face. The sparkling turquoise eyes, the curl of his lip: I had done something he liked.

"What's going on?"

"He's going to have me removed from my position as CEO of Sutter so he can take back the position I took from him five years ago."

"Your father used to be the CEO?"

"Right."

"But you booted him."

He waggled his head. "Yes."

"No wonder he's pissed."

"He's pissed because I had the board remove him based on job performance. I'm a better CEO, I'm the better businessman, and I'm the better leader. He would have ruined the company with his continual poor choices; we were well on our way."

"Until you took over."

"Yes. Since I've been in charge, we've had continual growth, a better market share, and business was up 27 percent last year over the previous one, even in this economy."

"Thanks for your résumé."

His smile was instant and blinding, and he crossed the room, tossed the helmet onto a chair, and then bent down over me.

"So," I teased, "will you keep that outfit on when we get back here?"

"I'm not going," he murmured. "My brother's going; he can be the Sutter everyone takes pictures of."

"Maybe you should let him do it all the time," I said thoughtfully.

"I was thinking that same thing myself," he said as he dropped down onto the bed and straddled my thighs.

"Were you?"

"Yeah," he murmured, his hands sliding over my chest. "Like maybe the amount of traveling I've been doing won't really work anymore."

"Why is that?"

His eyes searched mine.

"Tell me."

"I don't want to be away from you for two and three weeks at a time."

"Me neither." I exhaled sharply. "I would miss you."

He cleared his throat as I put my hands on his thighs and squeezed tight. "I was already missing you in that short—"

It took a minute before I realized he wasn't going to say anything else. "Aaron?" He was unsure, and I got that. I lifted my hands to his face and he leaned just enough so I could touch him. "You don't have to hide from me, and you're not the only one feeling it."

"No?"

"No," I promised.

He bent close.

"I have morning breath," I said, but clamped a hand around the back of his neck anyway.

"That's okay," he said weakly and slanted his mouth down over mine.

I had him rolled over onto his back and pinned to the mattress in seconds. He threw a leg over my hip and I grabbed it tight, savoring the feel of the strong muscles cording under my hand as his arms wound around my neck. No doubt about it: I could stay in bed with Aaron Sutter for the rest of my life.

"Oh." He was happy about something.

"What?"

He tipped his head to stare up at me. "Can I take you to lunch, Detective?"

"We can't just stay in bed?"

He studied me.

"What?"

"This is going to sound strange."

I grinned. "I love strange."

"I'd like people to see you with me."

Normally, those words meant the end for me and whoever. I had no idea what it was about me that brought out that need in the men I dated. It was probably flattering, the desire in them to publicly claim me, but I had never thought so. Until now.

Aaron Sutter wanted to basically hold my hand and have other people see it, and instead of being terrified like I normally was, just the thought of it felt right, settled. I really liked the idea of belonging to Aaron Sutter. "Isn't that dangerous for you?"

"I don't know." He seemed confused.

"You're playing with fire with your dad being on the rampage, aren't you?"

"Yeah," he agreed.

"Then why do it? We can hole up here," I said suggestively, waggling my eyebrows.

His eyes searched mine. "Because you deserve to be with someone proud to be with you."

"I think my ex said something similar about himself right before he broke it off with me."

"And now the shoe is on the other foot." Aaron grinned.

"Yes, but neither one of us can be out. Not really."

"Are you sure?"

I was, wasn't I? Or was I just too scared to find out?

"Do you know any other gay policemen on the force?"

"No," I answered, starting to feel cornered.

"But there have to be some."

"Well, yeah, of course."

"Is being gay something you can be fired for?"

"No, but you can be frozen where you are because of it."

"How?"

"Just not be promoted."

"And what is your rank now?"

"We call it a grade, civilian."

He arched an eyebrow.

"I'm a sergeant now."

"And you might never make it to be a lieutenant if you come out."

"Or captain, someday."

"Okay, then," he said, trying to roll away from me.

I held tight.

"Let me go, Duncan."

But I didn't.

"You don't like ultimatums, and I started this whole thing with you, and now—"

"I don't want you to pick someone else," I said bluntly.

He stilled and his eyes met mine.

"Do you get that?"

"Yes," he assured me.

"Then act like it," I said, crushing him with my bigger body, pressing him down until I felt the fight run out of him, and he wrapped me up, arms and legs holding tight.

"I don't want you to sleep with anyone else but me."

"I already promised," I reminded him.

"I know," he sighed, "I just wanted to hear it again."

I lifted off him only to shove his shirt up and kiss down his flat stomach. His breath caught, his hand fisted in my hair, and he shuddered as my mouth closed over the crown of his shaft, which strained to reach me through two layers of cloth.

"Please."

The request was unnecessary.

FIVE

AARON left on Monday morning, which was good because I had to get my game face on and get back to work with Joaquin and the others. It was really difficult to walk out of the suite knowing I wouldn't see him at the end of the day. In that short time, I got used to him and the hotel.

Benny came to pick me up at my new apartment in Joaquin's tricked-out Escalade, and we made the usual rounds. He and Andre both seemed exhausted.

"What the hell's with you guys?"

Andre had his sunglasses on, head back, and Benny, who was driving, had his on as well. But it rained with no bright light from anywhere.

"Party at the Mayan last night," Andre muttered in explanation. "Stop at Starbucks, I need water and coffee."

"My mother wanted me to eat eggs this morning," Benny grumbled. "Fuck me."

They were supposed to be scary. They were drug dealers. But right now they were both simply hung over.

"So what did you do?" Benny questioned me ten minutes later as we rolled up to Starbucks.

"When?"

"This weekend," he clarified. "Me and T rolled by your place, but you were gone. You hole up with some bitch all weekend?"

It was Aaron's fault. The separation was a fresh wound, and I wasn't ready to lie. "No."

"No?" Benny pressed.

"I don't sleep with girls."

Two sets of glasses came off; two sets of bloodshot, narrowed eyes stared at me.

I sat there and waited.

"Okay," Benny shrugged after a moment. "So less of you gettin' in my way. That's cool."

"I don't give a shit," Andre muttered, putting his glasses back on, shoving his phone at me. "Just go get my Venti Quad White Mocha, and that's nonfat, you got it?"

I was confused.

"The phone has my Starbucks card on it."

"I need a Venti Americano, and I want half and half in it, not milk." Benny chimed in.

"One of you guys go. I don't know what any of that shit is."

But since the daystar wouldn't fry me, I got elected. When I was back with their drinks and bottled water and coffee cake neither of them wanted—food bad—Benny explained we had a ton of cash to pick up that morning.

I was sipping my very regular cup of coffee, listening to a traffic report on the radio, when Benny disturbed my thoughts.

"Maybe we don't tell anyone else about you bein' a fag, huh?"

I gave him my attention.

"Yeah, that'd be good." Andre yawned from the backseat. "It might be a problem for some of those guys, and I don't wanna hafta shoot anyone today. I like this suit."

Priorities were important. "Sure," I agreed.

The first three stops were uneventful: just show up, take the money, give the dealer his cut, and walk away. At the fourth one, when we reached the door, it was already ajar and swung wide with just a gentle nudge from the tip of Benny's boot. I saw the blood spray on the walls from where I was behind him and stopped him before he stepped inside.

"Awww, what the fuck," Benny groaned from the doorway, pulling his phone from his breast pocket, as Andre and I tried to see how many guys were dead from the hallway.

"Freeze!"

Of course, the cops were there. Someone had to have called them. At least Benny and Andre had both finished their coffee.

THE question was simple: why were we there? At the police station, each of us got put into a different room with a different set of detectives, and we all said the same thing: we were there to see Pablo Guzman and nothing else.

"You a friend of Pablo's, are you?"

"Sure," I replied nonchalantly, waiting to be attacked with what they thought they knew: I worked for Joaquin Hierra, and Joaquin worked for the Modella cartel, which supplied half of the narcotics in the city.

"What is this, Ross?" Detective Craig asked, holding up a snub-nosed revolver.

I squinted. "I don't know, Detective. I carry a 9mm, as you know from your records."

"You have a permit for that?"

"You know I do."

It was hours before all three of us were standing in front of the police impound yard, waiting for them to bring the Escalade around.

I pointed at Andre. "Your eye is swelling shut, man."

"Fuckin' cops," Benny griped, licking at his cut lower lip. "You ain't looking too much better, Tuck."

I had gotten the elbow to the eye myself by accident, emphasis on the accident part. Not that I wasn't guilty of doing the same to suspects in my custody.

The interrogation had eaten up our day, so I was not surprised we had to work well into the night to catch up. We had a lot of driving to do, a lot of places to visit, a lot of people to see, and a lot of cash to bring back to Joaquin's bar, Jimmy Rig.

Once we were there, one of Joaquin's hostesses led us back toward one of the rooms in the back.

"Why aren't we going to the office or the VIP room?" Andre questioned as a man I had never met before, or even seen, opened the door.

Inside the sparse interior we were led to, a couch had been left vacant for us.

Joaquin stood with five men in the corner, and only then, stupidly, did it occur to me I had not checked in with anyone all day long. I had a 9mm strapped to my side, but I couldn't get to it without risking someone putting a bullet in my head. I was at Joaquin's mercy, and I had walked right into the fire all by myself. I had not done anything quite that stupid in a really long time.

"Get on your fuckin' knees!"

So the couch was actually not for us.

Me, Andre, and Benny were all grabbed by the back of the necks and shoved down onto the cold concrete floor. As I watched, one man separated himself from the others. It only took me a second. I had seen a lot of pictures of Esau Modella; I had just never seen him in real life.

"Apparently we have a cop in our midst," the man in charge of security for the Delgado cartel informed us. "And we're about to find out who that is."

INTERROGATION or torture, it was impossible to differentiate.

The first thing that happened was, I lost track of time. It was tough to tell one day from the next when you were locked in a dark room. It was impressive, really, what Mr. Modella knew about inflicting pain, but being on the receiving end of it, of his ingenuity and patience, was grueling. The worst part of it was they suspected one of the three of us: me, Andre, or Benny. Someone, they thought, had been wired for sound for six months, feeding the feds information. I wanted to point out I hadn't even been with Joaquin for a month, but it came down to the fact that somebody was a cop and the other two knew or were covering. Or only one of us was covering. Mr. Modella didn't know. Joaquin didn't know. But they were determined to break us to find out. What that told me was that either Benny or Andre was on the job. I just didn't know which. As the days slipped by, it was difficult to focus enough to figure it out.

I was beaten unconscious the first day, and then, because they took my watch, it was too hard to figure out how the days bled into each other. It was a kindness my shirt wasn't ripped off so no one saw the stitches, or I was certain those would have been pounded on. Joaquin didn't mention it, but still, occasionally, someone caught me there. It winded me instantly, the acute, splintering pain, and on my drop toward the floor, my face took some more damage.

My left eye was swollen shut, my nose broken, again, and between the piss and blood and vomit, the cell where they kept me reeked. We had been transferred at some point, or I was, having by then lost complete track of Benny and Andre. I couldn't hear the others screaming anymore. I had been proud of myself for not yelling, but when they broke my right arm, I didn't have a choice. The howl was involuntary and loud.

The questions were always the same: Was I the cop? Did I know who the cop was? What had I told him?

They only gave me water, nothing else, and when I saw no one for what felt like days, I thought maybe I had been left to die. My only regret was I had not gotten to live with Aaron Sutter. I would have really enjoyed coming home to him every night.

SINCE standing was no longer an option, I was dragged to an area of a warehouse and thrown down in front of Joaquin and Esau Modella. It was funny to see what appeared to be pain wash over Joaquin's face. We were his men, after all. It couldn't have been good for him to be the one with the weak links.

Andre had been beaten much like me. Benny was worse, and his breathing sounded wet.

"So," Esau said, striding forward. "The only person who has said nothing at all is you, Mr. Ross. Why do you think that is?"

It took me a second to find my voice, since I hadn't used it in however many days. "Because I've only been here a month," I answered him.

"And what have you seen or heard from Benny or Andre?"

Both men were looking at me.

"Nothing," I answered. "Absolutely nothing."

"Unfortunately," Esau Modella said, removing his gun from the holster under his Armani suit jacket and maneuvering around behind Benny and Andre, "that's not the case."

"No!" Benny screamed, and it was high-pitched and fractured before Modella pulled the trigger.

The blast splattered me and Andre before Joaquin moved behind us.

"Oh God." Andre was trembling and looked over at me. "I'm so sorry."

Which was basically a confession.

I gazed up at Joaquin as he pulled the trigger, and I was splattered with more blood the second time since I was closer. Both men were dead beside me.

"And now what?" Joaquin asked Esau.

He tipped his head at me. "Your man saw me. We don't leave loose ends."

"Sure," my fake boss answered and lifted his gun and pointed it at me. "I am sorry."

My eyes fluttered shut. I heard the gunshot, the sound followed by lancing pressure, heat. It felt like it tore open my left shoulder. Maybe all the blood was leaking out of my heart and that's what the draining felt like. Too much to know. Too much to care about.

One regret was not bad, and it was all I had. I wondered if Aaron would track down the truth or just ponder for the rest of his life what happened to me. I really hoped I was worth looking for.

"Shoot him in the head!" The command came, dark and murderous.

"I'm so sorry," Joaquin whispered under his breath.

I couldn't speak anymore. He really needed to just aim. Wounded and bleeding to death was not a good time. Better to just be done.

The bomb going off couldn't even get me to open my eyes and look.

Chapter SIX

I ALWAYS had a strange way of processing trauma. Like when I was eight, my stepfather came at me again. He used to beat the holy crap out of me all the time, but unfortunately, this time, my brother Ian was home from military school where my stepfather had sent him—I wasn't old enough to go yet—and got in the way. I had thought, we both had, that Philip Calloway was letting it go, but he came back with a bat and bludgeoned my brother to death.

He missed me by inches as I bolted out the front door. My mother had covered for the man since I was six and Ian was eleven. But my brother was murdered at thirteen, and in court, when I testified and cried, showed how my stepfather had held me down and punched me, and when the district attorney showed the huge 18x24 blowups of my bruises, it was done. He was charged, found guilty of murdering Ian and attempting to do the same to me. The sentence handed down came to thirty years. He never made it to the execution chamber at Utah State Prison; he had a heart attack and died in his sleep a year after his incarceration. The papers reported it was much too good for him. People who left letters and signs at the prison said it was far too easy an end for him. I, of course, could not have agreed more.

My mother was charged with child abuse, neglect, endangerment, the whole gamut, and sentenced to ten years. The death of any child is horrendous. For a mother to allow the murder of her child and still support the killer was completely beyond the comprehension of the jury. I was informed when she killed herself three years into her sentence. She never apologized or, as far as I knew, expressed even a moment of regret. I did not mourn her passing.

My juvenile records were sealed, and afterward, I went to live with my father and his new family in Detroit, Michigan. My old man was a mechanic and had his own shop. My stepmother, Susan, was a secretary at one of the largest Baptist churches downtown. Both she and my father were extremely religious, but whereas when she caught me doing something wrong, I got a lecture, when my father caught me, he got out his belt.

Henry Stiel's punishments were nothing like my stepfather's had been, and so I simply took them, dealt with them, and moved on. He only beat me when I did something wrong, not for sport. By the time I was the same age as Ian had been when he died, my father had put his belt up for good and simply roared at me and took things away. I had to sleep on the fire escape or go without dinner. The punishments seemed fair.

I learned to be sneaky and lie, and soon, once my two younger sisters hit fourteen and sixteen respectively, everyone forgot about me. I was wild in private; Lydia and Karen were wild out in public. As soon as I could, I signed up for the Army and was off to boot camp a week after graduation.

With my father and stepmother being ultraconservative, having grown up with faggot jokes under Henry Stiel's breath and Leviticus from Susan, I did not come out to them. They sent Christmas cards; I sent one of those Hickory Farms cheese and meat baskets every year. It was the extent of our interaction.

Mostly during the holidays, when I was alone at night after dinners with friends, I thought about my brother and what our relationship would have been like. And while I knew I over-romanticized it a bit, we had been close as kids, even though separated by five years. It was why he had rushed to my defense the night he died. He wasn't about to let me get hurt again.

So, because of losing Ian and all the events that went along with it, because of growing up hiding who I really was, hiding in the Army, losing friends in Iraq and Afghanistan, being a homicide detective and hiding who I was yet again, having two men I knew killed in front of me didn't send me over the edge or spiraling down a rabbit hole. I just went still.

An anonymous tip lead the feds to the warehouse in Hoboken, New Jersey, where they found me alive and Benny Aruellio and Andre Franks both shot in the head. They arrested Joaquin Hierra but Esau Modella got away. I didn't care. The fact of the matter was, through trauma, I was golden. Nothing else mattered.

THE second night in the hospital, I nearly passed out from shock. A man I had not seen in three years came breezing into my room.

"Oh shit." I grinned even though my lips cracked and my nose hurt along with the rest of my body. I felt like I'd been run over by a truck.

He moved fluidly to the side of my bed and took hold of my left hand.

"What the fuck, T?" I breathed out, gazing up at Terrence Moss, who I had been friends with from fifth grade until we graduated. We had even joined the Army together, but he had gone off and become God knew what else, while I had just stayed a grunt.

"You weren't where I left you." The man smiled at me; his eyes glowing. The contrasts were beautiful on him: his dark skin, white teeth, and the bright spring-green eyes. I always mentioned to him he could have done something on a runway instead of shooting people in whatever third-world hellhole he found himself. I knew he had become a mercenary, but there was no record of him anywhere, not even in the Army. I gave up looking, and just accepted I would see him when I saw him.

"You check on me a lot, do you?"

"I do," he said frankly, squeezing my hand and as his gaze ran over me, I got the feeling I looked like absolute crap.

"Oh, it's not that bad."

"Yes, it is," he said, and I saw the furrow of his dark brows.

That fast it clicked. "Anonymous tip, my ass."

He shrugged. "I'm sorry I couldn't save your friends, but the only way to do that was to kill everyone, and that would have meant them as well. Either way… it was a done deal for them."

"They weren't my friends; we worked together. But thank you for my life."

"'Course."

It was his way. He came, imparted some information, normally we had dinner, I got a hug good-bye, and that would be it for another year or four. It was no different this time. He had come to check on me for whatever reason, maybe even a hunch, not found me, and so had searched like only he could. I owed him my life, but he was not there to get an award or be thanked by anyone but me.

"How long was I there?"

"You mean how long did those thugs have you?"

"Yeah."

"Five days."

Huh. "Seemed longer."

"No doubt."

He stayed an hour; walked around the hospital room in that fluid, almost predatory way he had, and finally gave me a number where I could leave a message if I needed him. I laughed because it was so out of character.

"You going soft?"

"What?"

"I mean, really? An actual number?"

He flipped me off, didn't explain how he'd gotten by the police guard at the door, and then left without even a word. It was always like that. I could turn a corner and there he'd be; turn another and be alone. Funny we'd ever even become friends, as different as we were.

He was a soccer star in high school, a track star as well. I played football—defensive lineman—but only well enough to stay on the team, not enough to be drafted. He'd had his own drama at home: his father gambled, couldn't keep a job, and his mother drank. We had gone to his place one day and found his father on the front steps with a note in his hand. T never saw his mother again. What was good, though, was that after his mother left, Terrence's father stepped up and changed. He eventually became a bus driver, until he was killed trying to stop a robbery at the bodega close to their home. It was why Terrence joined the Army with me instead of going to school. He didn't want to be him anymore.

I was not a guy who questioned, and I didn't ask him to stay when he walked out the same way he'd come. I'd see him when he was ready; it wasn't my place to pin him down. He was my friend. It was really the only thing that mattered.

"Detective?"

The officer who leaned into the room, who had not checked with me to see if Terrence Moss could come in, was apparently back from his break—or the bathroom or wherever he had been—and ready to ask me if I wanted to see a Mr. Sutter.

"Please." I swallowed hard, wondering what I was going to say and what all Aaron had been told. Had he dispatched men to check on me, look for me, find out what was going on with me, or not? We were supposed to have kept in touch, but I had been held for five days. As far as he knew, I was just not taking his calls. Or had he been briefed on everything that had happened to me? There was no way of knowing what kind of information money like his could buy.

The question was answered when a version of Aaron, but not Aaron, walked into the room.

"You're the brother?"

"Yes. I'm Maxwell Sutter."

He was beautiful, too, golden like the original. But while Aaron had laugh lines in the corners of his eyes, a swagger to his walk, and a slow, sexy grin, Max resembled a model. Everything was perfect, not a hair out of place. His jacket and tie were perfectly creased, his manicure was shiny, and so were his teeth when he smiled. Really, he belonged in the Hamptons or on a yacht, welcoming guests aboard. Even if you didn't know who he was, you knew he was rich. His very presence screamed good breeding and money.

"Detective Stiel?"

My eyes narrowed as I wondered what in the world he was doing there.

He reached the end of my bed and stared at me, taking all of me in for a moment before he took a breath and began. "I don't know if you know, but my brother is fighting my father for control of Sutter Inc."

I was quiet a minute, sizing up Max before I spoke. "Yeah, I heard."

He cleared his throat and came around the bed. "Well, what started out as something very ordinary, just our father sort of throwing his weight around, has become much bigger."

"Okay."

He moved closer, and between the worry in his eyes, the furrowed brows, and the way he was crossing his arms, I got that whatever he was talking about was a really big deal.

"What did your father do?"

"He got a lot of people to vote their proxy shares."

"I don't know what that means."

"It means, that votes Aaron thought he had, because they would vote the way they always have in the past, are suddenly alive and need to be courted."

"And you're here why?"

"Because there can't be any reason for someone not to be swayed by Aaron," he answered. "It's vital that he not be involved in any impropriety or scandal."

I was tired and hurt, but my brain still functioned. "Your brother could lose the company to your father if anyone finds out about me and him."

"Yes," he said softly.

"Does he know you're here?"

Slowly, he nodded. "Yes, he does. He really wanted to come, but he simply can't. He's doing a charity fundraiser tonight with the mayor and then flying to Brussels tomorrow morning. I'm going with him."

I coughed, which hurt my broken ribs quite a bit. "So when will you two be back in Chicago?"

"I'm not sure," he said and sounded almost sad.

I understood, I did. Me more than most people. Aaron Sutter couldn't be gay any more than I could. It didn't go with the image, with the job, and now there was no reason for me to rock the boat. He was stepping away from me because he had to.

"It's really great you guys are putting up a united front," I complimented him. "Nice that you're on your brother's side."

"He's making me the public face of the company." He beamed at me. "Which he said was something he had talked to you about, actually."

"We were just shootin' the shit." I forced a smile. "I don't have any sway over your brother."

"So you say."

"What about Jaden whatever-his-name-is, your brother's old boyfriend?"

Max made a face as if it was beneath him to mention the guy's name. "Jaden Cobb has been proven a blackmailer. He was found with pictures of my brother and the wife of a married man. Of course, Aaron had to pay to avoid a scandal."

"You mean the appropriate pictures were planted on him to ensure that everyone goes on thinking Aaron is straight."

He nodded.

"I see."

It was nice of Aaron to save his ex, to give him pictures that helped him and removed him from his father's clutches at the same time. I hoped Jaden appreciated it and learned his lesson about who to trust.

"The board is not pleased with my brother's indiscretions, but it's not been proven he's gay. There is no proof."

"Sure."

"But you would be the proof if Aaron saw you, Detective. He seems serious about you."

"Which makes no sense, considering you're here," I said flatly.

"You're missing the point," he assured me.

"I don't think so."

The point was, Aaron Sutter did not want anyone to take pictures of me and him together. He couldn't. I was a cop. My presence in his life could not be explained away. When I had asked him that day about who I would be—a friend, his bodyguard—it had been only semiserious. But I understood, now, that to Aaron, his business had to be paramount. It had to take precedence over our affair, and truly, what had just started was now at an end.

No matter what our conversation had been the last time I'd seen him, the truth was Aaron Sutter was not in any position to step outside the closet. His father had made sure of that with his latest scare tactics. And while it would backfire—Mr. Sutter would not wrest his company from his son—the fact was what I had counted on was not happening either. What either of us wanted was not to be.

"Don't worry," I said to Max. "As soon as I get out of the hospital, I'm on a plane for Chicago. Once I'm home, I promise not to contact your brother again. You can count on me."

He appeared relieved. "I knew I could, Detective. My brother said you were an honorable man."

"Sure" was all I could manage.

"If there's anything I can do for you or—"

"No." I exhaled sharply, closing my eyes. "Now if you'll excuse me, I need to rest."

"Yes, of course. Thank you again, Detective."

"Please make sure you tell Aaron that he can count on me to keep his secret."

"I certainly will."

I heard him leave the room.

SEVEN

IT WAS early—not even eight in the morning—but my partner, Jimmy O'Meara, and I were in River North at an ultraexclusive nightclub called Posh. The upscale establishment, which didn't close until 4:00 a.m., had reported nothing amiss the night before. But when the cleaning crew came in at six, they found a dead man in the john.

"That is new," Jimmy told me as we both walked up to the stall where Ellie Chun squatted beside the man.

"How are you not barfing in there?" I knew she was a trained professional, but still, the smell was overwhelming, and I knew the paper mask she wore did nothing to block out the stench.

"Oh." Her eyes lit up when she pivoted, clearly amused. "Little smell gonna bother the big bad detective?"

I flipped her off, but she expected it, so I got the eyebrow raise and over-the-top cackle right back.

I had been medically cleared for active duty three months after being discharged from the hospital. Two months to fully recuperate and another month to work out, strengthen my body, and build up my left shoulder and my mended right arm. Once I was ready, I had been debriefed, my transfer completed, and I was back in the 18th District working homicide.

It was good to be back, doing the job I normally loved, and even better, to be reunited with my partner, James Vincent O'Meara. I'd left him after the one serious relationship I'd ever had went up in flames. It was too much to handle homicide without someone waiting for you at night, to hold you through the memories of the bad parts of your day. Major crimes wasn't any better, though. The time and effort people took to fuck each other over was painful to see. It had never been a good fit for me, and so I had transferred back to homicide.

Being back full-time—no more undercover stings or task force drama—was necessary, because putting Aaron Sutter out of my head was a hell of a lot harder than I thought it would be. I had counted on spending time with him, getting to know him, and the realization it was not to be was more painful than I'd anticipated. It was, in fact, quite acute. I felt broken, hollow, and usually, work fixed whatever ailed me, gave me purpose. Even after a month on the job, sixteen weeks total of being apart, I could not seem to get over him. The job, which I had always been able to count on in the past, had failed to take his place and make me forget. Worst of all, I was having trouble wrapping my brain around the fact that it wasn't working. At night, alone in my bed, my mind always dredged up Aaron Sutter.

That morning, though, no memory or yearning, nothing could stand up to the odor wafting through the bathroom. I was 100 percent focused because, Christ, the place just stank to high heaven.

"I need a gas mask," I complained to Ellie.

"Or something else to smell," she offered. "Aren't you glad you came back to all this?"

I was. I had missed the part where I got closure for people. And even though I was back, I kept up with the case I had left for.

Riley Evanston, the mob enforcer, faced life without parole and fought extradition to Texas for two murders committed there in 2010. Any deal with him was off the table once Joaquin Hierra rolled on the Delgado cartel instead of facing prison himself. I could testify to Hierra killing Benny Aruellio and DEA Agent Andre Franks, who had been undercover for a little over two years.

Mr. and Mrs. Gibson came to see me in the hospital, and Mr. Gibson held my hand, while his wife and their daughter, Raquel, cried all over me. I had done what I promised, had tracked down the man who killed their son and brother, and Evanston would face the maximum sentence for his crime. The idea that he might be transferred to Texas to die by lethal injection was something the family was sharply divided on. Mrs. Gibson would pay to watch a needle be put into the arm of the man who killed her baby. Mr. Gibson didn't believe in the death penalty, and life without possibility of parole was, to him, justice. I hoped whatever happened to Riley Evanston would not tear their family apart, but I had done all I could. I tracked down a killer, had lived, and so had prevented Joaquin Hierra from getting away with murder. As a result, Esau Modella was a wanted man. Everyone would face judgment; it was simply a matter of time.

For my part, everything had worked out. I had received a commendation—basically for not dying—and I made sure Andre Franks received a posthumous one as well. I gave a statement so his family knew he had done his job.

"Detective?"

Coroner Eleanor Chun was still waiting for me to decide whether I needed Vicks VapoRub. I made my smile big. "I'm good, thanks."

She laughed at me. "Then man up, Stiel. You don't remember when the cat lady died downtown in that loft near Halstead?"

"Oh God." I tried not to gag. "Yeah, all right… that shit was worse."

"Shit," Jimmy snickered as he rejoined us, having gone to check with the officers on site. "That's funny."

"You're a pig," Ellie passed judgment on him.

"You two, separate corners."

"Gotta love homicide," she said cheerfully.

"Shut up," I ordered.

She laughed again behind her mask. "Ask me, already."

"Just wait a sec. What is with that?"

"What are you talking about?"

"I mean, people do shit themselves when they die, but that doesn't always happen, does it?"

"No, you're right," she agreed. "I think our vic here was in the process of going when he was killed."

"Aw, that's just mean." Jimmy sounded repulsed.

"And how was he killed?" I asked her.

"GSW here, to the head," she answered, pointing at his temple for me. "It's a small caliber; I'm guessing a .22 maybe. I'll know more when I get him on my table."

"Anything else?"

"There's what looks like a muzzle burn, contact wound, here on his skin."

"So whoever did it got right up against him."

"Yeah," she agreed.

"Okay." I got closer. "So he's sitting there, pinching a loaf, and someone opens the door, shoves a gun in his face, and fires?"

Her dark brown eyes met mine over the mask she had on. "Yeah, that's what it looks like."

I threw up my hands. "Who leaves the door open when they take a shit at a bar?"

"Oh, you're asking the wrong girl." Her voice dipped low. "I only do my business at home."

"Only?" That was interesting. "How do you manage that? What if you get hold of some bad Italian and get the runs?"

Her face scrunched up. "You go home, Stiel. That's disgusting."

I circled to Jimmy. "Is that disgusting?"

"No." He pointed at the dead man on the toilet. "That is disgusting."

"O'Meara!"

"What?" he groused at her. "It is. Jesus, I need to make captain already."

Ellie and I laughed.

"What?"

"You have no patience," she informed him.

"You're a dick," I further educated him.

We both got flipped off.

"Detective Stiel!" came the call from the outer area.

"Back by the toilets!" I yelled.

"Not something you hear every day," Jimmy wisecracked.

"Nice."

"Well." He arched an eyebrow for me. "It is you we're talking about." And I was given the international sign for blow job, his fist working an invisible cock, his tongue making the sliding motion on the inside of his cheek.

"Charming."

"See," Ellie said, as she too knew I was gay, "that's why you'll never be captain. That's gross, what you just did."

"Awww, lighten up and get laid."

"Stiel!" she complained to me.

"You knew the job was dangerous when you took it."

Her exasperated growl was funny.

I was still amused as we were joined by Robyn Cohen and Seth Benoit, who both gagged and coughed when they reached me.

"Who is this guy?" I queried them both.

"This is Evan Polley." Cohen spoke up first, as was her way. I liked her; she was earnest and thorough. She passed me the victim's wallet, one latex-gloved hand pinching her nose shut. "He's thirty-four, owns—or I should say, owned—Rabbit Run Productions—"

"It's a record label, Boss," Benoit chimed in, fiddling with his own gloves.

"Thank you for that." I smirked.

"No problem."

"Suck up," Cohen muttered under her breath, and because her nose was pinched, she sounded like a cartoon bunny.

"When did anybody last see him?"

"The girlfriend saw him right around twelve thirty last night."

"Time of death?" I inquired of Ellie.

"Between 12:00 and 2:00 a.m."

"Do we like the girlfriend for it?" I checked with the two people who technically worked for me, at least this time out. My grade was higher.

"Probably not." Cohen shrugged. "She was pissed at Polley because he wouldn't get her bar tab, so she ditched him and picked up another guy, Artie Thompson, who would. Lots of people saw her and Artie going at it hot and heavy in the VIP room."

"Why wouldn't he buy her drinks?" Jimmy sounded annoyed. "That's so lame."

"Apparently, Mr. Polley was trying to, and I quote, cut the dead weight out of his life," she read out of her notebook. "End quote."

"And that's from?" I pried.

"His buddy Nick."

"Uh-huh."

"Apparently, Mr. Polley was desperately trying to get his life back in order before he went completely bankrupt," Cohen went on.

"Okay, lemme get this straight. He's poor."

"Yes," Cohen confirmed.

"But he's here at this high-end club last night? That makes no sense."

"No," Jimmy agreed, looking at the two younger detectives. "So what the hell was he doing here?"

"Not sure yet."

"Okay, so the girlfriend...." I trailed off, needing the name.

"Liz Guerra," Benoit supplied.

"Of course he talked to the girlfriend." Cohen rolled her eyes.

"Me too." Jimmy elbowed Benoit. "I always hit up the hot women while Detective Stiel was in the dumpster."

Cohen was grinning at me.

"Don't talk to them like they're people," I warned my partner.

"Oh yeah, true," he said, moving away from Benoit as if he were a leper.

I cleared my throat. "Okay, so Liz is pissed, and were they fighting?"

"Yeah," Benoit nodded. "They were loud, and suddenly Evan is screaming at her that he can't keep up with her spending."

"We have witnesses to that?"

"We do. And that corroborates Mr. McCall's statement about Liz being dead weight that we got from him."

"Do we like this McCall for the murder?"

"No," Cohen explained. "He left with some guy he picked up before midnight."

"Okay." I was piecing it together. "So buddy Nick is gone and Liz is...."

"Off with Artie," Benoit reminded me.

"Got it," I said, filing it away as I made notes in my logbook. "Now tell me about Rabbit Run."

"It's defunct," Benoit answered me; apparently, this was the part he knew about. "According to the same friend of his, Nick McCall, Evan sold the building Rabbit Run was in, and all the studio and engineering equipment, last month and was in the midst of paying off his loans."

"Wait." That made no sense at all. "If he's declaring bankruptcy, why is he paying off loans?"

Benoit waggled his head for me. "Not those kinda loans."

"Oh." I understood. "The kind of loans the bank doesn't give out."

"That's what Mr. McCall said, yes."

"Do we have names of people he owed?"

"No. McCall didn't know and neither did the girlfriend."

I processed it all.

Polley needed money.

What brought in the quickest payday of all?

He was in a bathroom in a club.

Buying?

Selling?

But if the club had a strict no drugs policy… which it did….

"So he needed a big influx of cash to get square with whoever-the-fuck," Jimmy threw out, pale-blue eyes meeting mine. "Why would he be here, then, at one of the most expensive clubs in the city?"

"You know why." I tipped my head toward him.

"Maybe he was networking?" Benoit chimed in. "Maybe he was looking for someone to help him out with another loan."

"His buddy said his credit was so shot no legitimate bank would touch him," Cohen added. "If a bank wouldn't take the risk, then we're talking about somebody less on the up and up that he was trying to wrangle into helping him out last night."

"No." I shook my head because I already knew the answer. "Think about it. He would be trying to pay off his loan any way he knew how, not find someone new to hit up. And if he owed a bad guy a big chunk of cash, then he probably tapped out his friends and everyone else in his social circle. I bet there was nobody else to mooch from."

Walking out of the stall, I crossed to where I saw faucets. There were no sinks, though, just a slanted marble slab. It was tilted downward in the back with a long trough behind it. Strange not to have sinks, but why did I care?

Sometimes my brain works backward. Trying to tell me something, make me think about something—

"Ellie," I said, pivoting, leaning back, and crossing my arms as I gazed at her. "You won't actually know cause of death until you get him back downtown on your table, right?"

"No, but why?"

"I feel like the gunshot wound is just a cover."

She walked out of the stall and fastened me with a look. "Cover for what?"

"Easy." Jimmy followed my train of thought like he always could. "Drug mule."

"Yeah, makes sense, right?"

"It does."

"I'm not following," Benoit complained.

"Think about it," I said, eyeing him. "What scenario would put Polley in this bathroom?"

Everyone stared at me in silence.

"He was hooking up," Cohen offered. "That would explain the door being open."

"He's not gay, though," I pointed out. "If he's straight, he's having sex in the women's bathroom."

"Hey, that's sex—"

"It is not sexist," I cut her off. "There are more stalls in the women's bathroom."

Ellie chuckled. "He's got you there."

"So, no sex but the door is open," Jimmy went on. "Because someone is there to collect."

"And gross as it sounds," I said, thinking as I spoke, "whoever it is wants to see him pull the balloons out of his ass so they can make sure he didn't fuck with anything. They wanna know that whatever they're supposed to get is all there."

"So we need the contents of the bowl as well," Ellie sighed, her gaze dropping to the toilet.

"Yes ma'am."

Jimmy grinned at me.

"I thought homicide was supposed to be glamorous," Benoit grumbled.

"No, that's vice," I assured him. "They have theme music and flashy cars."

Cohen was shaking her head.

"We need a wet vac in here!" Ellie yelled.

Oh yeah, homicide was charming.

IT WAS two days of interviewing people, looking at surveillance video, running down phone numbers and license plates, and talking to the club manager, bartenders, security, and wait staff. We put everything on the board, listed names, ran down leads, scanned pictures, and spent a ton of man-hours cross-referencing events and people from Facebook, following tweets, and checking phone records. It was tedious, and in the midst of it, I realized I really needed to get laid.

I came to that conclusion while questioning Nick McCall. Sitting across the table from him, having just delivered him a cup of coffee with cream, I noticed, more than anything else, the divot under his nose. The fine sheen of sweat above his upper lip, the freckles on the exposed patch of throat, and his collarbone were also a treat. His skin was a sort of warm nut-brown color my own paler version would have contrasted well with if, say, we were naked. He was younger than me, beautiful and hot, and the way he stared at me from beneath his thick lashes, I got the idea that maybe I was a little interesting myself. I was at least appealing in the one-night stand kind of way. It was all I really wanted.

My body, which was now finally healed, but forever altered, was ready to be used or to use another's. Unfortunately, since Nicholas McCall had not been cleared from our suspect list, I couldn't take him up on what he was offering.

"So tell me about the drugs," I said.

His eyes were dark, rich, warm brown and they were locked on mine. "You know about that?"

I'd had confirmation from Ellie, but I knew even before that. Evan Polley was someone's mule, and I needed to find out whose. "I do. Is there any possibility that you have a name for me? That you might have seen him with someone?"

"No," he confirmed but hesitated.

I sat there listening to him breathe, watched him worry his bottom lip. "But?" I led him.

"But," he said, slouching forward, never breaking my gaze. "That's because we really weren't that close for the last couple of years. He got to be the kind of guy that, if you couldn't help him, if he couldn't get something from you, he didn't have time for you anymore."

"Sorry."

"No, it's fine; I got over that a long time ago. But if you really want to talk to someone who knew him, you should talk to Max Sutter. He and Evan have been friends since prep school—I mean, we all have—but Ev, he hit Max up for a lot of cash when the business started bleeding money."

"Okay." I smiled, closing the file and pushing back from the table.

He cleared his throat. "So am I still a suspect, Detective?"

"Until we rule everyone out, I'm afraid so."

"Okay." He sounded disappointed.

"Why?"

His sudden grin was really nice. "You know why."

And I did. Pulling a card from my wallet, I passed it to him. "If you think of anything else, don't hesitate to call me."

He seemed so relieved as he ran the card across his lips. "I won't."

I was up and out of the room seconds later.

Once I was back at my desk, I called Cohen and relayed the message for her and Benoit to go talk to Max Sutter.

"He's just going to lawyer up."

"Maybe not. Just go see what he knows."

"Shouldn't it be you and O'Meara?"

"No," I said, making sure there was a tone in my voice that let her know she was not allowed to question me.

"On our way."

I grunted and hung up.

"You sent them to bother the rich people, didn't you?" Jimmy solicited from his desk across from mine.

I waggled my eyebrows.

"That's a dick move."

"I care."

"They're just gonna crash up against the lawyer wall."

"Probably. Let's eat."

"You're buying," he informed me.

"If I buy, I get to choose."

"As long as we don't have to go to that same hot dog—no." He sounded serious. "I'm not twenty-two anymore. I can't eat ground up—D! Are you listening to me?"

I wasn't. Didn't he get it? Bad cop food was part of the gig. "What cops eat salads? Do you know any?"

"Do you have any idea what my cholester—D!"

But I was out the door before he could say anything else.

IT WAS never easy. Nothing ever was.

My phone rang as I shoved a chili dog piled high with sauerkraut into my mouth. Jimmy was revolted and shook his head as I answered.

I made a sound of greeting since my mouth was full.

"Duncan."

The voice sent a roll of heat through me that was surprising. How was I still having a reaction to the gravelly voice of Aaron Sutter? Why did my breath hitch, my stomach drop, and why on earth was my body flushing cold right after burning up with no problem at all? What the hell was with that?

"Aaron," I managed to choke out.

"I need to speak to you."

"About?"

He coughed. "Max called to tell me that your detectives were at his townhouse wanting to talk to him."

"And did they?"

"Yes."

"And was he helpful?"

"I believe so."

"Okay. I'm confused, then. Why the call?"

He cleared his throat. "I was annoyed that you hadn't bothered to show up to speak to him when I learned you were the lead detective on the case."

"Yeah, but—"

"And then Max said, 'Oh no, Duncan would never come to my home or yours.'"

I made a noise of agreement.

"Duncan," he said my name coldly. "Not Detective Stiel. But just Duncan, like you two are old friends."

"Yeah," I said dryly. "We're not friends."

"But Max was just so sure you would never show up at his home, let alone mine."

"No, of course not," I agreed, annoyed suddenly. As though I were not a man of my word. Who did he think he was talking to?

"Of course not," he repeated.

Long silence that I wasn't sure what to do with. "Aaron?" I finally said to check if he was still on the phone.

He inhaled deeply.

"What's this all about?"

"Well, it seems that you and Max both saw this as a foregone conclusion."

"You lost me."

"The fact that you would never come to my home; apparently, both you and my brother were certain it was impossible."

"Right. I would never. I told him to tell you that. I promised him and I promised you."

"I see."

"I would never put you in that spot. It would be reckless and selfish and—"

"But I didn't know that."

"I'm sorry?"

He cleared his throat. "I said, I didn't know that."

"Didn't know what?"

"That you and Max had spoken," he said, clipping his words. "Because you see, I, unlike you and Max, was not privy to that conversation. I wasn't part of that decision."

I got up and walked away from the food truck where I had been standing with Jimmy. "Listen, in the hospital, I—"

"You were in the hospital?"

"You know I was. You just—"

"That's why you didn't call."

"No," I flared. "I didn't call because I was held for five days, and I took a bullet, and had my arm broken and then I was in the hospital, and—"

"You were held?" His voice cracked.

"Aaron," I said gently. "We don't need to—"

"And someone broke your arm?"

"Aaron—"

"You were shot?"

"Why are you—"

"So let me get this straight. You were detained, bones were broken—"

"It was just my—"

"A bone was broken," he amended, "then shot, and then in the hospital. Do I have the sequence correct?"

"Well, yeah, but you have guys that could have reported all that back to you if you wanted. I mean, I get that you were busy fighting your dad and trying to keep him from taking away your company and everything else. You didn't have time to check on—"

"Stop," he ordered. "I was waiting for a call, and then I was pissed, and now I'm something else altogether."

"Yeah, but you don't hafta be anything. Everything's fine. Our timing was just crappy, and—"

"Duncan."

"No, come on, Aaron. We still can't be seen just hanging out. Your little brother was just looking out for your best interests because that's how he—"

"Duncan!"

"It's fine. I get it."

"You don't get anything, and neither does he!"

"But it's been a while, so—" I exhaled sharply. "—water under the bridge, right?"

Silence.

"Aaron?" I was shifting from one foot to the other, anxious but not understanding why.

"So the day my brother came to the hospital… they just let him in?"

It was a weird topic change. "What?"

"You were recovering, were you not?"

"Well, yeah."

"And the police just let my brother in to see you, opened the door right up for him?"

"No, of course not."

"Right." Quick sigh. "So that's my question. He was announced. They asked you if he could come in."

"Yes."

"And you thought what?"

"I don't get what you're trying to—"

"You thought that Max was there to see you or that I was there to see you?"

"What?"

"You're not dense, so stop pretending to be." His anger was there in his voice. "I don't like it, and I don't appreciate it. Answer the fucking question!"

"Aaron—"

"Answer!"

"They said Mr. Sutter was there to see me," I said flatly.

I heard him inhale. "And you thought it was me."

"Yes."

"Okay. Now this part is important. When you thought it was me, what did you think?"

No way was I answering.

"Duncan?"

"What?"

"Don't," he warned. "Don't hedge, just say."

"It was a long—"

"It wasn't. Speak."

"I'm not your dog that—"

"No. You don't get to pick a fight to deflect me either. Answer."

"This isn't important."

"I assure you, it's critical."

"Just—"

"Tell me now," he demanded.

"Aaron—"

"Duncan," he said my name sounding suddenly breathless. "What. Did. You. Think?"

I shook my head even though he couldn't see me.

"Please," he pressed me.

"Fine, whatever. When I thought it was you coming in, I was happy. That's stupid to even ask me!" I retorted, angry at him for making me go back and think about it. "Yeah, I wanted to see you; I was fucking dying for it. Does that get you off, make you hard?"

"You're an idiot!"

"Fuck you!" I yelled.

The call ended abruptly, and I was left to stare at my phone.

When I walked back to Jimmy, he seemed confused. "Everything all right?"

"It's fine," I growled.

"Yeah, it sounds peachy."

I flipped him off, and we at least made sense.

After lunch I went with him to talk to a couple of witnesses from the party, who both put themselves across town at the time of the murder. Back at the station, I made calls, checked their alibis, and then added them to the growing case file filled with dead ends.

I was going through the surveillance video from the club again when Jimmy's throat clearing made me glance up. He tipped his head, and I saw Cohen and Benoit leading Maxwell Sutter back toward the interrogation rooms. He had a man with him in a bespoke suit, topcoat hanging over one arm, a briefcase in his other hand.

"Oh, he lawyered up fast," I groused at my partner.

"Yeah, he did," Jimmy agreed. "They must have—oh."

My attention went back to Jimmy, who wasn't focusing on me but instead on Cohen as she crossed the room to me.

"Hey," she began. "Max Sutter says he's only talking to you."

"Sure." I gave her a trace of a grin and got up to follow.

"There's a mob of reporters outside," Benoit relayed when he joined us. "TV, newspaper, magazine—you name it, there's somebody out there."

"Have his driver come around back to where the jail transport normally picks up."

"Will do."

"Let's get Max back out of here without any pictures."

"We'll do our best."

"No," I insisted. "Not our best. Let's just make it happen."

"Yes," they both answered at the same time.

It was strange how the sounds bounced off the walls in the hall, how I noticed the cracks in the concrete floor, the rust on the vents, and the chipping paint on the doors. On the walls, I saw the framed pictures of police academy graduating classes, Medal of Honor winners, and the current police commissioner and various other officers. All the things I normally passed without notice suddenly came into sharp focus as I was reminded how much I still missed Aaron Sutter.

In the room, I took a seat across from Max Sutter and his lawyer. I didn't even glance at the little brother; my attention went first to the lawyer.

"Vaughn Holtz of Holtz and Maitland," he said as he eyed me.

"Okay."

"Against my better judgment, my client wants to share with you what he knows about the incident in the club, Detective, but I need—"

"No," Max cut him off, and I saw him take a shuddering breath.

"Max—"

"No!" he informed Mr. Holtz, staring at one of the best trial lawyers in the city, as well as probably the most expensive. "I'm innocent, but I have a name for him, and I need to do this before I'm completely disowned by my brother."

I couldn't focus on the words; only Max was important. And I thought good things about him. He was a stand-up guy, and also, he looked good in a suit. The way whatever designer he was wearing fit— the jacket accentuating the breadth of his shoulders, the way the sleeves rose to reveal the silver monogrammed cufflinks, and the pale-blue shade against his golden skin—all of it was stunning. But he was not his brother, and so even dressed up, he was a poor substitute once you had seen the original.

I got why Max couldn't really be the Sutter brand. Something was missing.

Max was so very pretty, but the smirk wasn't there, the rakish tip of the head, the wicked gleam in the eyes made even more noticeable by deep laugh lines and dimples. Max's hair fell forward into his face; Aaron's only did that after he'd been tumbling around in bed for a while. Even sitting completely still, Aaron radiated a sort of crackling vitality Max simply didn't have. Yes, they were brothers, but people wanted to be in business with the mover, with the shaker, with the man who kicked down doors and knew how to wheel and deal. Max was not the dealmaker; his big brother was.

"Me and Nick McCall and Lance Madison all went into business with Evan Polley."

"You guys all went to school together?"

"Yeah. We did. First Exeter and then Yale."

"And you all put money into Rabbit Run."

"Yes."

"How much?"

"Two hundred and fifty grand each."

Jesus. "And?"

"And nothing. Evan didn't do anything to build the business. I mean, he talked a good game, and it seemed like he was wheeling and dealing, but nothing came of it. He signed no one, no records were produced, and when he finally got a break with a really promising singer, he found that between what he put up his nose and what he spent on partying, he had nothing left over to launch a career with."

"Who was that?"

"Jenna Tate."

I knew the song. Her song. The one about the man who had beat her and left her pregnant and alone. It was a good song about finding your own power and love and doing what was hard because it was right. It had become an anthem against domestic violence and about the joy of motherhood. But it was also about respect and the right guy, and so with all of that, the song and the video had gone platinum and viral.

"Who is she with now?"

"Capitol Records."

"Good for her."

"Yes."

"So what did he do?"

"Like I said, absolutely nothing. He partied and made promises, and when Lance finally found his own calling in gay porn, Evan wanted nothing to do with it."

"So Lance did what?"

"Lance got his money back from Evan and used it to start his own company, Fielding James."

I had actually been on his site and seen Lance Madison's idea of porn. It was one of the classiest ones I had ever come across. His webmaster was gifted, and the guys who worked for him were all toned and gorgeous ideals of male beauty. I wasn't into rape fantasies or bondage or fetish gear, and his site had none of those ads or pop-ups. It was just straightforward categories of college-age guys fucking: no role playing, no bad acting, no fake scenery, scary outfits, or poorly engineered mood music. Every video showed two guys, sometimes three, a clean bed, laughing, touching, kissing, and lots of hot, sweaty sex. The man definitely knew what he was doing.

"And so?"

"So Lance started making serious money, but when Evan needed some, he refused to help him."

It was understandable. "So Evan hits you up next."

"No. He went to Nick."

"Nick McCall."

"Yes."

"And?"

He shrugged. "Nick couldn't make a go of his chain of sports bars, and once his entire trust fund was gone, he went to work for his father. They buy companies and then turn around and sell them off, either outright or in pieces."

"What about the money Nick gave Evan?"

"He's out that, just like I am."

"And neither of you need it back?"

"It's business," he said frankly.

"Okay," I sighed. "So after Evan gets nowhere with Nick, he comes and knocks on your door."

"Yes."

"And what did you say?"

He fell back in his chair. "I don't have money that's just mine, Detective. I mean, I have my trust fund, but it's locked up until I'm thirty."

"So how did you get the money to give Evan to begin with?"

"I borrowed against what's mine."

"From a bank?"

He shook his head. "No, from my brother."

"Aaron gave you the two hundred and fifty thousand dollars."

"Sure."

"And he didn't care what you did with it?"

"No. Why would he?"

Rich people. It was beyond me. I leaned forward. "Okay. So walk me through this. Evan's gone through his own money, yours, and Nick's."

"Yes."

"Lance was smart enough to get his back before the ship sank."

"Yes."

"And then what?"

"Okay, so then Evan needs money because he borrowed some from people who weren't his friends, and they want it back like now."

"And who's that?"

"I don't know who he borrowed from." He shook his head. "He wouldn't tell me. But he was really scared."

"Okay, then what?"

"Well, then he's gone, and I was worried and thinking the worst, you know, but then he suddenly shows up."

"Just like that."

"Yeah."

"And?"

"And the last time I saw him, he told me he was in real trouble, but that he had met someone who was going to throw him a lifeline. He said this guy was saving his life."

"Does this good Samaritan have a name?"

"Yeah. Clay Wells."

I had been taking notes and made a line for the brand-new name. "And do you know him? Does he travel in your social circle?"

"Not in mine. His money's too new. But he has a place in the Hamptons, and Evan took me there with him for the weekend."

"Drugs?"

"Drugs were just the tip of the iceberg. That weekend was insane. I mean, whatever debauchery you can think up, Detective, it was there. You could have it."

"Okay."

"And then Sunday night, he flew us to Vegas on his private jet, and we were there as his guests for a week."

"Okay. So while you were with Evan and this guy Clay, did you see any drugs change hands?"

"No. But Evan made a big production of saying that he had an even smaller plane than Clay's that belonged to his father's business but was his to use whenever he wanted."

"And so since you're not stupid, you got that he was offering to transport drugs."

"Yes."

I made some more notes. "So Evan started doing this that weekend?"

"Pretty sure."

"And this was when?"

"About a year ago."

"Did you hang out with him after that?"

"No, not really. As you know, my father and my brother were waging a war for the business. The first part of it is settled, but my dad wants Prentiss—he's another of my dad's sons—to take over Sutter now that the board has informed him that they unequivocally will not reinstate him."

"But Aaron makes the board and the investors' money," I couldn't help but remark. "There's no way they hand over the reins to someone brand-new."

"That's true, but a protracted legal battle would still be wearing on everyone."

"Sure," I agreed, because it was easy. "So you've been with your brother, which means that Evan Polley's drama was sort of lost on you."

"Yes."

"But your belief is what?"

"I think Clay Wells murdered Evan because he either didn't want to move the drugs anymore, or he thought he had done enough for Clay to be paid off. I'm not sure. I don't know how much of Evan's debt Clay took care of, but I do know that the drugs themselves were what killed him." His eyes locked on mine. "They were, weren't they?"

"Yes, they were," I told him because Ellie had confirmed it for me the first day. "Evan Polley was shot post mortem. He was killed by an overdose of uncut cocaine in his system."

"I figured it was something like that."

"Okay."

"Okay?"

I closed the file. "I think we're good, unless you have something else to tell me."

"No."

"Are you sure?"

He nodded.

"All right. Thank you so much for coming in."

"I don't feel like I've done anything."

"You gave me a name to run down, and you gave me the how with the plane. You've been a great help."

His eyes searched mine. "He's so angry with me."

I was not about to get into anything else with him. "Mr. Sutter—"

"I thought he'd appreciate what I tried to do, but he didn't, and now he's just so mad."

"That's all the time we—"

"Please could you go out to his house and talk to—"

"I can't," I shut him down. "I have no time at all."

Funny that he almost seemed hurt, but I went into hyper-efficient mode and got up, walked out the door, and barked for Cohen and Benoit.

Max came out of the room and started down the hall after me, but there was suddenly a swarm of uniforms behind him and a heavy jacket was thrown over his head before he could even react.

"What the hell is—"

"We have you, Mr. Sutter!"

He was grabbed by two officers and rushed down the corridor in a crowd of patrolmen, lost to the eye, which was the whole point. He was carried along by the sea of men toward the back stairs that led to the transport bay. Mr. Holtz shook my hand, thanking me for keeping him out of sight.

An hour later, after I was done adding information to the file as well as to the board that Jimmy, Cohen, Benoit, and I worked off of, I put both my minions on tracking down the plane and ran a record search on Clay Wells. My phone rang when I was waiting for information to pop up on my screen. "Stiel," I answered on the second ring.

"Tell me why you're doing a record search on Mr. Wells, Detective."

"I'm sorry, who is this?"

"This is Special Agent Carlene Summers with the FBI, Detective Stiel, and I need to know why you are looking into Clay Wells."

"We—"

"Now."

I cleared my throat. "We believe he either killed or had killed a drug mule of his on Saturday night."

"Oh?"

"Yes. Why?"

"I think you need to come see me, Detective. Do you know where the field office is?"

"Unfortunately, yes," I groaned.

"Oh, look here. Four months ago, you were with us on the Delgado task force in New York."

I grunted.

"Well now, Detective, have you ever considered a career with the Bureau?"

I made a noise in the back of my throat. "When do you want me there?"

"Now, Detective. Right now."

Shit.

Chapter EIGHT

MY CAPTAIN went with Jimmy and me to the Federal building to have a long talk with Special Agent Carlene Summers. She knew all about Clay Wells. She even let us listen to the chatter on the line of where he ordered one of his guys to go to Posh and deal with Evan Polley, who was freaking out because he felt strange. The next phone call was the guy calling Mr. Wells back.

"Due to unforeseen circumstances, a nonscheduled package has burst. Please advise."

"Repeat."

"A package that did not appear on the manifest has burst, sir, please advise."

"An extra?" Wells sounded surprised.

"Affirmative."

"Our cargo was not affected."

"No, sir, our packages are in transit."

"But the other has burst."

"It has. We await instruction."

He cleared his throat. "Alter delivery confirmation to suspend tracking."

"Affirmative."

I looked at Agent Summers. "That's Wells's guy shooting Evan Polley in the head."

"Unfortunately, yes."

"So then what we thought was wrong. Polley wasn't a mule."

"No," she shook her head. "He *was* a mule, just not the kind that normally shoved uncut cocaine up his own ass. He used a plane to move drugs for Clay Wells."

"But he got greedy and tried to make a little extra on the side."

"Yes."

"So you think what? Evan Polley died of a cocaine overdose?"

She sighed deeply. "No guess, Detective. We know from that brilliant recording you just heard, and I'm sure that your coroner already confirmed cause of death, did she not?"

"She did."

"And?"

"And, like you said, he OD'd and then got shot in the head to cover it up."

Her eyes never left mine. "Let's stop the second-guessing, Detective. You can safely assume that I know everything you do."

"But that's not quite true is it?"

"In what way?"

"Well, you guys didn't find Polley."

"We had no idea there was even a connection between Wells and Polley before two days ago. Obviously, we knew someone was dead, we just didn't know who."

Which made sense. "And of course, even Wells giving those vague orders on your wiretap doesn't give you anything to arrest him on."

"No, it doesn't."

I absorbed what she'd said and then made the next logical jump. "So are you sending someone in undercover to try and take Polley's place?"

"We can't."

"Why not?"

"The timeline is too tight."

"I'm sorry?"

"Mr. Wells lost a courier this week, and he needs a new one."

"Right."

"Well, he can't wait, and we don't have time to build a backstory and create a whole fictional identity in the time we have."

"Do you know what's going to happen?"

"Yes. Mr. Wells will fly to Las Vegas tomorrow night, and from the high rollers at the parties he attends, he'll pick out some candidates to go into business with."

"Then what?"

"And then he'll invite them back to the resort he owns in Sedona."

"Why can't you just put in surveillance at that resort? Catch him making a deal to move his product?"

"Because entry to the resort is by invitation only," she reiterated.

"No, I'm not talking about some rich guy he's looking to go into business with. I'm talking about a contractor or—"

"Wells has a private company that takes care of all the maintenance and security at the resort, and everyone who works there lives on site."

"What?"

"He's covered all his bases, Detective, there's no way to move people off and on the property."

"Okay, so you're saying really the only way in is by partying with Wells in Vegas and getting an invite."

"Yes, that's exactly what I'm saying."

"So you plant someone in Wells' path. What's so hard?"

"Like I said before." She was terse. "We don't have time. He's going back to Vegas this weekend already."

"But you could put—"

"He handpicks from the wealthiest, most powerful men, Detective, and everyone knows who those people are and what they look like."

I had to think. "So tell me about it."

"It?"

"The resort."

"We don't really know. Supposedly, it's Xanadu. It's Sodom and Gomorrah. It's whatever exotic, depraved wet dream you can think of. Apparently, the security and everything else is top of the line. They have military grade signal scramblers, and no electronics of any kind are permitted on the grounds. Everything remains at the gate."

It sounded like Wells had thought of everything.

"From what little we've been able to find out, they have facial recognition software on site and trap and trace on every incoming and outgoing phone line."

"Jesus," Jimmy muttered under his breath.

"No cameras, no phones… nothing."

"So you can't reach your people once they're inside."

"Exactly."

"And from what you're telling me, you have no play."

"Exactly. We would need to get someone invited in. Then he, or she, can insinuate themselves into Wells's group, and we can see if he asks that person to either take over the drug business or help bankroll it."

"It sounds like you have a golden opportunity right now to get someone in there."

"In theory, yes. But the problem is that you can't just create rich people out of thin air. Fabricating a background, planting media stories, and inserting fake information, all of that takes time, and really, with his resources, there's no way of knowing how easy it would be for him to discover the ruse."

I had a terrible idea. "What if we could get one of Evan's friends to go in undercover? That would make sense, right? I mean, they would have seen Evan getting paid, and Mr. Wells would have seen all of them."

"Yes. That would be brilliant, but you can't just ask a civilian to step into a dangerous situation. It's not something we do."

"It is," I contradicted her. "I know that it might not be standard operating procedure, but you do make rare allowances for one-offs if there's no other choice."

"Yes. We would make an allowance if there was an undercover detective present to protect them."

The room exploded.

Jimmy was not having it; I had a bad habit of getting shot.

Captain Gaines apparently liked me more than I thought. She wasn't having it either. She actually needed homicide detectives in her homicide department.

But neither of them had the clout and position that the special agent had. Twenty minutes later, it was just her and another agent in the room with me. My partner and my boss had been excused to the hall to wait.

"So you're thinking what?" She queried me. "Bodyguard?"

"I would think so. Or… do you know what Mr. Wells's take on gay is?"

"Better than bodyguard." She was blunt. "If you and another man went in as a couple, that would put him more at ease. The bodyguard thing would be a harder sell."

"Okay. Then let me talk to Evan's friends. Let's see if Nick McCall or Max Sutter will step up."

Her eyes were locked on mine. "Are you certain about this, Detective?"

"Who else can do it?"

She was silent.

"I mean, do you have an undercover agent to spare?"

"Honestly, no. Not that I can even get them up to speed in the timeframe we have."

"Well, then."

"You've already been vetted, Detective. If you can get some solid citizen to sign a waiver, we're good to go."

I had my marching orders.

MAX didn't pick up, so I left message on his phone, explained that I was going to try Nick next, and stressed the urgency of his returning my call.

I got my first choice for an undercover partner on the second ring and was deeply relieved. "Mr. McCall."

"Just Nick, Detective," he slurred, his voice thick like he'd been drinking. It was only six, but I guess he'd had a day.

"I need to speak to you; can I stop by your place?"

"I'm actually out. Did you want to come by Duck & Cover and pick me up so we could talk?"

"That would be great."

"Yes, it would," he murmured. "I'll be waiting."

My initial plan was to go home first, shower and change before I went and pitched my idea to Nick McCall, but I needed to talk to him before he did any more drinking.

I took a cab downtown toward Rush, the street Duck & Cover was on, and the driver dropped me off at the light a block from the restaurant/lounge. The place was new and trendy and loud, without any really good food that I knew of so, because I was hungry, I was disappointed. I needed to eat, but I wanted something good. A big, fat porterhouse sounded like heaven, or some good Italian, but I would have neither, and so walking in, I was grouchy.

Spotting Nick across the room where he was sitting at a table with three other men and a couple of women, I realized it might be more of a challenge to extricate him then I had first thought.

When I neared the table, he lifted his head and saw me. The smile I got was nice. "Detective." He exhaled long and deep when I was looming over him. "It's really good to see you."

I smiled back but realized suddenly what I had found alluring earlier no longer was. Or at least not for me. It was a problem I had been experiencing a lot lately: my complete and utter disinterest in any man who was not Aaron Sutter. I really needed to get the fuck over it.

"Let me introduce you."

So I stood there and met people I didn't give a crap about, not memorizing names, not even bothering to catalog them. Being as I was a cop, things stuck if I wasn't careful. Trained to recall details, see faces and memorize them, remember the smallest tidbits of conversation, I had to make sure I focused only on Nick.

"So can I—"

"Sit down and have something to drink. We're celebrating."

"What's the occasion?" I inquired but didn't move.

He didn't answer. Instead, he stood up and faced me. "We can get out of here, Detective. It doesn't look like you want to talk."

"Oh? What does it look like I wanna do?"

"Get laid." He grinned and it was sloppy, like he wasn't in complete control of it. He'd had more than I thought. "I can help you with that."

It didn't matter. We would go back to his place and fuck, and I would explain what I really needed. "Okay, come on. Say g'night to your pals."

He wheeled around and gave them all a quick wave before he was facing me again. "Lead on."

Outside on the sidewalk, I realized my phone was on death's door.

"Hey, I gotta run home and grab my charger really quick."

"I will follow you home, Detective." He leered at me, his eyes making the lap up and down my frame.

"Okay," I said, taking hold of his hand and walking toward the curb.

He squeezed tight. "That's, uhm, nice."

I glanced over my shoulder. "Holding hands?"

"Yeah." He shivered. "Most guys—don't."

And I was one of them. I normally didn't either. Not in public. It was funny he was thinking I was one of the good guys when that was not the case at all.

In the cab, he didn't let go of my hand, and at my place, I had the driver wait as I got out.

"Can I come up with you?" Nick questioned, holding the door open.

His eyes were blustery, so I relented. On the sidewalk in front of the stoop that led up to the security door of my loft, Nick recaptured my hand, lacing his fingers into mine.

"I need to talk to you about something important."

"Whatever you want."

So many people walk around who, from the outside, appear strong and capable and normal. But when you get up close—when you talk to them, listen to them—you realize they're broken. I had no idea until that moment Nick McCall was the kind of guy who was ready to dive into the deep end with the first person who seemed like they wanted to keep him. It terrified me that he was so fragile. If I took him on this scary undercover adventure with me, he would be mine afterward, and I wasn't ready to take possession of him. I didn't want him to belong to me.

"Hey." I made my voice gentle, reaching out right before the door closed. The cab wouldn't have to wait after all. I was putting Nick right back in. "I think maybe you better go home and sleep off whatever you took."

His eyes widened. "How did you know I—"

"I'm a police detective, you know."

He was scared as he pulled his hand away from me.

"I'm not gonna bust you for whatever," I apprised him. "But promise me you'll go home and not back out."

He coughed. "You don't want me to come up?"

"Not tonight," I said, holding the door for him.

As he got back in, I leaned over and gave the cabbie two twenties. "Just not back to where you picked us up."

I got the head tip from him but nothing from Nick; he ignored me completely. Watching them drive away, I wasn't quite sure how I felt. What was really screwed up was that the only option left open to me was Max. Hopefully, I could talk him into it.

"Detective Stiel."

I turned to find a vintage Lincoln Town car parked across the street on the opposite curb. There was a man there, leaning against it. It was gorgeous, the car; definitely someone's baby. It was in mint condition.

"Yes?" I called over to him, wary because the driver was not small. He was my age, maybe even a little older, but he was massive in comparison. Another huge red flag was using my name and me having no clue who he was.

"My boss would like a word."

"And who's that?" I didn't panic or reach for my phone or my gun. I was waiting to see if he was an actual threat or not.

"Mr. Sutter." He gave me a trace of warm eyes with crinkling laugh lines around them. "He's upstairs in your loft."

It was the best news I'd heard all night. Max Sutter had come to me. Now that Nick was out, I would need to convince the younger Sutter to help me. And yes, he'd have to pretend he was sleeping with me, but I was hoping he would be willing to try and pull that off for the greater good and to avenge his old friend.

"Thank you," I acknowledged the driver before vaulting up the steps and going inside. I was surprised to see the man get in the Lincoln and pull away.

Upstairs in my loft, I made sure to announce myself when I walked in, calling for Max as I shut the door behind me and locked it. "Must be nice to be rich," I snickered, hanging up my topcoat, then the suit jacket underneath, before loosening my tie. "People just let you— Max!"

He came up from behind and drove me face-first into the living room wall.

"What the hell are you—"

"Not Max, you stupid ass."

Aaron.

And Aaron apparently in great need, as evidenced by the hard groin shoved against my ass, the hands tearing at my clothes, and the knee wedged between my thighs.

"Get off me," I ordered weakly.

"Fuck no."

He sounded frustrated and mad and, God, it was sexy.

I flattened my hands on the exposed brick and dropped my head forward, struggling to stay still and not turn and ravage him. He tugged my shirt out of my pants and lifted it, and the T-shirt underneath, up between my shoulder blades.

"What are you—Aaron," I croaked out, because his mouth was on my skin, open and wet, sucking, tasting and kissing, and it was all I could do not to beg him for anything and everything all at the same time.

"I want you," he said flatly, his front pressed all along my back, arms suddenly tight around my abdomen, lips at the nape of my neck. "And I know you want me."

"Oh yes," I agreed, my cock already painfully hard even before his hands slid down my stomach, dropping lower to my belt buckle. His intent was deliberate, and everything was unzipped and loosened, the whole works shoved to my ankles at once.

When one strong, long-fingered hand wrapped around my shaft, I jerked back against him, shuddering just from the feel of him, of the possessiveness and dominance. "Hurry."

"Who have you slept with since me?"

It would sound like I had been waiting, but I couldn't help that. "No one."

"No one?" he repeated, stroking my leaking dick with his right hand, the other lifting up under my shirt to my nipple. When he pulled first gently, then harder, rolling my sensitive skin between his fingers, I let my head fall back onto his shoulder. "In four months?"

"No. Can't you tell?" I ground out; because just the reaction, the welling lust and need, should have told him I was telling the truth.

"I can," he assured me, his teeth tracing down the cord on the side of my neck, making my knees wobble. "And so you know—no one else for me either."

I cricked my head to look him in the eye. "That says something, doesn't it?"

"It says everything," he promised, pulling back, letting me go.

I spun and had my back against the wall I'd clung to, abrading my shirt, not caring that it snagged.

We stood there, staring at each other.

"What the fuck was Nick McCall doing in front of your place?"

"It's about work."

He was furious with me, and it was there on his face, the anger and jealousy.

"I wasn't gonna fuck him."

"No?" he challenged, advancing on me, brows furrowed, jaw clenched.

"I put him in the cab. Weren't you watching?"

"I was watching," he said, staring at me with raw, wounded eyes.

It hurt to see him like that, vulnerable and aching, simmering with rage, all at the same time. I wouldn't let him stand there alone, and so reached for him.

He lunged at me, and I realized he was not going to let his rage go, wasn't going to just melt into my arms, so I twisted my head away. This was not the Aaron I remembered—instead a cold, angry lover.

The growl that came out of him was full of frustration as he caught my jaw, his teeth grazing my skin. "Duncan!"

I didn't look at him, and when he moved to the other side, wanting my mouth, I tipped my head away again.

"Kiss me!" The demand was aggravated and desperate and sounded like fear to me.

"I'm not going anywhere," I soothed him, though still refusing to meet his gaze.

"Duncan!"

His voice shook and I saw that I was right. He was terrified.

"Look at me!"

When I did, he leaned in and his teeth closed on my bottom lip. He bit down, the guttural snarl not from the gentle man I knew. Our time apart, that had left me feeling unsettled and ungrounded, had done something darker to Aaron, and now he was frantic to reclaim it.

Everything about him was spoiling for a fight, and it was my place to soothe away the uncertainty in his head that I could hear and see. Wrapping him up tight, I used strength I had never shown him before and crushed him tight to my chest.

"Duncan!"

"Stop," I whispered, bending to kiss him.

"Let go."

"That's what you really want?"

With his arms pinned to his sides, all he could do was tip his head up and meet my gaze.

"Aaron?"

Eyes rimmed in red were locked on mine.

"It's okay," I gentled him, grinning as I tipped my head to seal my lips down over his.

He pushed up, his tongue sliding into my mouth, and I met him eagerly, deepening the kiss so I could taste him.

The first led to another and another, and then he shuddered and I lifted back just enough, my lips still hovering over his. "Let it go."

He exhaled softly, and I released his arms, smiling as he coiled them around my neck. "You think you know me so well."

"Yeah," I growled, rubbing down his sides, to the small of his back, and finally grabbed hold of his beautiful, round ass. When I squeezed tight, he arched into my touch. "I do."

He nuzzled his face into the side of my neck, and then his tongue ran behind my ear and it was my turn to shiver for him. "I know you too."

It wasn't supposed to happen like that, that fast, that hard. No one fell like that. I didn't believe in love at first sight, first fuck, or first anything. So why did I feel like Aaron Sutter had just been walking around waiting for me his whole life?

"Aaron, just let me have—"

"Shhh," he quieted me, untangling himself before dropping to his knees.

"You don't—fuck."

My cock was not small; a lot of guys gagged giving me head, but not Aaron. He opened his throat and took me in, swallowing my length, sucking, laving, his face buried in my groin.

My fingers threaded through his thick dirty-blond hair—darker than mine, golder. I was pale in comparison to the bronze of his skin, all of me not the rich color he was. The contrasts between us were beautiful, and I noticed and relished them, savoring the feel of his mouth, his skin, and how I controlled him as he sucked my dick.

He traced over the muscles in my thighs, rising higher until his hands were on my ass, squeezing tight.

"Aaron," I huffed, forcing his head back, breaking the suction so I could gaze down into his eyes. "I wanna do this in my bed. I've been hoping." And I had, along with waiting. It was why there had been nobody else. I wasn't ready to give up on the idea of him and me, no matter what I said out loud.

"I thought of you too much," he confessed.

The weight of passion on him was beautiful to see. His blown pupils, flushed cheeks, swollen red lips, and rasping breath sent a jaw-clenching shiver through me.

"I don't wanna do this next to the refrigerator."

"I just want you, the where hardly matters."

"It matters to me," I said, hauling him to his feet, hands under his armpits, yanking my pants up and bumping him as I walked by. "Follow me."

He did as ordered, and when we reached my bedroom, I rounded on him and shoved him back into the wall.

"What do you want?"

"What can I have?"

"Anything," he promised, his eyes locked on mine.

"Get the lube," I directed. Heart pounding, skin hot, I wanted him all over me, because I felt like I was going to fly apart if he wasn't.

He was silent, moving where I pointed, going to the nightstand and retrieving the bottle as he yanked at his clothes with one hand.

The second he was within reach, I grabbed him and pulled him forward, going to work on his shirt, getting the buttons, and undoing them fast.

He leaned as if he was drunk, rubbed his nose along mine and then under my jaw. His hands were on my hips, fingers following the line of my pelvis, licking my collarbone even as I heard the pop of the cap.

"No condom."

"No," I agreed. I didn't plan on there ever being anyone else. And it was stupid romantic bullshit, but I felt it in my heart, and I could barely stand it.

Slick fingers slid between my cheeks, two at once, no gentle opening but instead the immediate press inside. The familiar burn and the sound that came out of me—pleading, begging—was, but wasn't, me. It was strange because before the man putting bite marks all over my skin came into my life, I had never sounded like that. I had no idea

I would want to submit so often. With the nameless twinks in the bars, I only topped. And when I had been with Nate, I had fought to fuck, not be fucked. But Aaron inside me, moving, filling, stretching, was something I would beg for.

"What do you want?"

I scrambled away from him and gasped when his fingers were gone, spun, and braced my hands on the wall, bending forward, the invitation clear.

"I thought fucking in bed was what you wanted?"

"It doesn't matter."

"It matters to me," he said, hand around the back of my neck, guiding me to the bed. "You need to see that I—" He wiped his other hand on his leg, the lube stain glistening. "You're not simply some trick, and I'm not leaving after."

My heart hurt looking at him.

"Come here," he said gently, drawing me forward, pulling my shirt and T-shirt up over my head and off.

"My feet—" I chuckled because they were still caught in my pants.

His smile was warm, loving. "Get on the bed, Stiel."

I went face-first down onto it and pulled off my shoes and socks before he unbunched the slacks gathered around my ankles. "Just fuck me."

"No," he growled, and I vibrated under him when he kissed along my spine, sucking the skin inside his mouth, his hands reassuring and tender as he stroked over my sides. He was soothing all the fight out of me, the tension, and the worry.

I lifted to my hands and knees, arching my back for him.

"You have to stop," he warned me, hands on my hips, holding tight. "You're way too much of a temptation, and I want to go slow and show you I'm serious in this, and I don't care what anyone—"

"Tell me later, fuck me now."

Instantly, he was reaching for the lube he'd dropped on the bed, and then his hands were on my ass, grabbing me roughly, spreading my cheeks before his cock pressed against me. "Duncan," he said, his voice low and husky. "I have things to say after."

"Yes. After."

His breath caught, and it was nice that I was doing that to him, and then the push, the breach, left me the same way, holding, not moving, frozen there on the bed, feeling him, thick and hot, inside me.

Sex isn't supposed to fix anything. It's an act, a primal one. There's no emotion tied to it, and I had always been able to separate it.

"Fuck," Aaron moaned as he pulled out only to drive back in, harder, faster, the lube allowing for the slide but not lessening the pressure, the clenching of my muscles around him. His hips against my ass, his thighs pressed to mine, his hands digging into my shoulders as he held on, all of it so needed and craved, I knew whatever he wanted or asked, I would do. "You should see your hole stretch around my cock, baby," he groaned. "It's so beautiful."

The words, *his* words. No one else's had ever mattered in bed, but his flushed me with prickly heat as my balls tightened, the first throb of orgasm rippling through me.

"Duncan," he uttered; his hand slid between my shoulder blades, pressing me down, his cock grazing my prostate with the new angle as I fisted my hands in the blankets. The pounding was endless; he pistoned relentlessly, and I could hear him panting, rough and hoarse. "I don't want anyone else to see you like this," he almost snarled. "Just thinking about it… swear!"

I had to think? He wanted me to form words and make promises?

"It would kill me," he let slip, taking hold of my cock at the same instant.

It was too soon, too fast, but I had been dreaming about him, missing him, wanting him, and trying to be rational about moving on and practical about the reasons. But always, in my heart, there'd been hope because I couldn't let go of Aaron Sutter. And now, he was there, in my bed, with me, saying the best things, making promises because he felt all the same things I did. He was my reward for living and not giving up and holding out for what was real.

Heart, head, and body all aligned—finally—at once. He annihilated me.

I spurted into his hand seconds later, my body giving me no warning, just the rush of euphoria, the release, my world washing white for a moment, the pleasure too much not to shout his name through.

I came apart.

"Duncan!" he cried out and then emptied inside me; my muscles spasming around him as he kept up his hammering rhythm, not stopping, wanting it to last.

"Here," I soothed him, dropping down onto the bed, carrying him with me, his weight driving him deep again. He didn't move, just stayed there, buried to the balls in my ass, covering me, and I was still under him, sated, lying in my own come.

"You're all used up," he said before he kissed my shoulder.

"Yeah, it's good."

"I'm crushing you."

I snorted out a laugh. "I'm bigger than you; no way you're crushing me."

Slowly, carefully, he eased from my body and then slid sideways, thigh still draped over my ass, hand in my hair, as I rolled my head to look at him. The softness in his eyes was like a punch in the gut. I couldn't dance around it. I wanted to keep him.

"Oh man." He grinned, taking hold of a corner of the flat sheet and wiping come off my abdomen. "That should not be so ridiculously hot."

I waggled my eyebrows, as he laughed and yanked the sheet up, untucking enough so he could wad up a portion and cover the wet spot.

"Thanks," I teased, leaning forward to kiss him.

His hand went around the back of my neck as he guided me to him, our lips locking together, melding, each inhaling the other in the frantic dance of reconnection. It was ravenous and sweet and building, but suddenly he jolted back leaving me gasping for breath.

"What?"

His hand was on my right wrist and he rolled it so the long scar was visible up my forearm. "This is new."

"Yeah," I agreed before trying to kiss him again.

He tipped his head away. "Why is there a scar?"

"I want to kiss you."

"I want an answer."

My sigh was loud. "They had to put pins in it because after it was broken I was cuffed in a stress-position instead of just a normal one so the angle jacked up how the bones lined up and—"

"Okay," he cut me off, letting me go before tracing over the scar on my left shoulder.

I grinned. "Why'd you ask me if you didn't want to—"

"This is a bit close to your heart."

He was definitely preoccupied with my injuries. "But it wasn't and I didn't die, so can we drop it?"

"You could have died."

"But I didn't so could—Aaron!" The yell was caused by the pouncing, by having him all over me, pinning me under him on the bed, wrists over my head, held down tight.

"Could have lost you," he murmured against my mouth before he claimed it, kissing me hard and deep.

All his longing, worry and pain were translated into heat and need as he mauled me, biting, tugging on my bottom lip, sucking and rubbing his tongue over mine.

His hands moved to my face and he held me immobile as he feasted. I lifted one of mine to the small of his back, the other closing around his thickening cock.

"Duncan," he gasped. "Please."

Grabbing him, I rolled us both over so that our positions were switched with him on his back. "Aaron."

He shivered, and I reached for the lube and slicked my cock before sliding a slippery finger deep inside him. The way he arched up off the bed, reaching for me at the same time, made my dick leak.

"I want *you* inside," he moaned as I added a finger, two inside, scissoring, rubbing, massaging, and then curled forward and slid over his gland.

"And I want you ready for me."

"Always ready for you, always want you," he rasped, almost angry. "Almost lost you and I can't... it's all I can feel."

"Not anymore," I promised, and his eyes fluttered as I added a third, a fine sheen of sweat breaking out over his neck and chest.

"Have me."

I eased my fingers free of the grasping channel, shoved a pillow under his ass, and lifted him, grabbing his thighs and opening him wide, spreading him out in front of me.

"Duncan," he cried as I pressed against his entrance.

He was gorgeous in his submission, out of his mind with want. He didn't tense up when I pushed forward; his muscles sucked me in.

"You're just massive," he moaned but there was no pain in his voice, no complaint, simply a statement heavy with need.

I stilled even though it killed me, his muscles milking my length, spasming as they constricted.

"Take the fear away," his voice broke.

I thrust forward, slamming into him, and his hands skidded over the smooth surface of the bed, needing something, anything, to hold onto.

"I'm not going anywhere," I promised, leaning forward over him, and sliding my hands between his, as I slid back inside in one long smooth stroke. "And you can hold onto me."

He held on tight, his legs wrapped around my hips as I fucked him, hammering, pounding, needing him to feel it, to know that it was me who'd used him. It was beautiful the way he bowed up under me, completely lost in the sensation of what I was doing to him.

"You feel so good," he ground out, and the tears there, welling, ready to overflow, almost undid me.

I slammed into him, over and over, my thrusts jarring, and he accepted each like a gift and begged me to not stop, never stop.

When I fisted his cock, he went rigid under me, frozen for a second before he spurted over my hand, wrist, and his abdomen.

My orgasm wrung me out a second later, and my balls ached with the force of it. When I tried to pull free, his legs tightened so I couldn't move.

"Aaron?" I asked gently, unlacing my fingers from his, lifting my hands away.

"Just… let me kiss you," he said, reaching for my face.

I bent my head down, and he smiled as I kissed one palm and then the other, rubbing my stubble covered check and chin on his hands.

"God, you're beautiful," he sighed, grabbing hold of my thick, coarse hair and tugging. "I wanna kiss you all over."

He started with my eyes and I chuckled as I held myself braced above him.

"Lay down on me, I won't break."

"You must want me out of—"

"No," he cut me off, easing me close, my face in the side of his neck. "I want you," he murmured into my sweat-dampened hair.

I would have rolled free but he wanted me on him, crushing him, pressing, sliding together. He wanted to be wrapped around me like a second skin, wanted to somehow push inside me and live there. I wasn't strong enough to say no to something I wanted just as badly.

When I finally slid from his body and propped over on my side, facing him, he moved fast, snuggling into my shoulder.

"What happened with your dad?" I asked because I wanted to know.

"He lost," he said, raking his fingers through my hair, pushing it out of my face. "But he's got a son from one of his wives; I can't keep track of them."

"Prentiss."

"Oh yeah," he said, grinning, running his thumb over my eyebrow. "Maxie told you about that, huh?"

"He did."

"Well, so he thinks he's going to start the whole thing up all over again, but the chairman of my board already instructed me not to concern myself. I'm in, I make money, and they know me, trust me. It's done."

"But what about the gay part?"

He cleared his throat. "I need to get married."

It took me a second. "I'm sorry, what?"

"It's weird," he said, cuddling closer. "I have just recently found out my board is extremely progressive and fiercely traditional both at the same time."

"How are they managing to do that?"

"By strongly recommending—and when I say that, think twisting my arm—that I get married right away."

"To a woman?"

"No," he clarified, his smirk just decadent. "To a man."

My mouth dropped open.

"I know. Turns out I can be gay. That's okay with them—they can work with that. Indecisiveness shows weakness, and that they can't have. Unsettled playboy doesn't play well to the board or to the investors."

My mouth closed as I stared.

"Me, sleeping around, being seen as a playboy, that's bad for business. I need to be settled. They want me settled. They need me to grow up, have a home, and share it with someone. They want to see the same person come to events with me, stand at my side, and be accountable for me and to me. They want to know I won't just jet off to Paris on a whim, not because I can't but because I'm expected for dinner."

"They want to see you all domestic."

"Basically, yes."

I took a steadying breath. "You can tell them to fuck off, it's your life."

He nodded slowly. "I could. Luke Levin, the chairman of my board—"

"Luke Levin?"

"Yeah?"

"That's the name of a chairman of a board?"

"Yes. Why?"

"I dunno. I just imagined chairmen of the board having names like Reginald or Buckley."

He laughed.

"What? Levin—I had a buddy named Levin in high school. What is that, Jewish?"

He laughed harder. "He can't be Jewish?"

"You know what I mean!"

He fell back and laughed until tears rolled down his cheeks.

After shoving him off the bed, I heard a thump and more laughing. The man was insane. I got up to head into the bathroom, scowling as I walked by, and was under the water minutes later. It felt good, the heat on my skin, and even better when I heard the snick of the glass door being opened and closed.

"So Levin," I said, picking up the conversation. "He wants you to get married."

"Yes, he does," Aaron said, unhooking my removable shower head and pushing me into the wall.

"What're you doing?"

"Just shut up and take it."

I leaned my forehead on the cool tile, widened my stance when he directed me, and enjoyed his free hand sliding over my flank. "Aaron," I gasped.

"We need to talk."

"We are talking."

"No, I mean really talk, about everything."

Christ. I couldn't think of anything worse than that. "Really? We have to?"

"I'm not like this," he said, kissing the back of my neck, as the hot shower spray ran down the crease of my ass.

"Not like what?"

He spread my cheeks and the water bathed my tender opening. I shivered at the sensation.

"Feel good?"

I grunted.

"Don't move."

I stayed where I was and heard him bumping around in the stall, opening shower gel, and then the mesh sponge was gliding over my back, down over my ass, and between my legs. He took his time washing me, making sure he missed nothing, and then did my hair, massaging my scalp until I put my head down on his shoulder.

"Let me rinse you off and we'll go get some dinner."

I lifted up to look in his eyes. "I actually need to talk to your brother."

He shook his head. "No."

"I—"

"Just let me get this soap off you."

I closed my eyes and put my head back as he combed his fingers through my hair.

"Okay, you're good," he rumbled, kissing my throat. "Now get out so I can shower. You smell all clean and I smell like sweat and come."

"I'm not complaining," I said, my eyes drifting open. "And I should return the favor and bathe you."

"I'm not the one who never gets any tenderness thrown his way, Detective. It should always be me taking care of you."

"That doesn't seem fair."

"It is. Believe me it is."

I found myself frozen there, unable to leave him.

"What's with the look?"

"I didn't hurt you, did I?" I was checking.

"No, Duncan, you never hurt me."

"You're sure?"

"I'm sure," he sighed. "Now go already."

I got out, dried off, ran product through my hair, put on lotion because otherwise my skin got really dry, had to hunt a minute for the deodorant because it wasn't where it was supposed to be, and left the bathroom for my bedroom.

"You need to loan me some underwear!" he shouted.

And it should not have been hot that he was going to put on a pair of my briefs, but just the thought of it made me hard.

"Or I can just go commando!"

In a two thousand dollar suit, now that was practical. Out of the corner of my eye, I noticed my phone, which I had forgotten to plug into the charger—like I was going to think of that when being mauled by Aaron—was now plugged in. He must have done it when I first got in the shower. When I checked, a call had come in, which meant he'd answered it, seen that the battery was about dead, and had hunted around to try and help me out. That part was thoughtful; the privacy part was odd.

I had on jeans and a pale-gray henley, and I was threading my belt when Aaron came up behind me and wrapped his arms around my chest. "Your skivvies are on the bed," I let him know, twisting my head so he could reach my mouth. "But they're just a loan. I want 'em back."

The noise he made was a purr and moan mixed up together before his lips slid over mine. I opened for him, shifting in his arms to face him, and took his face in my hands.

Kissing the man was a religious experience. He tasted so good and I wanted more, I wanted to devour him, but my brain kicked in and I shoved him off me.

"What?" he panted.

"My phone." I swallowed. "Who called?"

"Nick," he coughed out, reaching for the briefs. "Your phone rang when you went into the shower, and it was him."

"And?"

"And I made it clear he couldn't come back over here, that he wasn't welcome."

"You don't even know what I needed to talk to him about."

"It doesn't matter. Whatever you wanted him for, I'll take care of it."

"It's not what you think."

"Again, whatever it is, if it involves you, it's my business, nobody else's."

"You just went ahead and answered my phone?" I put him on the spot, getting to the heart of the matter.

"Yes."

"You didn't think that was an invasion of my privacy?"

"Yeah, maybe," he agreed. "But there was no caller ID, so I had to see who it was."

"Why?"

"You know why."

"I don't," I pressed even though I sort of did, or hoped I did.

"Because I don't want you to date," he snapped, obviously annoyed.

"I'm not dating anybody," I fired back, not wanting him to get the wrong idea. "And I wanted to talk to Nick about work."

"Yeah, I got that."

"I need either him or Max to be my cover."

"I have no idea what that means." He exhaled sharply. "But I'll do it instead."

"Again, you don't even know what *it* is."

"So tell me."

I smiled because his possessiveness was really a big fat turn-on. "I have to go undercover to a resort and try and bust the man who killed your brother's friend."

"And you were going to ask Nick or Max to go with you?"

"Yeah. We need someone who actually is rich because we don't have time to make a background up out of thin air."

"Why Nick?"

"He's rich."

"He's really not," he said snidely, pulling on my underwear, which stupidly sent a ripple of arousal right to my dick.

"No?" I tried to cover my reaction. "He's not?"

"God, you're easy."

"What?"

He searched around for his pants and found them on the other side of the bed.

"Aaron?"

Bent over, all I saw was his muscular back and round, tight ass for a second before he shucked on his trousers. "Just me putting on your tighty-whities got you all horny."

"What?" My voice went up a bit too high.

"What?" He mocked my tone, coming back around the bed to plant one on me. Hard.

His hand around the back of my neck, the other on my hip, and his tongue stroking over mine made it impossible to stand. I sank down onto the bed and pulled him into my lap, my hands on his ass, gripping tight and yanking him forward.

His legs folded in half and squeezed around my hips, his groin shoved up against my abs as he crossed his arms loosely behind my neck.

"You find me wearing your clothes incredibly sexy," he said against my lips.

"Yes," I agreed before I kissed him.

We sat there on my bed and made out. His mouth was hot and wet, and I couldn't get enough of it. I had to wonder how the man was still dating at thirty-six. Why wasn't he taken? How was he walking around without a ring on his finger? But the answer was right there if I just thought about it.

"Hey," I rasped, breaking the kiss, my hands coming up to frame his face and push back his hair. "It's because of your family, right? Your father?"

"You lost me," he huffed, licking his bruised lips.

"The reason you're not settled down. It's because you never could. You were thinking you would lose the company if you came out."

"Yes," he agreed. "My father's views on homosexuality are well-documented, and without the support of the board, he could have removed me."

"But now you have the board's support."

"Yes, I do." His eyes softened as he spoke.

"And so, what are you going to tell your board?"

"About?"

"You said they actually more than support you: they want you to settle down."

"Yes."

"Like I said earlier, you can tell them to go to hell."

"I could do that." He nodded, and then his breath hitched as I yanked him forward again, grinding my groin up against his ass.

"But?"

"But," he picked up the conversation as his eyes fluttered. "They really do need to know that the CEO and the man who now owns 46 percent of the company—since I bought out my father's shares—is a grown-up."

"How did you get your father's shares?" I was interested to know.

"Max had some proxy shares from his mother that he couldn't afford to—"

"You and Max have different mothers?"

"Yes. We're ten years apart after all," he explained, as he traced a fingertip over the cord down the side of my neck. "Not that there weren't wives between my mother and his."

"Wives? Plural?"

He chuckled. "My father's been married seven times."

"Holy shit."

"God, I love talking to you. Things I take for granted, you find so interesting."

"Seven times?" I went on. "Imagine the alimony!"

"Oh baby, only my mother got that. She was the only one he married without the prenup. He learned his lesson."

I digested that. "Sorry I interrupted; go on about how you got the 46 percent."

"Well, like I said, I bought Max's mother's shares since she had some investments she wanted to make, and some board members had shares my father didn't know about because they were held through shell corporations and other third-party sites. Because he needed capital last year to finance some real estate purchases, he sold some of his personal shares to people he thought were loyal."

"But they sold those shares to you without him knowing."

"Yes."

"Out of the kindness of their hearts?"

"No, love," he said, curling sideways to kiss along the line of my jaw, his nose brushing over my stubble-covered cheek. "It's business and it's not pretty."

"You're evil is what you're telling me."

He shrugged, his hand cupping my chin as he nibbled on the patch of skin under my ear. "I'm determined to get what I want."

"And so now your investors own 51 percent of the company, that's what your board oversees, and you own 46—wait, who owns the other 3 percent?"

"Max."

"Oh." I was confused. "Why didn't Max's mother just sell him her shares?"

"He didn't have the money to buy them off her."

"I see."

"No, you don't," he said, his smile warm as he gazed into my eyes. "You're thinking, that's her son. She should have just given her shares to him."

"Yeah," I agreed. "I guess that makes me pretty naïve."

"No, it makes you kind. But Joanna Sutter needed money for her own dreams, and so when I offered to take those shares off her hands, she couldn't say no."

"Okay, so the investors own the fifty-one, you own forty-six, and Max has three."

"Yes."

"And you get to be CEO."

"I do."

"Because the board elected you." I was trying to keep it all straight in my head.

"And voted unanimously to keep me there, yes."

"So you're kind of a big deal."

Instead of answering, he pushed me down on the bed, so I was flat on my back under him and then shoved his tongue down my throat.

The man really knew how to kiss. It was sweet and filthy at the same time, and even though we'd just recently finished having sex, twice, my dick took notice of the heat rolling off him, the way his body moved, and his thrusting tongue. My cock thickened and strained against my zipper.

He was working on the button, and once open he shoved a hand down the front of my jeans. I was already leaking, and when he fisted my cock, I bucked up off the bed. "We're never gonna eat." He broke the kiss, heaving out a breath, hot and heavy, on my face. "And I should feed you."

I rocked my hips under him, dragging my shaft back and forth in his grip.

"Open your eyes."

Having not realized I'd closed them, too lost in the flare of urgent need running through my body, it took great effort to comply with his request.

"I don't want to hurt you," he said as he stood up and went to my nightstand, where he had apparently returned my lube. "I was rough before."

"You weren't," I said honestly. I felt good, replete, languid, and now simmering with renewed lust.

He moved back to the bed and peeled my jeans down my legs, followed by my briefs. The henley he left alone, rucking it up, before he flipped open the cap on the lube. His eyes stayed locked on mine the whole time.

I shuddered as he parted my thighs before leaning forward, pressing our cocks together, and coating them in lube.

"Aaron," I moaned.

"God, Duncan, I don't get you." He sounded pained. "How do you not belong to anyone?"

"What's your plan here?"

His grin was wide. "To jerk us off together."

I shook my head. "That's not what I need."

The smile fell away as he got serious. "You can't want—"

"I do want."

"But—"

"I missed you," I huffed out. "And it was like I was starving the whole time."

"Me too," he whispered.

"So, then, dinner can wait."

"Yes," he agreed. "I need to see you so... on your back, all right?"

I would have answered, but the sizzling heat shorted out my brain.

"Hold on, baby," he said gruffly.

I was big and strong; I was covered in scars from knives and bullets, my nose had been broken more times than I could count, and people said all the time that I seemed scary and moved dangerously. But somehow, some way, Aaron Sutter, suave Wall Street billionaire, gazed into my eyes and thought *baby*. It was overwhelming and made me all the more desperate to cement the man in my life. He needed to stay because he actually saw me.

His hands went behind my thighs; pushing forward, opening me, and pressing down, the head of his cock sliding along my crease before it slipped inside a fraction.

"Hurry," I barely got out, the shudder tearing through me.

I was still relaxed from earlier, so my muscles didn't clench or fight him; no shove needed, just a long stroke, all the way in.

"This is right; it's supposed to be like this."

"Yes."

He curled over me, my legs on his forearms, making sure he had me supported before he eased out.

"Aaron!"

His hips snapped forward, and he was buried in me hard and deep.

My hands scrambled for purchase in the sheets, because I had to ground myself so I wouldn't move. I didn't want to move.

Again, he drew back slowly, and I could feel how slick I was with lube and precome before he rammed inside, the plunge not careful, all about hunger and power and urgency. He liked me where I was: open for him, under him. His narrowed eyes, clenched jaw, the cording muscles in his arms, his hands gripping my legs—he wanted me, badly, and the knowledge sent tremors of pleasure surging up my spine.

The retreat followed instantly with the breach, again and again; the pounding onslaught, furious and fast, propelled me quickly over the edge.

My climax came too quickly to warn him, and what there was spurted over his smooth, flat stomach. The sound he made when I did it, the moan torn from his chest, made me shiver as he froze above me, his own release just as unexpected.

I saw him shaking and lifted my hands for him. "Come here."

He wanted to, but it was almost like he was afraid.

"Aaron," I coaxed him, reaching out.

Closing his eyes, he leaned into my hands, kissing the palm of my left before he gave me his weight.

"Let me have you."

As he slipped from my body, the gush of fluid was a worry. "I should go get a towel or—"

"Who cares," I said, my voice soothing.

"But you just got clean and—"

"I wanna hold you."

Easing my legs down on the bed, he moved, straddling my thighs, still not falling over on top of me.

It was taking too long, and whatever he was feeling, I didn't want him to shore himself up. A wall had come down; I didn't want it rebuilt. Grabbing him, I rolled him to his back and pinned him to the bed under me.

The tears were there, leaking from his eyes.

"It's okay," I promised.

"I almost lost… so stupid…."

"We're good. I feel good."

His eyes were stormy, so I did the only thing I could think of. I slammed my mouth over his and kissed him with everything I had, letting him know my heart was right there for the taking. After several minutes, I felt him surrender, and only then did I lift my lips from his.

"No," he whispered, arms wrapping around my neck, hand buried in my hair as he pulled me back down.

The scorching, mauling touch of lips and teeth and tongues went on until one of us had to break for air. The only sound in the room was sucking and grunting and groans and whimpers. I finally broke the building, brutal rhythm and took hold of his head and held him still. "What do you want?"

"I want to see you whenever I want, and I don't want you to see anyone else."

"Done."

One dark-gold eyebrow arched for me. "Just like that?"

"Yeah."

A shiver ran through him, before I wrapped him in my arms and held tight. It took long minutes for the trembling to stop, and I nuzzled against his ear and whispered all the filthy things I wanted to do to him.

"Oh yes, please," he husked after several minutes, chuckling and squirming in my embrace.

I let go and propped my chin on my hand as I stared down at him.

"Something you want to know, Detective?" He sighed, the hooded gaze so very sexy.

"Yeah," I broached gently. "What else did you say to Nick?"

"Nothing."

I tried not to smile. "Nothing?"

He coughed. "I told him not to call again."

"Oh."

"You sound sad." He was studying me.

"No, I just feel bad for the guy. I think he needs a keeper."

"Yeah, well, it's not your job," he said frankly. "And leading him on is a shitty thing to do."

"I didn't lead him on." I got defensive.

"You let him hold your hand."

"You saw that?"

"Yes, Detective, you have a lovely view of the street from your front room."

I had done that, and it was a mistake.

"You're a good man, and it is a cliché, but they are hard to find."

"You're good too," I made known.

"No, I'm really not."

"Yes, you are," I maintained. "And I'm just lucky that I caught you between men."

"There hasn't been anyone serious in a while. I stopped moving people in."

"Why?"

"I guess I'm like my father. I get bored too fast."

I squinted. "I don't get that from you. I get the 'I want to come home and eat with my boyfriend' vibe off you."

"That's because all I want to do is spend any time I can with you."

"You just wanna get laid," I teased.

"That too, though usually it's quite a bit tamer than this."

"What do you mean?"

He tipped his head and stared at me. "I'm normally nicer."

"In what way?"

"In bed."

"Why the hell would you wanna be nicer in bed?"

"To make sure I never forced anybody to do something they didn't want to."

"You're talking about two different things. You already have all the trust issues squared away before you take off your clothes."

"Well, I don't normally do anything without asking, and I check in bed too, not just out of it. Not just before."

"I don't recall being asked what I wanted."

"No, you weren't, because you're the first man I've ever been in bed with who could make me stop if he wanted to."

"So what then? My strength is bringing out your bad side?"

"No." He lowered his voice as he moved under me and slid a hand around the back of my neck. "Lie down."

I sank over him, my head in the hollow of his throat as I wrapped my arms around him.

He rubbed his chin in my hair and stroked his hand over my bicep. "You're so beautiful, you know that?"

Only to him.

"I dream about holding you down and making you do whatever I want."

"Sounds kinky."

"Normally, yes," he admitted. "And normally I don't like to be the only one doing it."

"Meaning what?"

"Meaning that I really get off on seeing other guys fuck the guys I'm sleeping with."

"You like to watch," I husked, kissing his collarbone.

"I do."

"Okay."

"It only happened one time before that I didn't."

I could guess. "Jory?"

"Yeah."

"I'm not him."

"No, you're not," he agreed. "And that's good because that didn't work."

"Can I ask why not?"

He tangled his hand in my hair and tugged gently, so I tipped my head back to look up into his eyes.

"I wanted to change him. I wanted to own him."

"And you're not like that anymore?"

"I am partly," he said, his voice full of gravel. "I'd be lying if I said I didn't want to own you."

I was all aboard the possessive train. "And the changing?"

He was staring into my eyes. "I kind of like you how you are."

"Yeah?"

"I feel like you would let me show you some things my money can do."

"Like?"

"Like take you to some of my favorite places in the world."

"You want to travel with me."

"Among other things, yes."

"Yeah, sure. Why not?"

He bit his lip, and I could tell the answer had excited him. "And as long as I don't try to buy you everything, you might stick around?"

"I don't need anything but you in my bed," I said bluntly.

"What about out of bed?"

"Not sure what I can ask for."

"What about you? How much of me can your captain see without it becoming a problem for you?"

"I was actually thinking about that."

"When?"

"When I thought we were gonna be something."

He tensed in my arms, and I nuzzled into the side of his neck and sucked on the skin there, giving him a zerbert that made him laugh.

"Ohmygod, that was so not hot!"

Sometimes funny was better than sexy. I did it again and then kissed hard.

"Jesus, you just turned me into one giant goose bump!"

He was very huggable, and so I slid higher and drew him close, cuddled him tight, tucked him against my chest.

"Duncan."

I grunted.

"Can you go out with me?"

"Like, be seen out with you?"

"Yes."

"For your board or for you?"

"For me, you idiot!"

I laughed softly into his hair.

"Am I thrilled that I don't have to hide who I am anymore?" It was a rhetorical question he posed. "Oh hell yes, I am. And do I feel like a weight has been lifted off me?"

"I'm guessing yes."

"Yes!" He was belligerently happy. "Do I wish I could have just had the balls to live my life this whole time? Oh hell, yeah!"

I let him go because he squirmed, and he sat up beside me.

"I'm so pissed that I went from being afraid of my father, afraid of my board, scared of what my brother would think, and concerned over my mother's disapproval to not caring about any of it."

"That's not true. You care."

He sighed heavily. "My brother thinks I walk on fucking water no matter what, and I should have known that."

"Yeah, you should have," I agreed. "I've heard how he talks about you."

He scooted back until he hit the headboard, moved the pillow so he was comfortable. "I was pissed at him today."

"And I'm sure he thinks you still are."

"Because I still am."

"Maybe you should fix that."

"Perhaps," he said under his breath.

"Don't be an ass."

"I never asked him to step into—"

"He was trying to do a good thing," I interrupted.

Sharp inhale from him. "You were almost gone. One more hour, one more day… if you had slept with someone else…."

"Or if you did," I mumbled.

"Why didn't you?" Aaron wanted to know.

"I was hurt."

He wasn't buying it as evidenced by the squint I was getting.

"Fine, I'm a romantic sap." I shrugged. "I wanted it to be you."

I wasn't expecting him to lean down and kiss my forehead.

"Get off me," I complained.

His laughter was warm.

"So now you have a board that wants to see you with only one person."

"Yeah," he said, sliding down beside me. "And so they're going to see a lot of you."

"Are they?"

"Oh yes."

"Your father will have a seizure."

"I give a fuck."

"Tell me about your mother."

"She lives in Paris."

"That's cool."

"She's been there since I was six. She went back to live with her family after my parents got their divorce."

"You never visited her or anything?"

"I did, but it's not like you think. You're going from nanny to nanny, not from parent to parent."

"Sorry."

"It's okay."

"So," I broached the subject. "You were worried what your Mom would think if she found out that you were gay too?"

"She's very conservative; I know what she'll think."

"But it won't bother you anymore?"

"Honestly, I needed her stocks, her shares, but nothing else. We've never been close. We do the Christmas gift exchange, but she plants a tree somewhere for me, and I have my assistant send her something from Cartier or whatever."

"You have an assistant?"

"I have ten."

"Huh."

"But my personal assistant is Margo Dayton. She'll be the only person you'll liaison with."

"That sounds dirty."

He shook his head. "Peasant."

I scoffed. "Hey, look at me."

His bright blue eyes locked on mine.

"I'm sorry about your folks. Really."

He was trying to figure something out.

"What?"

"You have sealed juvenile records, Detective."

"I do." I nodded. "You bump up against that wall when you were doing your background check on me?"

"I did."

"And?"

"Do you think you would ever trust me enough to tell me about that?"

I didn't even have to think about it. "Yes."

He was very pleased; it was all over his face.

"No secrets between us."

"No." He was adamant. "Nothing."

"Okay," I said playfully. "Can I take you to eat?"

He whined and it was adorable.

"Are you by any chance hungry, Mr. Sutter?"

He flopped over. "Ohmygod, I'm fucking starving."

"Would you like me to feed you, since it's already a little after nine?"

"Please, kind sir. I'll blow you for food."

"I think I can get you to do it without payment," I taunted.

"Ass!"

Yes, I was.

NINE

HIS driver's name was Miguel Romero, and he had apparently worked for Aaron a long time. The only reason I hadn't met him before was he'd been on vacation when Jory set me and Miguel's boss up on our blind date. He had a month off every year, because otherwise, even when Aaron traveled, Miguel was the one there, driving him. He was pleased to meet me but also surprised, which I kind of liked. Apparently Aaron had a normal type I did not fit at all, and that I was different, was a source of interest.

I wasn't stupid. I got that beautiful, small men were his usual fare. I'd met Jory Harcourt, Sam Kage's partner, on a number of occasions. He was five nine, slender, fragile, and the kind of beautiful that you stopped on the street to watch walk by. How Sam had swung that, I had no clue. He had muscles and height going for him, but not much else. There was no way Jory had traded up when he picked Sam over Aaron Sutter. It amazed me that after having a Jory, or some of the others, that Aaron would have ever looked twice at a guy like me.

"What are you thinking?"

I rolled my head on the seat and my eyes slid over him. "Just trying to figure out what you see in me."

"What?"

"No, not like 'poor me, I'm so repulsive, what the fuck were you thinking'," I snickered. "But more like, I am so not your type. You like cute little twink boys."

He reached for my hand and I let him take it.

"You don't hafta tell me."

He lifted my hand and put it on his thigh. "It's just you. I saw you, and I can't see anybody else anymore."

"That's kind of romantic."

"Yeah."

"Maybe it's 'cause of Jory," I offered. "He introduced us, after all."

"He's not magic, I assure you."

"He seems nice."

"Yeah, he is. But it's funny: now that I'm not looking at him through rose-colored glasses anymore, I have to tell you that he would try the patience of a saint. It's a wonder that neither Sam nor his brother has thrown him off something high."

"He didn't strike me as particularly annoying."

Aaron's glare was funny.

"Okay, I take it back."

He rolled my hand over and examined it.

"What are you doing?"

"You have a scar on your palm."

"Junkie put a knife through it."

His eyes flicked to my face.

"What?"

"You're covered in scars."

"I know." I shrugged, glancing away. "Not hot."

"Duncan."

The streetlights outside had all my attention.

"Look at me."

I followed his direction after a moment.

"I get the feeling you've been in bed with some men who did not find the scars sexy."

"Not bed. Only two men have ever been in my bed, but yeah, guys fuck me because I'm scary lookin', all broken and marked up."

"They're idiots," he said frankly. "I want to know the story of each and every one, and yes, I promise you, they make my dick hard just looking at them."

I was surprised.

"Am I being clear?"

"Yes. Very."

"I just want to lie on top of you and feel your bare skin under mine. I could do it for hours if you let me."

He got a kiss for that, and the way he opened for me, melted against me, I was very tempted to pull him into my lap and forget about food. My stomach had other ideas, though, because the growl was loud and long, like I was possessed. It was not sexy to have the man you were kissing collapse in a heap of raucous laughter. Apparently, I was very amusing and would be kept around purely for entertainment purposes.

At the restaurant he chose in River North, we were walked in through the back and brought upstairs to the second floor that overlooked the street. The lights of the city were beautiful, and the spring rain had washed everything clean.

"Pretty," I remarked.

"Gorgeous."

It was not lost on me that the only thing he could see was me. "Kind of cheesy, wasn't that?"

"Yeah. I don't care," he said, sliding a small key ring with a couple of fobs on it across the table.

"What is this?"

"The gray one opens the gate that surrounds my home in Winnetka. The black one will get you on the elevator of Sutter plaza in Streeterville. Above the offices, at the very top, is the penthouse. That fob will get you there."

My eyes flicked to his. "That's fast."

"No. You're not moving in. That would be fast. I'm giving you access to my homes because my work and yours are not going to just magically align," he explained, reaching over to take my hand. "So if you can, or I can, even if it's late, we could see each other."

"I like the sound of that," I said, squeezing his hand before he pulled it back. "So I'll make you a key for the outer door and my loft."

"I would like that."

"Okay."

The chef himself came out to talk to Aaron at our private table. A partition had been put up so no one could see us, and with Miguel there, no one was getting anywhere close to try and take a peek. I had no clue what anything was since they were speaking Italian, so it was nice that Aaron translated for me.

"What sounds good?" he offered.

"I don't care. Just don't make me eat brains or, like, veal or lamb or something." I shrugged. "I'm easy."

The grin made his dimples pop.

"Get your mind out of the gutter."

"I can't help it."

The red wine was heavy and thick, and I liked it a lot. The appetizers he ordered were good. I loved bruschetta, and the other— dates filled with goat cheese and wrapped in prosciutto—was amazing.

"I've never eaten a date before," I told him. "I thought people only ate them in the movies. Ya know, like *Indiana Jones*?"

"I see that I'll be broadening your horizons in all kinds of interesting ways, Detective."

"Why does everything that comes out of your mouth sound filthy?"

He laughed at me before settling back in his chair.

After a minute, I realized he was still staring at me. "What?"

"Nothing."

"Something."

"No. I just didn't think I'd be here with you when I woke up this morning."

"But that's a good thing, right?"

"It is. Very good."

"Okay." I grinned, pointing at the last date. "You want that?"

"It's all yours."

Once I was done thoroughly enjoying the last morsel, I washed it down with some wine. He was staring again. "Jesus, what? Did I not eat that right?"

"No, I just really liked watching you do it." His smile, the way it lit up his whole face, was good.

"You like to see people enjoying your money," I said truthfully. "You like treating."

"Yeah, I do, and it usually goes one of two ways."

"Sure. You have people who want to take advantage, or people who take it to the other extreme and don't let you do anything for them at all."

"Yes."

"Well, guess what," I said, admiring the way the suit that had previously been on the floor of my bedroom fit him. "Tonight, it's your treat. Tomorrow, wherever we are, I'm buying. I hope you like burgers."

"I do." He flashed me a grin. "And your sense of compromise is stunning."

"Is it?"

"You have no idea."

I took another sip of wine.

"And from now on, I'm only treating you."

"Good," I confirmed. "'Cause I'm a jealous prick."

"Oh? Well, that'll be novel."

The way he said it was weird. "What does that mean?"

"Normally, that's me. I worry about people being taken from me, not the other way around. I'm normally the jealous one."

"Not anymore. Never with me. I'll never give you cause."

"Thank you," he said, and meant it.

After the appetizers were cleared, and he poured me another glass of wine, I noted his fixed regard. "What?"

"Nothing. You're just out with me, and people could see you."

"Yeah? And?"

"When we go to more crowded places, it will get harder to hide that we're actually on a date."

"I know that."

"Well, I bring it up because you've been closeted your whole career, and now you're just going to kick the door down and step out into the light?"

I returned his stare. "I'm not going to take out a front page ad in the *Trib* or call a press conference, no. But I do feel different, and I'm not gonna lie about that."

"I have to ask."

"G' 'head."

"Your last serious—"

"Only serious," I corrected.

He cleared his throat. "Your only serious relationship; was that the reason you broke up, because you were in the closet?"

"I'm sure there were other reasons as well, but that was the main one, yeah."

"So why now? Why this time and not then?"

It was hard to explain because it made no sense. "I dunno. Maybe almost dying gives you a new perspective? Maybe deep down I knew I was kidding myself with Nate for two years, because I was never really what he needed? And maybe it's just simply that I want to."

His lip curled up in the corner.

"I mean, it would bother me if people thought, after all this, after us deciding to date—"

"Exclusively," he reminded me.

"Yes, exclusively." I smiled.

"Sorry."

"No. It's nice to be reminded."

"I told you, I'm territorial."

"So am I, and that's what I'm getting at. It would bug the shit outta me if, after you've given me these fobs, people would still think you're available just because they don't see you with anyone."

He nodded. "You want people to know we're together."

"Yeah."

"Very brave of you."

"I think it's just human of me. That's a pretty basic desire, kinda primal, right?"

"To claim a mate?" he baited me.

"Don't be an ass."

He laughed softly. "I'm just worried about you; we had this talk before about your job."

"Yes, we did."

"And nothing's really changed."

"I have. I've changed."

"Okay."

I leaned forward. "Am I gonna get shit—probably, most likely. Will someone spray my locker pink and write faggot on it?" I had to think a second. "Doubtful. But will there be a thing, like an unspoken wall I can't get over? Yeah, I think so."

"So this is career suicide for you."

"Suicide's a little dramatic."

"But what you are now might be as high as you go."

"Yes."

He scowled at me. "Then what?"

"Then what nothing," I said, taking hold of his hand. "I figured you were gone, and I was basically settling back into my life."

His eyes searched mine.

"But it didn't feel right. I want us to do this. If it doesn't work out, it won't be for a lack of trying. I'm gonna give it my best shot."

"I like how you think you have a choice."

I let his hand go. "Don't start. I gotta tell you about the job now."

"Tell me about the job, be my guest, but the rest of it is a done deal."

He was so arrogant, but what was funny was I knew, just knew, what he was rambling on about. "You've just decided that, no matter what, I'm gonna belong to you."

"Yes. Exactly. This is done, Detective. You're never getting rid of me."

I didn't tell him how much I liked his certainty.

AFTER dinner I took Aaron to the FBI field office and realized the one thing I could offer the man no one else ever had.

Intrigue.

Watching him listen to Special Agent Summers, the way he absorbed every single word out of her mouth and bounced in his chair with excitement, I realized that even if I failed with him, I would be a tough act to follow.

"Do I get a cool code name?" He was dying to find out.

Who knew millionaires could be giant nerds too?

Chapter TEN

IT WAS a blur. I could see where a person could lose his head hanging out with Aaron Sutter. The company plane was amazing, and the limousine that picked us up from a private airfield and drove us downtown to the Vegas strip was luxurious and stocked with more alcohol and food than I thought was possible.

"Hey, I forgot my sunglasses," I said, holding out my hand. "Loan me yours."

"Why?" He was confused. "I thought we were going for full disclosure here?"

"Once the op is over," I explained, pulling my Chicago Cubs baseball hat on. "I will show my face to everyone, and whatever pictures get taken now, they'll know it was me. But right this second, no one but Clay Wells, and whoever is in your inner circle, can know who I am."

"Makes sense," he agreed, passing me his oversize sunglasses and then grinning suddenly when I gave him my attention.

"What?"

"I like you in a baseball cap. It's hot."

I shook my head. "You have it bad if this is doing it for you."

"Kiss me."

The man was a bit smitten, and I was sort of crazy about it.

Once we reached the hotel, I wondered how it worked with people wanting to be close to Aaron, but Miguel's presence answered my question. He was, in fact, not just Aaron's driver, as I had previously surmised, but was also his personal bodyguard. He kept lookers from turning into touchers. Normally, at home in Chicago, it was just him. In Vegas, he had a team of four others accompanying him.

Aaron Skyped with his executive assistant, Margo, and when he turned his phone toward me, I got to meet her. She reminded me of Trinity from *The Matrix*, except she smiled a lot and talked really fast. I had no idea one person could do all she could and never leave her office. I was thoroughly impressed.

"I am thrilled to meet you, Detective," she gushed. "Anything I can do for you, you just say the word."

"Quit it," Aaron muttered.

"Oh, Boss, he's gor—"

He cut her off by ending the call, and I poked him in the ribs with my elbow.

"Go away," he groused at me.

A member of the staff of the Wynn met us when we drove up, and I was fine to just follow along with the rest of the entourage, but when Aaron stopped to point something out to me, everyone else did as well. I wasn't used to that, seeing him in leader mode, but it was natural for him. I was uncomfortable with the attention and scrutiny, but he didn't even notice. The only thing that kept me grounded was his hand in mine.

The man had grabbed hold of me when we got out of the car, and not once, even for a moment, had he let go. I saw the photographers, the paparazzi, stalking him, and was surprised when he made no effort to shake or hide from them.

"You said you were ready," he reminded me.

Turning the corner, we ran into a wall of flashing lights and sound: so many cameras clicking at once. It didn't last, though. Miguel herded us into the elevator, and we rode straight up for several minutes before we reached our three-bedroom, duplex, Encore Tower Suite. I had no idea you could have a two-story suite, but Aaron had insisted on it. We stayed upstairs, as did Miguel, and the four-man security team slept downstairs. In the room, surrounded by the panoramic view, it took me a second to get my breathing regulated.

"Are you all right?" Aaron checked.

I nodded before taking off the cap and sunglasses.

"You look a little freaked out there, Detective."

"Did you see all the photographers?"

"I did." He smiled warmly.

"So, I mean, that's was good for our case, but those pictures, they're gonna be waiting for us at home too."

He shrugged. "If anyone from work recognizes you, you can tell them that you were undercover. That will take care of all of this."

"No," I said, walking to the window. "Hey, uhm, we don't gotta stay in this kinda place every time we travel, do we?"

"We can stay any kind of place you want," he replied quietly.

"Okay." I crossed my arms. "That'd be good."

Aaron was suddenly behind me, hands on my hips, his chin on my shoulder. "We're going to do this, and then we're going to get invited to Arizona, and then we're going to go home together and have keys made for your loft."

That sounded good and normal. "Yeah."

"All of this—" He kissed the side of my neck. "—is nothing. I hardly do this anymore, and now… with us… why would I?"

I was uncomfortable, and I got how the whole money thing could so easily become an issue. "You're making a lot of changes for me so quickly."

"I don't think so," he disagreed, sliding his arms around me, his chest pressed to my back, his lips doing sinful things to my earlobe. "We need time, just us, and then if you want me to take you gambling in Monaco, I will. I have a villa in Italy on the Amalfi Coast that I'd love to show you, and I'd like to walk you around the left bank in Paris and take you to Hong Kong and—"

"And what about just being there when I get home on Monday nights when it's raining?" I inquired, worried, holding onto his arms.

"You mean just lying around on your couch after we eat dinner?"

"Yeah?"

"That sounds like the best part of being with you, Detective."

I inhaled deeply.

"Don't second guess me, all right? The thrill of going to all those places is for you to see them with me. I've done all that, and while I've loved it all, what you don't get—what no one ever has—is that I just want to share it and not have the other person thinking about anything else but how much fun it is."

"You don't want someone thinking either 'I wonder how much this costs' and worrying about it, or thinking 'I wonder what else I can get out of him'."

He tried to pull away.

"Stop."

"I would never think that you—"

"It was an example, dumbass."

He immediately calmed and wrapped back around me.

"It would be impossible to have another rich guy be with you 'cause he probably already did all the stuff you've done, and vice versa. To impress each other, you'd just have to keep upping the ante, and that would get crazy."

"Yes, it would."

"But a guy you keep, like that Jaden, that can't last long-term."

"No."

I twisted in his arms and took his face in my hands. "So you really are stuck with me, Sutter. Sorry, man."

He took hold of the front of my dress shirt. "Yeah, well. What am I gonna do?"

I was smiling as I bent to kiss him, and he met me halfway, the clench tight and hot, and another piece of my heart left my chest to go live in his. I couldn't stop the inexorable falling anymore. Aaron Sutter was the one, and no other would do.

After we changed, him into what appeared to be just another suit, and me into something a bit outside my comfort zone—the dress pants way too tight, the silk shirt hugging my chest and abdomen—we left the room and walked the strip to another hotel to show up at a rooftop nightclub that had more rooms than I could imagine they needed. We sat in the back of one of them; Aaron had reserved the space, complete with bottle service. I wasn't surprised he had friends there, or acquaintances. He knew people everywhere.

"I called and made sure we had a big crowd so it would look more natural," he explained in my ear as we were joined by ten people.

"Good idea," I replied, sipping on my bottled water. Technically, I was on duty, and no matter how much I wanted to loosen up and drink, it wasn't a smart move.

"You need to have at least one," Aaron cautioned before standing up to offer his hand to a guy coming around the table.

I smiled and shook hands and was going to just forget all the faces, as I normally did, but Aaron took a breath and everyone went quiet, even in the middle of the noisy club.

"This is my boyfriend, Duncan. Everybody say hi."

It was all over their faces, the surprise and interest and sudden scrutiny. When he sat down, his hand went to my knee, as he gestured for the two hostesses and instructed everyone to order whatever they wanted.

He never took his hand off me.

When I reclined, his hand was on my thigh; when I leaned forward, on my lower back. He had to get up to go walk the room, and when he did, he bent and kissed my temple. Returning, I got fingers sinking into my hair until I tipped my head up. The kiss on my forehead was my reward for following direction.

More people came, and a couple of guys, with others in tow, sat on the edge of the table in front of Aaron.

"I wrangled invites for us to a private club," one of them said, glancing over at me, his gaze missing nothing, moving slowly. "You can bring the flavor of the week."

Aaron cleared his throat and both men turned to him. "Go ahead and go. Have a great time."

"You're not coming?"

He shook his head.

The man who had checked me out was startled. "It's exclusive?"

"It is."

"Aaron, I didn't mean any dis—"

"It's fine," he cut him off, which just illustrated the fact that he was upset. Even I could tell. "Have a good time." They were being dismissed. Aaron really didn't like what he'd called me.

"I guess we'll go, then," one of the guys mumbled.

Aaron didn't say another word, just completely ignored them.

"Here," he said when one of the hostesses put a dirty martini down in front me. "Try this. I ordered it for you."

Gin wasn't my favorite, but this had more brine in it, which made it saltier, so I liked it better than martinis I'd had in the past. "It's good," I said, leaning in and kissing him. "Do I taste salty?"

"Open your mouth and let me really taste you."

I grinned. "You're kind of insatiable."

"I seem to be somewhat addicted to you."

Our eyes locked and everything else sort of stopped.

"You should go," Aaron suggested suddenly. "See if you get any bites."

"I was just thinking that." I winked before I stood up.

His hand in mine stilled me for a second, and he made sure to squeeze it before he let go.

I really had to wonder how in the world someone had not wanted to sit and soak up every drop of his attention before me. How could you not want Aaron Sutter all over you?

I went to stand at the edge of the dance floor, and after being there for a few minutes, sipping on a coke, I felt a hand on my back. Turning, I found a man I had never met before in my life.

"Duncan?"

"Yes."

"Duncan what?"

"Who's asking?" I requested of the handsome younger man. He was pretty: all delicate and perfectly styled. The hair, the tan, his manicure, the make-up: it all said boy-toy to me.

"Clay Wells."

Bingo.

I offered him my hand. "Duncan Ross."

His smile was bright as he took my hand but not to shake. Instead, he curled his fingers into mine to lead me away. "I'm Kian."

"Nice to meet you."

"And you, Duncan," he said, stopping to wrap both his arms around my one. "So tell me what you're doing here?"

I cleared my throat. "I was actually hoping to see Mr. Wells. I wanted to talk to him about something."

His grin was wicked. "I'm sure you did."

Clay Wells was sitting in a different room, at a table where it was obvious Kian belonged on his right. When we walked up, the man, who I had only seen in pictures up to that point, tipped his head and smiled at me. "Welcome, Mr.—" He glanced at Kian.

"Ross," he supplied, unwinding his left arm from mine and sliding his hand up under the back of my shirt. He was probably checking for a wire, but his search was thorough, his fingers dipping into the groove of my spine.

"Mr. Ross," Clay Wells addressed me, getting up and coming around the table. "Would you like to take a walk with me?"

"I would."

He snapped at Kian, and he was instantly off me and going back to his seat.

"Wow," I said, falling into step with Wells, walking out toward the patio. "He's certainly well trained."

"Yes, he is, and if you'd like a demonstration of his talents…," he trailed off salaciously, "do please let me know."

"Not right now, but I'll keep it in mind." I winced. "That's my whole problem."

"Tell me."

It was just the two of us outside by the railing with the blazing bright Vegas strip below us. Funny, but under different circumstances, I would have found Clay Wells alluring.

He was a little shorter than my own six four, built solidly with wide shoulders and a narrow waist. Unlike me, he was not bulked with muscle, more like Aaron, with a swimmer's build. His hair was a warm chestnut-brown, cut short, and his eyes were a lovely shade of hazel under thick lashes and brows. He was handsome in that sort of classic way, where he could easily be a pilot or a doctor or a newscaster. It still surprised me when I met career criminals because so many of them didn't look like you ever thought they would in a million years. Mr. Wells definitely would have flown far under my radar.

I turned to face him. "Let me get right to it."

"I wish you would."

"You don't know me, but I know you."

"How?"

"Evan Polley was my boyfriend's brother's friend."

"That's a lot of people in there."

I shook my head. "Not really. I knew Evan through Max Sutter, and Max Sutter is—"

"Oh." His brows lifted. "You belong to Aaron Sutter."

I squinted at him before pivoting to walk away.

He caught my bicep tight. "Mr. Ross?"

"If you're just gonna fuck around with me, I'm wasting my time."

His face hardened and his eyes closed to slits.

"We both know that Evan Polley is dead. When you got wind that Aaron Sutter was going to be in town you thought, *What the fuck is that about? Why is a friend of the guy I just got rid of showing up to play in my sandbox?*"

"I have no idea what—"

"I know you need someone to take over what Evan was doing for you," I explained. "And since I have access to a jet, as well as a helluva lot more money than he could have ever dreamed of, I thought I would throw my hat into the ring."

"And why would I ever consider even talking with the kept man of a billionaire?"

"Because I've got bigger plans than that," I said icily. "All I need is some startup capital, and I can walk away from spoiled little rich boys."

He was quiet a minute, circling, looking me over from every angle before turning to face me. "It's a good story, but I'm not sure I buy it. How close were you and Evan Polley?"

I made a face. "Not like that. Evan wasn't gay."

"No, no he wasn't. And you are?"

"I'm whatever keeps me in clothes and cars and off the street," I answered flippantly.

"And what makes you think I'd deal with you and not your handler?"

But I knew why, and technically, it was the same reason Aaron himself couldn't date another rich man. "'Cause you'd have no control over my boyfriend. He could buy and sell you if he wanted. But me... me you know I want out. Me you know I want something, and I'll do anything to get it."

"Really?" He sneered, stepping close, two fingers under my chin. "Anything?"

All of them were the same, and it never failed to disappoint. You said the word "anything" and all thoughts went south to their dicks. Why not something more creative?

"Get on your knees."

I did it instantly, without thought. He had to see I was serious.

He exhaled sharply, nostrils flaring. "Well, I very much see the appeal of having a man like you at my disposal. I'm sure Mr. Sutter enjoys ordering you around."

"Do you want me to blow you or not?" I groused irritably, my heart hammering in my chest, wondering how the hell I was going to get out of it if he said yes.

"No, not here," he insisted. "I just wanted to see if you would."

"And so, what?" I griped, standing up. "I'm just gonna get tested over and over?"

"You're not the only game in town, Mr. Ross."

"I'm the best option you have, Mr. Wells."

He studied me. "We'll see."

"What does that mean?"

He got close and started unbuttoning the front of my shirt.

"More tests? You think I'm wired or something? Undercover?"

"No," he said with a huff as he opened my shirt. "I've tried all my life to have a body like yours, but I just can't do it. Not built right."

I stayed still and quiet.

"All this definition, the carved six-pack.... I've done everything," he murmured, sliding his fingertip up the deep groove in my abdomen. "And I bet it comes effortlessly to you."

"No" was all I said.

"Are you hard all over?"

"Touch me and find out."

His nostrils flared. "I would love to, but again, not here."

"So if you like big men, why not have one?"

"So far I have yet to find one willing to submit."

"Really?"

"Yes. They're either body-builder types that I don't find particularly appealing, or men far too dangerous to house-train."

"I see. You keep lap dogs." I shrugged.

"Yes, men like Kian."

"Well, he's beautiful."

"He is, but he's a boy, not a man."

My body washed cold, because even in the middle of an op, I had to know if the pretty puppy was legal. "Yeah, but he's what: nineteen, twenty?"

"He's twenty-four, but that's what I mean." He sounded disgusted. "He looks so young. Too young, really, for my taste."

I was relieved; twenty-four, you made your own bed. "So you like to fuck men?"

"Yes. Not just male. Big, strong, rugged... does it for me." He was gazing at me like I was food. "Does Aaron Sutter fuck you?"

"'Course."

The tremor ran through him, and I watched his pupils dilate. "I want to."

I gave him my best smile. "Let's make a deal, then."

"No. As a sign of good faith, you come by my room around midnight and we'll talk again."

"I can't do that. I'll be missed."

"Then make it so you won't be." He bit off the words, reaching up and pinching my nipple. "And make sure you have a plug in your ass when you show up. I want you stretched and lubed so I don't have to mess with it."

I was annoyed, but I stood there and watched his eyes widen as he noticed the scar close to my left pectoral and then the next and the next.

"You're a gladiator, huh?" His groin brushed my thigh and I could feel his erection through his slacks. He was rock hard with desire.

"It's not what you think."

"I want to bareback," he whispered.

"You've lost your mind," I said, taking a step back.

He grabbed hold of my belt buckle, fingers sliding down into my jeans. "Fine, but you will be ready for me, and there will be others there to help hold you down."

"Like I said, midnight won't work. It's too late. We should go now."

He pushed my shirt further open and bent forward and sucked my nipple into his mouth. I jolted away before I even thought about it, years of training deserting me in an instant, drowned under the overwhelming wave of ownership. I was supposed to let him manhandle me if he wanted, but… I belonged to Aaron, and no one else was supposed to touch me.

"What the fuck is going on?"

We both pivoted and the man—my man—charged across the patio toward us, moving easily through the thin crowd, a Thursday night not quite as busy as it would be on a Friday or Saturday at the same time.

He reached us and immediately stepped in front of me to drive two fingers into the chest of the man we were there to talk into working with us. "Who the fuck are you, and what the hell are you doing putting your hands on what's mine?" Aaron shouted.

Criminal or not, scary or not, Clay Wells was intimidated by the man in front of him, that much was exceedingly obvious.

"I asked you a question," Aaron demanded, and his voice was hoarse with anger.

"Clay Wells," he answered, his eyes flicking to mine.

"Don't look at him," he snarled. "Look at me!"

Clay was back to giving Aaron his full attention.

"I don't know who the fuck you think you are, but I've never heard of you, and since I didn't give you permission to touch my property, you need to get the hell away from him!"

Clay was freaked out—it was all over his face—but he recovered enough to speak. "It's just a misunderstanding, Mr. Sutter. I was just talking to Mr. Ross and explaining that I'd like to invite both you and him to my resort this weekend in Sedona."

Aaron glowered, and it appeared very real from where I was standing. "I saw what I saw. Your hands were all over him."

"Again, a misunderstanding. Please accept my sincere apologies. He didn't say he was with you."

Aaron rounded on me. "You didn't say you were mine?"

I opened my mouth, and he backhanded me across the face. "Shit." I groaned for effect, because he'd pulled the punch, of course. I felt a light sting, but he could have split my lip if he'd wanted to.

I had to give it to Aaron; he was a natural.

"Come here," he growled, grabbing hold of my shirt and tugging me after him. "You too, Mr. Wells."

Aaron led me to a small bungalow on the other end of the deck, shoved me inside, waited for Clay Wells, and then zipped the tarp closed after he was in.

"Get on your knees," he snapped out the order.

I did as I was told.

"Do you have things you own as well, Clay? May I call you Clay?"

"Yes, please, and I do," he whispered, visibly amazed at what was transpiring right in front of him. He didn't know who to look at, me on the floor, or Aaron flopping down into a heavy wooden chair with a thick pillow on the seat.

"And do you have to discipline them when they do stupid things that could get their asses sold to others who would not treat them as well as you do?"

He nodded in a daze as Aaron slowly opened his belt and slacks, shoved his briefs down under his balls, and wrapped his long-fingered hand around his cock.

"Crawl over here and blow me," he ordered.

I started to move.

"Slow."

It was humiliating, but when I looked up into Aaron's eyes, I saw the heat in them, his blown pupils, and the way he licked his lips. Role or no role, he was into exercising his power over me, and it was turning him on big time.

I made a show of it, moving languidly, and when I reached him, I slid my hands up his thighs, leaned forward, and licked the wide head of his long, thick cock, tasting the precome on my tongue.

Clay Wells made a strangled sound, but Aaron's sharp exhale was a million times hotter.

"Suck me."

Lifting up on my knees, I bent forward and took him down the back of my throat in one smooth liquid slide.

"Oh," I heard Clay Wells gasp softly.

"Yes," Aaron croaked out. "He's a champion cocksucker."

"That must feel amazing."

"You have no idea," Aaron said under his breath.

I made the suction hard and licked and laved every inch of his thick, gorgeous length.

"So, your resort?" Aaron asked, trying for bored. It would have been more convincing if he could get his voice to even out and stop spiking.

"I—yes," Clay moaned, and I suddenly felt him behind me, his hands on my hips. "Would you consider letting me have his ass while he sucks you off?"

Aaron's laughter sounded barbed, filled with thorns, too sharp and staccato. The acting was tough for him to pull off with all his possessiveness seeping through. "I only share with friends, Mr. Wells. Are we friends?"

"I would love to be your friend, Mr. Sutter."

"Then tell me what you two were talking about."

This was a test to see who Clay Wells wanted more, trusted more, me or Aaron.

"Nothing," he replied, and I had my answer.

It wasn't just the promise of sex—even though I knew what Clay wanted as part of any deal with me—but it was what I had said to him. He couldn't own Aaron Sutter. The same was not true of the man he thought I was. Me, he could get his hooks into, and I would be working for him for the rest of my life. Aaron could walk away at any time, or even turn around and take his fledgling drug-smuggling business away from him. I would belong to him.

"So you just, what?" Aaron questioned, reaching inside my shirt and rolling the nipple that Clay had sucked on between his fingers. "Thought he looked good and wanted a bite?"

"Yes."

Aaron stopped me, lifted me off the end of his cock, and ran his thumb along my lower lip. "Is it the clothes, Clay? Is he dressed like a whore?"

"Yes," he said roughly.

"Good." Aaron smiled, gripped the back of my neck, and eased me down to his dick.

He shoved himself in, thrusting until he hit the back of my throat. "Fuck," he muttered as I hollowed out my cheeks and sucked hard.

"Mr. Sutter, you—"

"Call me Aaron," he said tightly, and I eased up before all his concentration deserted him. "And no, Clay, you can't have his ass. Not yet."

"Whatever you—"

"Tell me, Clay," Aaron began, his voice hitching as he squirmed under my mouth. "When you're done with your toys, where do they go?"

"I give them away."

Aaron tsked to cover up the hiss that crawled out of his throat. He was enjoying my fellatio skills a little too much. "I don't do that. I sell them. Normally, a year is about all I do before I get bored, but Duncan here has been so much fun to break. You should see him take cock now. It's beautiful. When he first showed up, owing my brother money, I knew he'd make a great submissive as soon as I taught him to love being dominated. Small men can only take so much punishment before they break under the cane or the lash."

"You—" Clay began. "I saw his chest. You're responsible for all that damage?"

"Of course," Aaron assured him.

"Jesus." Clay sounded both horrified and impressed at the same time.

"I enjoyed it."

Clay couldn't keep his hand from my crease, or from sliding it under me to grope my cock through my pants. "He's really hard. May I suck him off?"

"How about this," Aaron countered. "You have me out to your resort this weekend, and I might let you come in his ass."

He squeezed my right cheek before he got up. "Is he tight inside?"

"What do you think?" Aaron scoffed. "I'm the only one he's ever had. He was straight before we struck our bargain. Of course he's tight, and when he wraps those muscular thighs of his around you... I swear to God, I've never come like that in my life."

I felt a hand graze my back.

"Invite me to the resort, Mr. Wells," Aaron said coolly. "And don't touch my things without permission. It makes me edgy."

Wells's hand was gone immediately.

"We leave tomorrow morning on my plane," Clay said after a moment.

"No. I only fly on *my* plane. You can join me if you like. If not, my man Miguel is just outside. Give him the details, and we'll join you there tomorrow afternoon."

"Yes," he sounded breathless. "I will, and thank you."

"Please leave us and zip—"

"Could I watch him finish you off?"

"Certainly," Aaron sneered and snapped his fingers at me.

He couldn't possibly last. Already he was like velvet-covered steel in my mouth, and between my hand and my lips, he filled my throat in seconds.

"Take it all," he ordered.

I swallowed and then licked him clean, finally wiping my mouth on his thigh.

"Come here."

Hands on the arms of the chair, I pushed up to meet him.

Cupping my face in his hands, he kissed me savagely, devouring my mouth, tasting himself on my tongue.

"I'll see your man, Mr. Sutter," Clay Wells rasped.

Aaron moved his left hand from my cheek and gave him a dismissive wave. I saw the gesture out of the corner of my eye.

Once he was gone and I could hear the zipper being dragged down, I pulled back and grinned at Aaron. "That was kickass, Sutter."

But something was very wrong. Aaron looked shell-shocked. He was trembling, looking almost like he was going to cry, and gulping for air.

I grabbed him and stared into his eyes. "Aaron?"

"I'm so sorry," he said, his hand tracing over my cheek where he'd hit me.

"Are you kidding?" I beamed. "You were fuckin' brilliant."

He suddenly yanked up his pants and did the zipper but nothing else before launching himself at me.

"Honey?"

Head down on my shoulder, arms around my neck, legs wrapped around my hips, he wasn't talking, just shaking.

"You're scaring me," I said into his hair. "What's wrong?"

"I used—I treated you like a whore and I didn't… I would never… Duncan."

I chuckled and squeezed him tight. "You were being what he expected. You were amazing. For someone who was winging it, you certainly channeled your inner asshole."

He whimpered deeply, and his mouth opened on the side of my neck.

"You did it, Aaron. We got the invite, and he's going to go behind your back to talk to me now because he thinks he's getting one over on you. He'll think that big bad Aaron Sutter didn't see him coming, and he got what belongs to you."

Aaron's hand slid inside my shirt over the same nipple, again, that Clay had sucked.

"He's an arrogant prick and he wants what's yours."

"Well, he's not getting it," Aaron growled, pulling back, sliding off me to his knees before bending to lick over my pectoral.

"What are you doing?" I asked, because it felt good.

"Cleaning him off you," he said, gently putting his hands on my sides as he swirled his tongue over the pebbling nub.

It felt so good, and when he eased me up into the chair, I went readily.

He moved from my right nipple to the left, and then kissed down my exposed abdomen to my belt buckle. "You're hard."

"Have to be dead not to be."

He got into my pants, shoved my briefs down, and when my cock bobbed free, deep throated me with practiced ease.

I bucked up off the chair, and his hand closed on my base as he used the flat of his tongue, his teeth, and the suction to make my balls ache with the need to come. "Aaron," I whined when he stopped, unable to hold the sound in.

"Forgive me."

I made a noise, which he took as yes, and his lips clamped down over the end of my shaft.

"Fuck!"

It was fast and dirty, the way he sucked cock, and I dumped come down the back of his throat, thick and hot, and watched him swallow it down.

As I sat there, panting, heart pounding in my ears, I realized he wasn't seeing me. Fisting my hand in his hair, I lifted his head to meet my gaze and found those beautiful eyes swimming with tears. "What the hell?"

"I almost lost it," he confessed, and I could hear how nasal his voice was. "I can't have that man, or anyone else, put their hands on you. I thought I was going to throw up."

I couldn't stop smiling.

"I hit you!"

"Yes," I said, laughing softly.

"Duncan!" He was incredulous.

"You did so great," I praised him, standing quickly to tuck in my dick, zip up, and do my belt before sitting down and reaching for him.

He moved quickly, scrambling into my lap, and searching my eyes—for what, I wasn't sure.

"You were perfect," I went on.

"Holy shit." He burrowed close, and I felt him shiver. "I always thought I was a badass, but that was so scary."

"What was scary about it?" I rubbed his back hoping to soothe him.

"I thought you were going to be pissed."

"No. It was like we planned it," I murmured in his ear, inhaling his scent, the sound making him squirm in my lap.

"You're driving me crazy. I'm getting chills."

"It was hot how you ordered me around," I teased, kissing up his throat, nibbling, knowing I would end up leaving a bruise on his beautiful bronze skin.

"Was it?"

"It was," I crooned, loving that we were absolutely plastered together, as close as we could be, only thin layers of fabric between us.

"I got my dick out because I'd rather him see mine than yours."

"He didn't see much of it; you had it shoved down my throat."

His moan made me laugh.

"You didn't have to reciprocate," I said softly.

"You wanted it."

"I'm a guy, aren't I? I'm breathing, aren't I?"

He laughed and pressed tighter against me.

"Just realize that you have absolutely nothing to be sorry for," I said.

"Duncan, I—"

"Stop second-guessing me. Why would I lie to you?"

Instantly, he settled against me, heavy and wrung out.

A few minutes later, when I got him to his feet, I had to buckle his belt and straighten his clothes so he was ready to move. I had my arm around him, my hand in his hair as he walked beside me, leaning heavily.

The adrenaline that had to have been pumping through his system the entire time had completely dissipated. He was barely on his feet. "I'm sorry," he said, sounding worried—not like him at all.

"There's nothing to be sorry about."

Miguel was there at the door that led from the patio back inside. He had directions and a code to get onto the property in Sedona. We were expected the following afternoon. I explained to him that we all had to go back to the room and talk.

"Right away, Detective."

I had a feeling Miguel and I were going to get along just fine.

"I'll take care of the bar tab and be right behind you. Shall I include the tab for your friends for the rest of the evening?" he questioned Aaron.

"No." I shook my head, answering for him. "Close it out."

"Yes, Detective."

Aaron turned to me. "My friends won't understand."

"They better fuckin' start," I informed him. "And if they really are your friends, they won't be expecting you to buy all night, especially since you're not even there."

And instead of arguing, he let his head thunk down against my chest, sort of sagging against me. All of it, the last day, going undercover, the excitement, the adrenaline, me and him…. Aaron Sutter was wiped out.

"Corporate giant, huh?" I said, closing my eyes, leaning my cheek into his hair.

He grunted something in response before he gave up all his weight to me.

AARON had people trying to get up to the suite all night long. After I stripped off everything and put him in sleep shorts, I covered him with the comforter and cranked up the air conditioner. There's nothing better than sleeping in a cold room, all warm and snuggly on soft, clean sheets under a thick down comforter. I was hoping he wouldn't wake up.

When the calls came to the room, I had Miguel take them. He said "no" really well. When the pleas for entrance reached Aaron's cell phone, I explained he was asleep. No one believed me, and I finally just let everything go to voice mail. Everyone was going to need to be educated very shortly. The days of taking advantage of him were over. There would be no more coattail riding. I would make sure of it.

It was still early as far as nightlife in Vegas went, just a little past ten, so I tried Agent Summers to give her an update. I got her on the second ring.

"You keep late hours, Agent Summers."

"It's the job, Detective."

She was thrilled with our progress, and I gave her times when we would be moving the following day. I clarified how Aaron had tweaked the plan on the fly and how his quick thinking had suckered the mark right in. She was very impressed with him.

I spoke to Jimmy after that, not caring about the two-hour time difference where he was concerned. I had hoped I woke him up and was disappointed I hadn't.

"That's such a dick move, D."

But I didn't give a damn.

It was nice that he was both concerned and happy about what was going on with me.

"I want you to have a life. You know I do."

"I'm sorry that you're gonna be labeled as the partner of the gay detective. That's just how it's gonna be."

"Yeah, well, it's never bothered me before. Only difference now is that more people'll know."

"Jim."

"Like I give a fuck." He sounded disgusted. "Whatever happens, happens. If guys down at the precinct care who you're fuckin', there ain't shit I can do about that. What I will say is that everybody better keep any stupidass comments to themselves or I'll punch their teeth in."

"This is your adult response?"

"Lemme think about it a sec," he quipped. "Fuck, yeah."

"Thanks" was all I said because the thank-you for having my back didn't need to be spoken. This was my best friend; it was pointless to drag the conversation out. I would do anything for the man, and of course, it went both ways. That was never a question. Ever.

"So," my partner grunted at me over the phone.

"What?"

"Imma tell Lise about Sutter, all right?"

"Yeah," I sighed. "Before she sees it in the news somewhere and gets all hurt."

"Okay."

Silence reigned for a moment.

"Jim?"

"Yeah."

"You're still on the phone."

"I know."

"What is it?" I prodded.

"So Sutter… you think, uhm… you think we can see his place in Winnetka?"

It took me a second. "Are you kidding?"

"No, I'm not kidding," he barked at me.

"Really?"

"Yeah. What the fuck?"

I coughed. "Sure, yeah. I got a key. I'll show you around."

"Oh? You've got a key. Ain't that the shit!"

I hung up on him, and he called back laughing so hard he couldn't breathe. I made sure to tell him to go fuck himself before I hung up a second time. The third time, he was still chuckling but was in enough control to listen about the case. I promised to call him before we went into the compound the following day.

After Jimmy, I called to leave a voice mail for my captain and was surprised when she picked up the phone in her office. Apparently, she was working late, trying to clear out some paperwork, and was pleased to hear from me. I caught her up on the case and then got to the heart of the matter.

I started by explaining how sorry I was for not coming clean with her in person, but that I had to talk to her about me being gay before I returned and before it got back to her. She surprised me by thanking me for my openness and honesty, and then informed me it was not her business in the least.

"Have you spoken to someone with the Gay Officers Action League, Detective?"

"Uhm, no."

"Well, you should. Would you like me to shoot the GOAL rep for our department an e-mail?"

I had no idea what to say to that. "Sure, I guess."

"You guess or you're sure, Detective?"

"I'm sure."

"Excellent. It's very important for you to know your rights. Equality can be a rocky road. Just know that when it is, I will be there to support you. You're one of mine."

"Thank you."

"Of course."

When I hung up, I sat alone on the second floor and stared out the window. It made me almost sick that I had waited so long to be brave and stand up. And it was crazy, but I felt like I owed someone an apology.

It seemed like the natural thing to do to call my ex.

He picked up on the third ring. "Hello?"

Of course he wouldn't know it was me. My phone number wouldn't be in his phone anymore, not after so long.

"Hello?"

And it was late. My brain sometimes just didn't kick on.

"Is there anybody—"

"Nate."

After a moment, he said, "Duncan?"

"Yeah, shit, sorry. I just realized it's late there." There was a two-hour time difference and it was a quarter to midnight where I was.

"No, it's okay. I'm up feeding the baby."

That was news. "Baby?"

He chuckled, and as always, it was a warm, deep tone. Dr. Nathan Qells always sounded good. "My granddaughter."

"Oh." I smiled into the phone. "Congratulations."

"Thank you. I'm giving her folks a break before they start shuffling down the hallway looking for brains."

"Little bit of *Night of the Living Dead* going on at their place?"

"New parents. It happens."

I could imagine the scene.

"So, Detective Stiel," he said kindly. "To what do I owe the pleasure?"

"This is gonna sound really stupid."

"I doubt it."

"I just wanted to call and apologize to you."

"For what?"

"For not having the balls to come out when we were together. I'm so sorry, Nate."

He caught his breath. "You came out?"

"Yeah."

"To who?"

"To my captain, to my department, and there will be pictures, somewhere—I suspect in one or more of those horrible gossip magazines next to the checkout stand at the grocery store—about me and Aaron Sutter."

"Who?"

"Aaron Sutter," I began. "He—"

"Aaron Sutter the multi-millionaire hotel guy?"

I coughed. "Yeah."

"Wow." He sounded stunned.

"How do you know him?"

"I don't know him," he huffed. "I know of him. You'd have to be dead not to know who Aaron Sutter is. This is the man who said, 'Hey, why don't we build in the Pacific Rim? I hear it's gonna be big someday.'"

I started laughing because it was funny to hear him kid and even funnier that my ex, the academic, knew even a little about the minds of millionaires.

"So damn," he said with a laugh. "When you come out, you come out guns blazing, huh?"

"I didn't plan on—"

"Duncan."

"Crap."

His sigh was deep. "In or out of the closet, Duncan, you were never the right man for me. We both know it. We're both sort of similar, and while that can be a good thing, it really wasn't in our case. You being closeted at the time, I think, didn't let us see the big picture. But now you can, and damn… I'm so happy for you."

"Not everyone has to be out and proud to be happy, Nate."

"I agree. I do. I think it's a choice everyone has to make for themselves. But for you, knowing you, I swear if I didn't have this cute kid on my chest, I would dance around the room for you."

"Thank you."

"Are you happy?"

"So far," I said honestly. "It's brand-new, and the shit's gonna hit the fan when I get back, but I talked to Jimmy and my captain so… you know."

"It will be what it will be, and that has to be okay."

"Right. It will."

"Wait, back? Where are you?"

"I'm on an FBI task force."

He choked.

I laughed.

"What?"

"I forgot you were funny," I replied.

"Jesus, Duncan."

"So I just wanted to call and thank you for being a really good part of my life."

"You're welcome," he sighed.

"I'll see ya."

"I hope so," he confided and then hung up.

Nothing like closure.

ELEVEN

"DUNCAN?"

Lowering the newspaper I was reading, I glanced up at Aaron, who had come to stand next to the dining room table, rubbing his left eye and looking very confused. "Good morning," I snickered.

He was trying to focus. "What are you wearing?"

"My suit. Well, my suit pants, the jacket is right over—"

"No, I mean—" He rotated his head back and forth. "—what's going on?"

"Well, you have to shower and have some breakfast, I need to coordinate our exodus from this hotel, and—"

"No." He sniffled. "Why are you dressed?"

"Because I ran this morning, came back, used the gym, used the pool, showered, shaved, changed, had breakfast, and was reading the paper waiting for you." I answered, very amused by his complete confusion. "You want some coffee?"

He came around the table, and I pushed away from it so he could sit down in my lap, which was apparently where he wanted to be. "What happened last night? Why didn't you sleep with me?"

"I passed out on the chair after I talked to Nate."

"Who?"

"My ex."

"Why were you talking to your ex?"

"Just some things needed to be said. It's good."

His hands slid up my chest as he scrutinized me.

"What?"

"Whenever we're together from now on, I want you to sleep with me."

"Okay, I will. I just didn't wanna accidentally attack you in the middle of the night."

"Maybe I would have liked that," he grumbled.

"You're really cute, all bleary and out of it."

He would not be baited; instead he slumped forward and nuzzled under my jaw.

"You need to eat."

"Tell me what's going on?"

"We're leaving in about two hours so, really, you need to get a move on."

"How come I passed out? Did someone roofie me?"

I snorted out a laugh. "No, you passed out because once the adrenaline goes, you're pretty much done."

"Adrenaline?"

"Just the racing around you've been doing is crazy. Plus, think about all the changes in your life over the past few days, and then last night and today… you just wrung yourself out."

"That's ridiculous," he snapped, getting up and stalking to the window. "I'm not weak. I'm not the woman in this thing."

"In this thing?" I repeated.

He crossed his arms but didn't look at me.

"In our thing, ya mean?" I laughed, standing up and following him, feeling like humor was my best option. "Just so we're clear, there's no women in this thing, our thing, at all."

He spun around to face me. "Don't make fun of me."

"I'm not."

"Listen, I don't get taken care of or handled, you understand? I'm the one who does that. I fix things. Me. I'm the guy who makes all the plans. Not anybody else."

"Or," I said gently, amazed at my own patience. Normally, I would have yelled, but something about Aaron made me want to talk to him, soothe him, give him comfort. "We could take turns, ya know, since we're partners and all."

He was staring at me.

"If that would work for you?"

Still silent.

"Since that's what people do. Relationships are a team sport," I instructed him. "Or so I've heard."

His eyes stayed fastened on mine.

"Food?"

He coughed. "Yeah."

I walked back over to the table, and he followed me. I pulled out his chair, and he sat and even let me push it back in for him. Once his eyes were back on me, I poured him some coffee, served him up some eggs benedict and fresh strawberries with powdered sugar, and then asked him if he wanted any orange juice.

"No." He shook his head.

I went back to reading the paper, and after a few minutes, he said my name. My gaze returned to him immediately.

"Yeah, let's do that."

"Let's do what?"

He squinted. "Let's play a team sport."

"Okay." I grinned.

He looked better as he took a bite of his toast.

LEAVING the hotel would have been more easily accomplished with a battering ram or a snow plow. So many people, so many reporters, and every one of them wanted to know who I was, since Aaron was holding my hand. I had on his sunglasses again, which were way too fancy for me. We agreed to stop at a mall on the way out of town to pick me up a pair. We probably could have gotten through the paparazzi quicker, but when Aaron was asked point blank if I was his boyfriend, his answer—his clear and honest "yes"—started the whole onslaught all over again.

It was deafening: the sound of the flashes going off, the yells at me of "Over here"; the calls of "What's your name?" were crazy. Aaron smiled, held court, and then stuffed me into the back of the limousine.

Once we were safe behind tinted glass, I took off the cap that didn't at all go with my Italian suit and only then noticed his liquid eyes and the warmth in them. "What?"

"Why is that stupid cap so ridiculously hot?"

"Because you want me," I said flatly.

"Yeah, I think that's it."

I took off his sunglasses and held them out to him.

"You know you can just keep those if you want."

"They're not really me."

"No?"

"No," I said. "I just need a boring pair from some kiosk in the mall. I have no idea why you'd need them to be this fancy."

"Those are Moss Lipow."

"I have no idea what that is," I assured him. "Drive me to the mall."

But we ended up at Louis Vuitton, and I picked out a pair that would work. I pulled out my wallet, but Aaron grabbed the glasses, and my hand, and ordered Miguel to take care of it. We were headed back to the car in minutes.

"You can't just buy me everything," I cautioned him.

"Right," he agreed. "But a seven-hundred-dollar pair of sunglasses, I should be allowed to take care of for you."

I stopped walking and took off the sunglasses I had just put on. "These are seven hundred dollars?"

His grin lit up his face. "That *was* Louis Vuitton, baby, not Walmart."

"Holy shit," I said, holding them out to him. "I'll get something at the airport."

"No, you won't." He chuckled. "There's no more airport for you, don't you get it?"

I tensed because, really, the money thing was weird. You had the feeling it was quicksand, and if you got too close, you wouldn't be able to get out.

He squeezed my hand tight, and once we were back in the limousine, twisted in the seat to face me. "You look like you're freaking out."

"Just gimme a sec," I directed, staring out the window.

"Hey," he said, and I was surprised when he threw a leg over me and straddled my hips, in my lap when I wanted some space.

"You don't listen all that well." My eyes flicked up to his face.

He put his hands around both sides of my neck, and I was stuck looking up at him.

"Duncan, honey, listen to me." His voice dropped low as he stared into my eyes. "You ride in a private jet now. A car picks you up and takes you places. You have expensive sunglasses and tailored suits, and when it's time for me to get you a ring, the store will be closed when we pick out what we want. That's how this works."

It was how it worked for him. It was his world, but it didn't have to be mine. I—wait. "Ring?" I coughed.

"Yes," he said, his eyes rock solid on mine.

"You said when, not if."

"Because it's a when, that's why, not an if. If is gone."

"Someday," I said.

"Yes. Someday."

"Okay, but you get that—"

"I get that you're not going to quit your job and stick around my house all day or travel with me whenever I want. I understand that *kept* is not something you'll ever be. I know that. But what you have to wrap your brain around is your life now includes staff and charity fundraisers and events. During the day, at work, you're Detective Stiel. Nights, weekends, you're Aaron Sutter's partner, and you have to look the part."

I had to give. I never had, and it had yielded me nothing and no one. Letting the man go because I had too much pride was just a bonehead move.

"You can't manscape me," I threw out after a minute.

"Do you have any idea what that even means?"

I thought a second. "No, not really."

He bent close. "Stop spooking over every little thing."

"Stop saying what I can and cannot do," I cautioned.

"Okay," he said.

"Okay," I agreed.

And then he kissed me.

ON THE jet, Aaron was immediately on the phone and his computer at the same time. I was basically at a standstill until we got to the resort. Everyone knew where we were: all of us in a holding pattern until the next step of the adventure.

I spotted some magazines on the small table by my chair, although none that I normally read. But I picked up the *Forbes* because Aaron was on the cover. The inside article had a cheesy title, "Here Comes the Son." With Gordon Sutter on the left side of the page and Aaron on the right, Gordon with his arms crossed, Aaron with his hand out like he was ready to shake, you got the idea the two men were not close.

It was interesting reading all about Aaron's recent battle with his father for control of Sutter. The article cited many reasons why the company was better served with the son at the helm and not the father. Aaron was quoted as saying his father's tenure as CEO had been fraught with mismanagement, plagued by poor investments, and riddled with scandal. Gordon volleyed back with his son's lies about his homosexuality.

Luke Levin—I really was crazy about the man's name—was on record as saying that what mattered to the board and investors at Sutter were results and results alone. Under Aaron's supervision, the Chicago-based brokerage company was apparently on course to finish up a fifth straight year with a net return in excess of 20 percent. That was apparently very good.

I had wondered vaguely about Aaron's status, millionaire or more, and finally got my answer. The man was listed as a billionaire in the magazine, 11.2 billion altogether. He was not the richest, but neither was he the poorest of the exclusive club. His money was diversified, coming from hotels built all over the world, other properties, and the value of his shares in Sutter. All there in black and white was a lot of reality in a short timeframe.

"Hey."

I put the magazine down to survey him in his crisp blue whipcord suit and to admire the contrast of the white dress shirt, open at the collar, and his deep gold skin. The man just did not know how to go slumming.

"Are you all right?"

"I'm reading," I said instead of meeting his eyes. "Go back to what you were doing."

Seconds later the magazine was gently taken away and Aaron was on his knees in front of me, his hands on my thighs, holding tight.

"We're not alone," I informed him.

"No one would dare come in without buzzing to check if they could. That's understood," he said hoarsely, fingers sliding over my belt buckle.

I took hold of his restless hands and stilled them.

He was confused. "Duncan?"

"We're gonna land soon."

"But I just told you that—"

"Yeah, but I don't feel like having everyone know what we're doing in here. Do you get that?"

His eyes narrowed. "I get it, but who cares?"

"Just because you haven't in the past, doesn't mean I don't."

"Where is this coming from?"

"You've had a lot of men on this plane."

His eyes narrowed. "Like you've been celibate."

"Get up," I ordered softly.

He opened his mouth to say something.

"Please," I cut him off. "I'm not comfortable with having everyone know we're fucking on the plane. I'd rather skip that scene."

His eyes searched my face. "What's wrong?"

"Nothing's wrong," I said, because it was hard to articulate exactly how I was feeling, and if I couldn't figure it out, how was I supposed to explain it to him? "I know I need to get used to the being on display like all the others, but—"

"For starters," he snapped, his voice rising, "the others were hidden; I was very careful that no one ever saw them. Even Jory and I were never photographed together or—"

"That's not the—"

"And what I said was that you have to get used to people *wanting* to see you," he clarified, drawing out the word, sitting back on his heels, no longer touching me. "But no one gets to know private things between us."

"Good." I tried to smile but couldn't. "Then let's not screw around, all right? And you don't have to entertain me or talk to me. I'm fine. I know you have stuff to do. No worries."

He squinted. "So I'm being dismissed?"

"Aaron, for crissakes." My anger flared. "I can see you trying to get a crapload of shit done before you're forced into spending a weekend at a place where you're completely cut off from the outside world. You have responsibilities. You have a business to run, and I know you've got everything covered, but you're basically doing this for me and the feds."

"Duncan—"

"It's great that you're performing your civic duty," I stopped him. "And I appreciate it, but I know you have things to handle, so g'head."

It seemed from the look on his face he wanted to say something else, but instead he got up and went back to where he'd been. I peered out the window and tried to figure out why I was annoyed with him. Wanting to fool around with me was a good thing, so why didn't it feel that way?

In Phoenix another limousine waited for us, and once we landed, I got on the phone, which was better because it gave me something to do to occupy my time.

"God, this is like déjà vu," I said to myself.

"How so?"

"I was just here," I made known.

"Here in Phoenix?"

"Yeah. I was on vacation, and then I helped Sam out."

"Sam who?"

I turned to him. "How many Sams do we have in common?"

"Oh, yes, that's right. You all talked about that when we had dinner with them the night we met. You helped Sam watch over Jory. I had no idea that was here in Arizona."

"Yeah."

"Funny how small the world is sometimes, isn't it?"

"It is," I agreed.

"Did you see Sedona when you were here last?"

"No, I didn't."

"Well, at least that will be new."

And for no good reason, I kissed his cheek. His hand covered where my lips had been when I leaned back. "What?"

"You're a very demonstrative man, Detective."

"Not really. You bring it out in me."

His eyes clouded fast.

"Oh, wrong thing to say?"

"No." His voice dropped low. "Best, actually."

"Come on, let's go."

The drive was ugly, a lot of brown until we were outside of Sedona. Red Rock Country was gorgeous, and I rolled down the window to smell the air and feel it on my face.

"Should we talk about anything?"

It had been a long silent car ride.

"I don't think so," I answered the stunning scenery instead of him. "We just have to get him to commit to one of us that we're in, and then we set a time and place for the deal, outside his pleasure palace here, and we've got him."

"Right, but we're not going to get separated, are we?"

"I don't know. I don't think so. I mean, the fact of the matter is that he knows damn well he can't do anything to you. If he's gonna shoot someone in the head, three guesses who it will be."

No response, so I figured what I said made sense to him.

"Duncan."

I ignored him, which was a dick move.

"Duncan," he said, sharper the second time.

Twisting in my seat, I realized he was furious. "What's with you?"

"Oh, I don't know. Could it be that you're so fucking nonchalant about your life! About your safety! You think that's funny?" His voice rose.

"It's the job," I explained. "This is what undercover is. I've done this many times. Last time out, I got the shit beat out of me, I got shot—it happens. I mean, we're not actually on vacation, right? There's the potential for this to go extremely bad. Clay Wells is not connected to a drug cartel like my last job. He's basically a trust-fund rich boy playing at midlevel narcotics smuggler, but he had Evan Polley murdered—he's not benign."

"No, I get that."

"Then wrap your head around this and remember that, come Monday, if I'm with you or not, you leave. You drive out of the resort. If I'm not there, and Clay gives you an excuse, whatever that is, however thin, however crazy, you leave. That's the deal. That's what Special Agent Summers is banking on. You make her send a team in to extract you, the whole operation is compromised," I stressed to him. "You know all this; you were briefed same time I was."

He nodded like he was thinking.

"So we should—"

"Why are you so angry with me?" he let slip, and the sound, hurt and splintered, was startling. "What did I do?"

"What?"

"Don't deflect," he demanded, and I could see he was shaking. "Just tell me what's wrong!"

"Nothing's wrong."

"You're lying."

I was silent and glanced away from him.

"Duncan."

"You gotta let me figure this out in my head," I finally said. "Because I'm having trouble."

"Trouble with what?"

I raked my fingers through my hair, tugging before letting my head loll sideways so I could see him.

"Duncan?"

"It's like a circus."

"What?"

"Being with you," I huffed out. "It's like joining the circus, and I don't know if I wanna be a freak show for people to look at."

He went very quiet; I could actually see the recoil. "My life is not some frightening carnival, and how dare you compare it to one."

"Do you even know the difference between a circus and a carnival? If you're gonna get pissed, at least know what you're pissed about."

"Yes, Duncan," he said implacably, "I do."

And the offense he took was normal and that sort of calmed my momentary terror over… not what we were about to do—not about the op—but us.

"How dare you—"

"Wait." I chuckled, which I realized instantly was not a good reaction. I hadn't meant to be patronizing; it was completely unintentional. The whole conversation was just stupid, but when I saw how big his eyes got, I knew I was in for one hell of a blistering tirade.

He slid his laptop sideways onto the seat and slammed his hand down on the free-standing console. Miguel's voice came from the front of the car.

"Raise the privacy partition and do not stop this car until you're instructed." He said as he pulled off his suit jacket and flung it back into his vacated chair.

"Yes, sir."

"Aaron," I coaxed faintly.

"No," he roared, and in the small space, it was really loud. "Do not handle me!"

He hit another button on the console near him, and my window whooshed shut so fast, I was lucky my hand wasn't outside.

"We're having a mis—"

"Stop." His voice bottomed out as he was suddenly there, pressed tight, pulling, tugging, wanting my clothes off.

The cotton dress shirt surrendered first, the buttons torn free and flying everywhere as it was roughly opened and then peeled free of first one arm and then the other. The white undershirt was yanked over my head without concern, before he divested himself of his own clothes as quickly as possible.

I realized that Aaron Sutter did a whole hell of a lot of his communication through sex, and I got it because I normally did as well. The thing was, though, with him, I wanted more.

"You're going to run. I can feel it."

That was my fault; I was scaring him for no good reason.

Most people could count on two things, some more and others less: we each had a personal life and a professional one. At any given time, at least one had to be working right for us to truly function in society. So maybe the job was shit, but your home life was solid. Or domestic bliss was not in the cards, but your career was moving along at a healthy clip. If it was either/or, you could get by. But unfortunately, in a span of minutes, I had taken both from Aaron Sutter. He was already missing work, and the pride that came with it, the identity it gave him, and then I had made sure he knew we weren't solid either. My timing was fantastic.

"Take off your pants!" It was desperate and beseeching at the same time.

I had created doubt and fear. It was all on me. I was so stupid sometimes.

Moving fast, I tackled him, pile driving him down under me onto the floor of the car, my hand behind his head so he wouldn't bump it.

"What are you—"

"I'm sorry," I apologized, bending to press my forehead to his, closing my eyes at the same time.

He was very close to hyperventilating.

I inhaled and exhaled slowly, my hand moving between us, over his heart, just there, pressing gently, letting him feel the weight as I breathed.

He trembled violently, almost jerking under me as if an electric current had passed through his spine.

"Forgive me," I said, my voice hoarse and low, as I lifted my head and stared down into his eyes.

His hands were suddenly in my hair, buried there, holding on.

"I know why you want us to have sex."

He said nothing, but his eyes were riveted on mine.

"You make me stupid with wanting you," I confessed.

He gently massaged the back of my neck. "When we're together, you agree with me. You're not scared, and you commit to everything and anything I want."

"Isn't that what I just said?" I asked dryly.

He laughed lightly and lifted his leg to rub his thigh over my hip. "You really like fucking me."

I settled over him, and he wrapped both legs around my hips, as I burrowed my face into the side of his neck. "I do like it—love it actually—but that ain't all."

"No?"

I lifted my head so I could see his face. "Not hardly."

My words soothed him, and I watched the softness return to his eyes.

"Aaron—"

"Stop. Just listen to me," he said gruffly. "We're going into that resort together, and we're coming out together. The whole time we're there, you stay right by me."

"You know that might not be possible," I began gently.

"No," he whispered against my temple. "I know it's not a vacation. If it was, I'd have you sequestered away on some private beach."

I made a rumbling noise into the hollow of his throat, and he arched up off the floor, rubbing against me, moaning softly as he clutched at my back.

"You like it when I do that," I said, pleased because these were little things I could build on, private things between us.

"It drives me crazy," he confessed before he caught my gaze. "But seriously, you're going to love being on the yacht with me, but there's always, always going to be other people. Miguel is a constant because he's not just my driver, right? He keeps me safe. But there are housekeepers, butlers, cooks—these people are part of my life, and we've been together a long time. I have surrounded myself with an amazing group, and you'll find that out. But seeing me with you, that's part of the gig. It's part of having ironclad confidentiality agreements, and you need to get comfortable with that part of your life."

Yes, I did.

"The people who work for me are not just anybody."

"I get it," I insisted, shifting over him, pressing my hard groin to his.

"Are you hearing it? Are you listening? They're my staff, I trust them, and they trust me. Are you getting it?"

"Yeah, I get it."

"Yeah?" he asked, bending his knees and lifting slightly so my cock slid along his crease. "Are you sure?"

"Yes."

"Then enough of this bullshit," he rasped, grinding against me. "Enough of you pulling away from me! I don't ever want you to pull away from me!" He sounded scared and pissed and frustrated all together.

And I felt like such an asshole. "Sorry."

"Don't apologize if you don't mean it."

"I do mean it," I said huskily.

"Then no more of you even thinking about being out of this," he barked, toeing off his black penny loafers.

And he was right because that's where my brain had gone.

He put a hand on my chest and pushed back. "Help me."

Once he had his belt unbuckled and his pants unbuttoned, I grabbed the cuffs and shucked them down and off his long, muscular legs. I smiled when I saw what was underneath. "A thong?"

"I like them. They're not constrictive," he teased.

"No, they're not," I agreed, peeling down the black microfiber underwear. When I bent to lick the pearly drop of precome from the flared head of his cock, he choked out my name.

My lips closed around the crown, and he whimpered low and sweet before I dipped my head and began slowly sucking him down my throat, inch by inch.

"In my bag," he directed, even as he wriggled beneath me, one hand fisted in my thick hair. "There's lube. It's there, right there."

I just wanted to suck him dry.

"Duncan." He tugged urgently, trying to get me off him.

Lifting my head, letting his hot, wet cock slip from my lips, I heard his painful groan. "Get the bag!"

Turning, I saw what he wanted, grabbed the strap, and yanked it from where it was on the floor over to him.

He tossed open the flap and shoved a small bottle at me.

"You just carry that around?"

His eyes met mine. "Never know when you'll decide you actually want me."

"That's crap."

"Prove it," he flared, putting his feet on my thighs as I sat back above him. "Because all I've heard so far today is 'no'."

His bright eyes were locked on me, but they were heavy-lidded with need. Curling over him, I took brutal possession of his plump, shapely lips, grinding my mouth down over his, invading and tasting, sucking on his tongue.

He squirmed under me as he got my belt undone, trouser stays open, and briefs shoved down enough to let my cock bob free.

"Before we go into the resort," he said, panting, "I need you."

I slicked myself fast and pressed against his entrance as I lifted my eyes back to his.

"Please," he begged.

Slowly, I sank down into the welcoming heat of his body.

"You have to belong to me."

I lifted his legs to my shoulders and we moved together with the fluidity of years between us instead of merely days. Plunging deep and hard, I felt his muscles clenching around me. I pulled out, only to slam back inside.

"Don't stop!" he gasped, and I could hear unshed tears in his voice.

"You want promises, but you're scared to ask for them." It was a statement.

"Yes," he cried, and I knew it hurt to answer because it was true.

"Because everybody leaves you," I uttered his fear.

"Yes."

"Not anymore."

"Duncan... you have to want me, need me, have me... you have to stay...," he whined, his voice cracking as I pounded into him, driving to his core. "Please."

He was so tight and hot, and the way his hands clawed at me to keep me close, keep me buried inside him, all that was sexy. But his eyes were the true revelation. Whatever pride had been there was gone. I could see clearly what I was being offered, and his beautiful body was only part of it.

"Stay with me."

I had no intention of going anywhere.

"Promise me."

I shoved in, slid partway out, over and over, like I owned him, and he writhed beneath me, wanting more of my swollen cock and the savage pounding.

"I want the words."

I was so close to giving up and giving in.

"Baby."

"I promise," I said, and we both knew what I meant.

I would stay. I would be patient. I would be strong and swear to keep the secret of what the man looked like when he completely came apart and offered his heart up for the taking.

"Duncan!"

"I won't leave you."

And all the worry and fighting flooded out of him because from that second on, he would stand secure of his place in my heart.

"I want to feel your words."

Grabbing his hips, I lifted him up and rolled to my back, impaling him as I felt the desire licking up my spine.

"Make a mess all over me," I goaded him. "I'm yours."

He rode my cock hard, pressing down, shoving me inside impossibly deep, and I learned right then that the pistoning was not what got him off, but the stretch and the push. His muscles milked my length, the pleasure edged with pain, taking me inside, the intimacy and the dominance: that was what flipped his switch and made him spurt hot and thick over my abdomen.

My orgasm ripped through me as I thrust up into him, loving the feel of the aftershocks that consumed him, his ass spasming around my cock and his head thrown back on his shoulders in absolute surrender.

He was a vision.

I gathered him close and held him tight until he went boneless in my arms. I couldn't move that much, my dress pants only pushed to my knees, but enough so he could lift up and have my cock slide from his slick, wet hole.

Fluid ran out of him and onto me, and since there was no bathroom, no way to clean up before we had to get out of the car, I sacrificed my undershirt to the cause and wiped us both off.

"Duncan," he began, and I saw that my sweet man needed me.

Rolling forward and taking his face in my hands, I kissed his forehead and his eyebrows, nose, eyes, cheeks, and then took his mouth, inhaling him, kissing him until he had to pull away to breathe.

"You're not getting away from me," he panted.

"Don't want to. I'm right here. Not going anywhere."

I didn't know his eyes could get that big.

"We're in this."

"I thought we were in it before?"

"I will punch you in the head," I warned him.

His smile was radiant before he was all over me.

"You realize we have to get out of the car that smells like sweat and jizz, right?"

"Try to get me to care."

We moved apart, each of us surveying the state our passion had left us in. My pants couldn't be salvaged, my dress shirt had buttons missing, and I had semen sticking to my abdomen.

"This is such a bad idea," I assured him after retaking my seat.

"What?" He had flopped into his, sprawled out, looking completely debauched.

"Us getting out of the car."

"No," he said, scrambling forward, closing the short distance between us, and climbing back into my lap. "We're going to see this through. We're going to do our jobs here and then go back to Chicago because I really want to take you home."

"Why?"

"I'm ready for my life to start."

He had a way of knowing the right thing to say.

TWELVE

THE instructions were: drive up to the main gate of the resort, get out, and punch a code into the box. Once the code was transmitted to the front desk, a car would be dispatched with security personnel. The guests would have their passports or other ID ready to show when they were asked for it, and then they would be wanded with handheld metal detectors. All electronic devices, including cell phones, tablets, and the like, would be left in a secured, climate-controlled locker near the front gate. The guest would place items in the locker and get one key, and security would have the other key, much like a safety deposit box at the bank. The building where the lockers were housed had twenty-four-hour video surveillance, as well as its own security guards, to insure the safekeeping of all surrendered technology. Once all steps had been completed, IDs verified, and items relinquished and stowed, then a Jeep would show up to drive the guests the rest of the way, a mile and a half, to the main building.

Sitting there beside Aaron in the back of the nicest tricked-out, custom-leather-seat Jeep I had ever been in, I was able to take a breath.

"I hope you enjoy your visit here with us at Buona Sera," the driver said, smiling into the rearview mirror.

I opened my mouth to answer him, just to exchange pleasantries, but Aaron squeezed my knee and spoke instead. "Thank you so much."

I turned to look at him, and he gave the slightest shake of his head.

Not sure what was going on, I stayed quiet anyway, enjoying Aaron leaning against me, the last moments of it being just us before we were on stage.

A bellhop met us where we were let off and carried the two duffel bags inside the main building, where we crossed a wooden footbridge over a stream complete with river rock. The way it was done, it seemed to be floating, and already I was impressed.

The reception area was an enormous open atrium, beautifully landscaped, complete with a waterfall. But the bigger surprise came when I saw a man leading a stunning blond woman around on a leash.

Aaron's hand on the small of my back propelled me forward, and at the desk, the clerk, an attractive woman, smiled and said our stay would be taken care of by the owner of the resort, Mr. Wells.

"Oh. That's very kind of him." Aaron gave the woman his killer smile, and I watched her swallow her tongue. "But please take my card for incidentals, as I plan to be ordering many."

She shook her head. "No, Mr. Sutter. He said that he knew you would insist, but no."

"Well, that's so generous and unexpected. Are you able to tell me, will we be seated at his table this evening?"

"Yes, you will be, Mr. Sutter. Cocktails are at nine in the Red Room."

"Excellent."

She furrowed her brow delicately. "I don't mean to in any way overstep, sir, but does your boy have his collar?"

"He does, and thank you for your concern."

"I just wouldn't want him to be mistaken for someone who's available."

"Of course."

She looked relieved and her smile returned. "Here are your keys, sir."

"Thank you so much. Could you please point me in the direction of our bungalow?"

She produced a trifold map and proceeded to give him precise instructions. Once she was done, Aaron took my hand and walked me away from the front, but instead of following the path the nice girl had instructed he take, he veered off toward the balcony.

"What's going on?"

In answer, he let go of my hand, bent to his courier bag, reached inside it, and brought out a large black velvet box.

"What is this?"

He cleared his throat. "Here's the thing: there are specific rules at this resort that I pretty much guessed at from how Clay Wells acted when we met him."

I squinted in question.

"This whole scene is based on BDSM, though from what I know of Mr. Wells already, I can tell you that the true scene is not something he knows anything about."

This was new. "And you do?"

He shrugged. "I tried it a long time ago, when I was younger."

"And?" I asked, interested.

"Like the idea of that do you? Me held down?"

"Yeah," I said frankly, the thought of it very hot. "Answer the question."

"I lacked the commitment and discipline for the lifestyle."

"So you were too big of a flake is what you're telling me."

He laughed and passed me the box.

"What is this?"

"It's your collar for the weekend."

"It's my what for the what?"

He added coughing to his laughter.

"You have so lost me."

"I know," he said, running the back of his knuckles down my abdomen.

"Aaron?"

"Sorry, I'm distracted by the thought that you have my dried come on you under this henley you changed into in the car."

I shook my head and his smile was wicked.

"And by the way, watching you get out of your dress pants and into these jeans was one of the highlights of my life."

"You're such a wiseass."

He waggled his eyebrows at me.

"Can we focus?"

"Oh baby, I am so focused. Open that."

I expected one of the collars I had seen at clubs I'd busted in the past, or something from a movie, or any of those I'd glanced at on the Internet. I was not anticipating a rustic, hand-forged treasure. It was a silver chain with heavy links, had what appeared to be an oxidized patina, and was polished and shiny. At the center was a thick square piece with rounded edges and on it was an engraved *A*. When I lifted it out of the box, I realized that on the other side of the *A* was a *D*, and that it could be flipped to show off whichever letter I chose. On each of the four sides of the square—channel set into the metal—were two long, clear stones, eight in all.

"Aaron?"

"It will go back after this weekend; it's just here on loan."

"You could have slapped any old leather—"

"No," he cut me off. "Never."

My focus returned to the chain in my hands.

"Here," Aaron said softly, "let me show you the clasp. It's tricky."

"The silver is nice."

He scoffed. "That's platinum, baby."

"And I suppose these stones on the side are real diamonds."

"Baguette cut, and yes, they are."

My head snapped up. "Are you kidding?"

"No, I'm not kidding."

"Jesus, what if I lose it?"

"It won't come off accidentally; you'd have to purposely remove it."

"But—"

"It's nothing. Now look at this."

It didn't have a clasp, it had a lock, and it was impossible to work. One piece had to be pulled back, twisted to the side and then the two halves slid together and notched tight. He was right, you could never get it off quickly, and two hands were necessary. No fear of it going missing.

Once it was on, it sat heavily, but comfortably, below the hollow of my throat. "Does it look all right?" I checked.

The muscles in his jaw corded as he nodded.

"You're so full of crap."

He had to drag his eyes from the chain around my throat up to my face. "I'm sorry?"

"You think I'm an idiot?"

"What the hell are you—"

"Our initials are on the lock part," I pointed out, sliding my fingertips over the deeply engraved letters. "You had this made."

He was silent.

"But the question is, when did you have it made?"

He didn't answer.

"Aaron? You like the idea of a collar on me, do you?"

He was quiet but he held my gaze.

"Answer me."

"Yes." His voice quavered. "I love the idea of you wearing something that says you're mine. I wanted to get a huge gold chain with some enormous, really obnoxious, gold pendant with my name spelled out in diamonds on it, but I figured you'd think that was gaudy."

What I was wearing was heavy, the weight of it substantial, but it was not flashy, and you couldn't see the diamonds unless you turned the lock to look at the sides. Plus any collared shirt would hide it; even the top button of a shirt open wouldn't reveal the presence of the chain.

I had to be stripping out of clothes for it to be seen, which I guessed was Aaron's intent.

As a chain went, or collar—whatever he was calling it—the piece had clean lines and was very beautiful in my opinion. And really, the weight was sort of grounding, comforting. "I don't know if I'll keep it," I said, glancing at him.

"Whatever you want, but maybe…. You know, Jory has a tattoo on his back of Sam's name, and I never understood the point of that. I always thought he was such an idiot for doing it, but will you let me do that? Could I ink my name on your skin? Or a brand? How 'bout a brand?"

I couldn't control my smile.

"Down the road," he murmured, crowding up against me, hands on my hips. "Along with the ring."

"We already talked about the ring."

"Yes."

"A ring is a serious thing, Sutter."

He lifted a hand to the chain and fisted it. "This is serious, too, make no mistake."

"But this is just a cover," I reminded him.

But his eyes didn't agree.

I moved closer, my body flush with his until we were breathing each other's air. "Thank you for the gift."

"It's only a gift if you keep it."

I felt over the lock, found the side with the *A*, and flipped it so that was visible. His tremble was obvious. "You're easy to please."

"But I'm really not." He grinned evilly, leaning in to place a kiss behind my jaw. "I just seem to be smitten presently."

"Presently?" I teased, as one kiss became another and another, traveling down the side of my neck. The trail of them was wet, and the nibbling that accompanied each press of lips was doing funny things to my stomach.

"Yeah," he said, his hand brushing over the copper dragon belt buckle the front of my T-shirt was tucked behind. "Where did you get this?"

"Why? You like it?"

"I do," he said, tracing over it, his fingers trailing upward. "I like what's under it too."

"And I like that I have you on my skin."

"Shit," he groaned. "I can't trade banter with you, you always win. I want you too much."

"It goes both ways," I promised him. "Now let's find the damn bungalow."

"It's an adobe-style casita, actually."

"I have no idea what that means."

He cupped my cheek in his hand for a second, like I was dear, and then he told me to follow him.

"Yes, sir."

"Don't do that," he growled. "You start calling me sir and we'll never leave the room."

"You like me."

"No," he said absently, studying the map. "It's a lot more than that."

But how much more would be too fast, so neither of us was going there.

I was overwhelmed and wanted time to think, but he was moving, intent on finding our room, and I had to hurry to catch up to him.

It turned out we had our own small house, complete with a private patio and pool, a hot tub, and an amazing view of the mountains.

The master bedroom had a roof that could, with the push of a button, be retracted so you could sleep under the stars with nothing between you and the sky. The shower was so big, it had no doors, just a drain depressed in the center.

"It'll be like having sex outside," I announced happily.

Aaron made a face like I had lost my mind, and then gestured me after him through the sliding glass door to the lanai.

"What?"

"Are you kidding?" He was horrified.

"I missed something. What are we talking about?"

"No sex," he whispered.

"Why?" I asked, being as quiet as he was. "You got a problem doing it without the roof on?"

"No," he shook his head. "I have a problem doing it here at all. Imagine how much surveillance there is here."

He'd lost me. "Video surveillance?"

"And audio," he educated me. "Any sex we have here is being recorded. That's why I wanted to do you on the plane or in the car; you think I was ready to go three days without you when I just got you back? I mean, yeah, I get it; we're here to get the bad guy, but… I needed to get laid."

His words finally sank in. "Wait, you're not planning to fuck me until we leave here?"

He smirked at me.

"Have you lost your mind?"

"This is serious, Detective," he said under his breath. "We're undercover."

I so enjoyed being placated.

WE SPENT the day doing random activities like everyone else. There was tennis, which I sucked at, but Aaron had godlike skills on the court; skeet shooting that I should have been able to dust him at, but he was better at firing a rifle; and finally horseback riding that was a complete blowout. I fell off during a canter, and the man of my dreams laughed so hard, tears rolled down his face. It was not romantic in the least, and I never knew that horses pissed and shit while they walked. Lots of delusions shattered all at once.

That evening we went for drinks in the Red Room, so named because of the color of the walls, the sheer curtains, and the mood lighting. The tables, marble floor, and low couches where everyone reclined were all the same color.

Clay Wells was thrilled to see us and sat Aaron at his right. As clothing went, I realized I was overdressed in my jeans and short-sleeved silk shirt. Most of the other people sporting collars had barely anything on.

"What can we get you to drink?"

Aaron got a scotch and water, and I got some whiskey to sip.

"It's amazing, you know," Clay said after a few minutes.

"What's that?" Aaron inquired.

His eyes flicked to me and then back to my man. "How many people requested a scene with Duncan until they learned who he belonged to."

Aaron's smile was absolutely sinful. "No one's stupid enough to touch something of mine."

"Oh no?"

"No." He shook his head. "I have hit men on my payroll, after all."

And that was crap. I knew it was, but Clay Wells didn't, and neither did anyone else sitting close. They made sure to not even glance my way.

"I'm a billionaire." He snapped his fingers. "I make people disappear at will."

I slid my hand over his thigh because he needed to control his inner alpha. When I leaned sideways to whisper in his ear, he cupped the back of my head.

"Don't have to go all possessive right here in front of everyone," I reminded him.

"Yes, I do," he whispered back.

"We want him to approach me," I said under my breath.

His growl was evidence that the very idea was not boding well.

"Be good so we can go home."

I straightened up but he moved with me, his mouth kissing over my jaw, nipping lightly.

"God, Aaron, does he taste that good?" Clay asked, and the whole table laughed.

"Yes, he does," Aaron said, turning away from me. "Not that you or anyone else will ever find out."

And no one said a word to contradict him.

It was going to be a long night.

As we sat there in the uncomfortable silence, I checked out the room, noticing a swing in the opposite corner. It took me another minute, but I realized I was looking at Kian, naked and trussed up in the contraption.

Squeezing Aaron's thigh to get his attention, I pointed.

"Oh." He squinted and then addressed Clay. "Your boy is up for grabs?"

"What? Oh, yes. Kian's leaving my employ, and unlike you, Mr. Sutter, I give my pets the choice to find new masters. So whoever wants him at the end of this weekend is free to take him home with them."

"I see."

"I had already taken his collar off when you saw us in Vegas, so some who saw us there are here and are now vying to be the one who takes him."

Aaron scowled. "So you removed your protection."

"Yes."

"I find that reprehensible," Aaron passed judgment. "Better to simply sell him so that he goes from master to master instead of leaving him alone until someone new claims him."

"I don't see how giving him the choice is worse treatment."

"Because he should know that he's wanted, especially if he's a true submissive. He should know he's safe and won't be shared and will be sheltered."

Wells gestured over at Kian. "If you are so concerned, Mr. Sutter, make him an offer. But I suspect your idea of putting him through school, as you did Mr. Cobb, is not what—"

"How do you know about Jaden?"

"Because he told me." Clay smiled, lifting his hand.

I had never met Jaden Cobb. All I knew was he was the one who had cracked and confessed to Aaron's father about their relationship. In person, he resembled a younger version of Jory Harcourt. The similarities were many, but the differences were more pronounced. Jaden had a sort of plastic look about him, from the overly tweezed brows to the collagen-pumped lips to the deep tan that must have taken hours in a bed to achieve. Jory was a natural beauty; Jaden had been created.

He was stunning, though, and many in the area where we were sitting were entranced, as evidenced by the buzz he created when he took a seat on the floor next to Clay's thigh.

Aaron's eyes narrowed, and from the look on Clay's face, it was not the response he had been hoping for. As if he could rattle the billionaire. "So," Aaron clipped the word, staring holes through Jaden. "What happened to the cooking career?"

"I realized I don't really much like working," he simpered, rubbing his chin over Clay's knee. "I mean, I like to cook for one, but that's it."

"And so, back to being kept," Aaron said bluntly.

"Back to being pampered and adored," he corrected his ex.

"I see," Aaron nodded, leaning back against me.

Something was wrong.

"Lemme talk to you a sec," I said, getting up.

Aaron held out his hand and I lifted him to his feet.

Crossing the floor to the balcony, when we passed by the swing, I saw Kian on his feet looking up at a very angry-looking man who tightened a collar around his neck. He also yanked his own lightweight sweater up over his head and pulled it down over the smaller, younger man.

"Oh, that's good." Aaron cleared his throat. "It looks like someone was just waiting to hear that Kian was free of Wells."

The collar was thinner, but what was interesting was that it had none of those rings to attach something to like a leash. And what was most telling was the twisted metal on the front.

"What is that?"

"It's an Infinity Collar," Aaron informed me.

"Is that a big deal?"

"It is."

I smirked. "How come I don't have one?"

"Because yours had to be special, Detective."

We were close to the railing, so I grabbed him and crushed him to me, kissing the side of his neck.

"But whatever you want," he moaned, hands on my back, clutching tight.

"I'm sorry Jaden's an idiot," I growled into his ear before I kissed him.

"It's all right," he sighed, nestling closer. "That wasn't my first thought."

"What do you mean?"

"He reminded me that I tire of people and lose them," he said, staring up into my eyes. "And I thought that I need to make sure I don't lose my detective. That I don't let him get lost."

"It goes both ways," I said before I kissed him again.

Reaching under his suit jacket, I tugged at his shirt, yanking until it was untucked and I could get my hands on his skin. He felt good. He was open for me, ready, and then he shoved me away.

"What?" I gasped, my entire body hard and needy and ready to throw him up against any flat surface.

"The surveillance."

I was lost.

"I said we can't fuck here," he reminded me.

"Yeah, I know."

"Because it's being recorded," he said, as if I should have been riding his thought train already.

"Right."

"Well, what do you bet there is some place where they collect all that stuff?"

The light came on. "Oh shit, you're kinda brilliant."

He squinted at me. "Kind of?"

"Okay," I said, first rotating and then giving him a slight push back toward the room. "You go and be chatty. I'm gonna go look around."

"What?" He whirled on me. "No. We should go together. The story will be better that way. We'll say we're looking for our cabana."

"Casita," I corrected him.

"Whatever!"

"No. I'll be lost and drunk; you go back and be entertaining."

His eyes that had been passion-glazed a second ago were concerned now.

"What?"

"Should we even be talking like this? And I called you by your title a minute ago and… fuck."

He meant the audio surveillance. "I doubt it's bugged out here, probably just the rooms. Wiring the whole place for sound would be crazy expensive."

Aaron arched an eyebrow for me like I was stupid.

"Just go."

He was not convinced; but he left me. I checked to make sure no one saw me go and simply flipped over the railing and dropped the six feet to the path below. I would have preferred to have my running shoes on, because my dress shoes weren't as flexible or quiet, but Bond did it, so I would try and manage.

The grounds were ridiculous, but I figured that chances were any kind of surveillance room would be toward the front. It made sense, since farther back toward the small canyon, any signals would be harder to get. Yes, the resort had no Wi-Fi for guests, and it was billed as a positive. Like being away from the distractions of the outside was a good thing. But in reality, it would have been hell to get Internet into the resort, so it was actually very clever marketing.

Since only people who were invited into the resort got past the front gate, there was no one to provide us with detailed information about the grounds. The FBI had e-mailed me satellite pictures from NASA, and I had searched the resort on Google Earth, but none of those photos had markers on the buildings because nobody knew what was what. What I had seen had been no help at all. And anyone the FBI went to could have potentially tipped off Clay Wells.

So I was sort of moving around blind on the grounds until I saw the small tower. The antenna was a dead giveaway, as was the dish on top. It was tucked behind some very tall flowering trees and was no taller than an average two-story house.

The door was locked, of course, and a key card was needed to get inside. My only recourse was to either wait for someone to come out—and not knowing when a shift changed or even if someone was on duty, that seemed futile—or find where the staff quarters were. I needed to get into the room and see how they stored data and fortunately, I wasn't worried about a search warrant. I had one to look, just not one to enter. But since I had been invited…. It was sticky but if I could identify Evan Polley on the grounds, from video surveillance, that would be enough to tie the two men together. That, along with a wiretap would elicit the kind of investigation that would ruin Clay Wells. I had to do some more looking around, but I was getting worried about Aaron explaining my absence.

Coming around the side by the footbridge, I saw Kian and his new guy. The man, easily six five to Kian's maybe five eight, had him in his arms, the younger man's arms and legs wrapped around him. I stopped to look at them because how could I not?

"They look beautiful together, do they not?"

I turned and confronted a very handsome man, older, silver at his temples, tall and broad-shouldered, powerfully built. His pale-blue eyes were like glittering pieces of ice, cold and empty. He appeared eastern European to me; his accent wasn't soft, as others I knew were, but sharp and precise. Although the words were benign, the voice was like a razor.

"They do," I agreed.

He offered me his hand. "Goran Begović."

I slipped mine into his. "Duncan Ross. Pleasure."

"No," he said, taking a step closer, his eyes all over me, finally stopping at the heavy chain around my neck. "It is very much mine."

It was not lost on me that he was still holding my hand.

It was hysterical, really. Back home, in my life, walking around, I never got this kind of attention. No one saw me outside of the club when I was trolling for a one-night, or one-hour, stand. But now that Aaron was suddenly looking at me, everyone else was as well.

I tried to ease my hand back, but he tightened his grip.

"That is a lovely piece," he said, lifting his other large, meaty hand to my neck, his fingers sliding over the surface of the collar. He lifted it and saw that the *A* could be flipped to a *D*.

"So the *D* is from Duncan. What is the *A* for?"

"Aaron," I answered, trying to take a step back, but his fist around the chain made that impossible.

"Wait," he said gently, calmly, releasing my hand but not the chain. "Don't be scared."

I glowered. "Let go."

And he got it because I saw the understanding fill his eyes. I wasn't afraid; I was annoyed.

"You look like you've been in your share of fights, Duncan."

"A few."

He nodded. "You've taken some damage. Your nose, your hands…. May I please see below the chain?"

"I don't think—"

"You need to show me, actually. You're away from your master, and I am returning you to him. While he's not here, you need to do as I say, within reason. Unbuttoning your shirt is a small request."

I had no idea what the protocol was, but I seriously doubted he was telling me the truth. The thing was, I didn't want the act—me strolling the grounds by myself—to have attention drawn to it, so I complied.

When my shirt was unbuttoned, he flattened his hands on my chest, sliding them over my skin like he was sculpting my pecs.

"Your body is beautiful."

I just stood there, waiting.

His hands ran down my abdomen and finally settled on my hips as his eyes lifted to mine. "Very beautiful."

It took a lot of concentration not to move away.

"These scars," he said, tracing a fingertip over one that bisected my collarbone, "are from some kind of service. These are not bondage scars. These were made to try and kill you, not for fun, not for punishment. I know the difference."

"How do you know?"

His smile did nothing for his eyes, infused no warmth. "I've inflicted some that look like this, seen more."

"You're in the service?"

"Not here."

"Where are you from?"

His eyes narrowed, and too late, I saw his gaze slip past me.

Hands gripped my wrists, the back of my neck, and I was shoved forward. Someone grabbed the chain and used it to choke me, and I was shown a knife before I felt the tug on my belt.

I was not small. I was strong and big, so the very idea of being overpowered and held down, having others force themselves on me... rape me... had never, ever, entered my consciousness. It was not something that could happen to me.

But there were so many hands, and my belt had been cut from the back and pulled through the loops, the buckle yanked off from the front. I saw the bench, just four steps into the bushes in a small clearing, like it was natural that it should be there under the stars. Rings were soldered into a cement base so chains could be attached, leashes fed through, and tethered. I was slammed down, winded, my chest smacking the wood, head thumping hard enough that, for a second, my vision swam. One of the men took that opportunity to show me the large hunting knife he'd used to destroy my belt, serrated and thick, and I wished I could see it better, but I could barely focus.

Fingers were inside the back of my jeans, sliding close to the top of my crease, and I heard the rip as the knife began slicing through denim. For a second, a beat of time, a rush of terror, of futility, swept through me, but I moved my right foot in reaction, just a slight jolt, and I realized it was free.

In law enforcement, there are two schools of thought. One says it's all you and your weapon. Your gun will get you out of any dilemma: become a marksman and learn the lethal art of bringing down any target.

My partner was very good with his firearm. You did not want to face him down in an alley if you both had your guns drawn. He would put a bullet in your head before you even thought to return fire. Sam Kage was the same way, as evidenced by the canon the man carried as his spare.

I had never been a great shot and so had to depend on the second protocol of self-defense, the whole *dive-into-the-fray* part most cops didn't much care for. I was the guy who tried to grab you before you could get the gun clear of the holster. It was not the preferred way for a policeman to conduct himself. It accounted for me being hurt more than Jimmy or Sam, the distance the gun created keeping you clear of fists, bats, brass knuckles, and knives. What I found, however, was that people who depended on their guns were not so great with the hand-to-hand stuff—except the special ops guys, of course—or the grappling. So when I drew back with my leg, pushed forward, and got it under me, my leverage got better, and I was able to twist sideways and kick out.

The sound of a knee popping, followed by a high-pitched wail, was music to my ears.

"You fuck!"

I lifted in time to get a fist in my face, my left eye feeling like it had liquefied and spurted out of my socket. There was blood, and I knew it was mine, but it didn't matter. I wasn't helpless anymore.

When he turned and swung at me with his leg, I threw myself back, clear of the kick, and dropped to the ground. When I rolled, my hand slid over my discarded belt buckle in the gravel clearing, and I grabbed it, wrapping the belt up fast as I got to my knees.

"No!" I heard Goran yell, but his man charged me anyway, and when he was close enough, he got a fist to his balls. With my belt wrapped around it, it had a larger surface, which doubled the force of my blow. He dropped like a rock.

My heartbeat was pounding in my ears as I sprang to my feet and kicked the guy in the head, rendering him unconscious. Then I turned on the other, who was still clutching his knee, and kicked him as hard as I could in the ribs.

I missed the guy with the knife, but the blade sliced and didn't stab, his angle poor.

Grabbing his arm, I bent his wrist and heard it snap, followed instantly by his scream, and then I shoved him down and off me, taking the knife as I whirled on Goran.

His eyes that I had found so dead were now wide and glittering.

I stayed where I was, wary, listening for anyone.

"That was magnificent."

Taking a step back, keeping all of them in my sight, I slowly straightened up from my crouch.

"I would like to speak to your master. Please show me to him."

"You're kidding?"

He took a step forward and I took one back.

"No," he lifted his hand. "Please. Let me talk to you."

"You just tried to assault me."

He smiled placatingly, as if my statement were insane. "It was a test. If you hadn't fought, we would have let you go."

"Or," I offered, "the whole nonconsent thing is your kink, and now that I'm here and you're there, you're giving me this line of bull."

"No, I—"

"You just let me hurt your men for a test?"

He made a face. "They're not my men; they're resort security. They work for Wells. We're not allowed to bring our people here with us. You know that."

"Emergency," the guy who's wrist I had broken suddenly yelled, and I saw the walkie-talkie on him, and when he moved, hanging from the inside pocket of his dress shirt, his security badge. "We need immediate medical evac."

"Duncan," Goran began. "Please, show me to your master. I must explain and offer recompense for damaging his property."

I heard people running, feet pounding up the concrete path, and in the chaos of the swarm of help, I bent and lifted the key card from the guy I had kicked unconscious and slid it down over my hip under my briefs.

A woman was suddenly in front of me, her hands on my face, looking at me.

"Your right eyebrow is going to need stitches," she informed me. "Will you come to the infirmary with me?"

"Sure."

"Who's your master?" she demanded, wincing as she examined my neck.

"Aaron Sutter," I said, and just uttering the man's name, I felt better.

The people in front of me did not have the same reaction.

My nurse—doctor? I wasn't really sure yet—her eyes popped open wide like I'd shocked the crap out of her. And big scary Goran Begović made a noise in the back of his throat. When I glanced at him, he was absolutely ashen.

I grinned. "Let me guess, do you happen to know Aaron Sutter?"

I thought he was going to faint.

Chapter THIRTEEN

HER name was Miranda, and she was, in fact, a medical assistant there at Buona Sera. She was very nice and gave me a local anesthetic before she closed the cut above my left eyebrow, five stitches in all, as well as the slice above my right nipple, which took six. My nose, amazingly enough, came through the assault unscathed, but my lip was cut and my left cheek rapidly changed color. I had blood on my shirt, my jeans were done for, and my shoes, which had been in fair shape before, were cut up from the gravel we had been fighting on.

"I'm really worried about your head." She winced. "Your pupils are huge and your neck is just raw. You need to take that chain off."

It was rubbing, and as much as I liked it, it did need to come off. But I had to wait for Aaron to do that. He was the one who could remove it, not me. It wasn't my place. And not for any other reason besides the obvious: it would make him wonder if he got there and it was on the examination table beside me instead of around my neck. I never wanted him to doubt I belonged to him.

I was sitting, being fussed over by Miranda, when Aaron charged in with Clay Wells and Goran Begović close on his heels. He was in front of me in seconds, hands on my thighs, gripping tight as he stared at my face.

"Hey." I smiled, reaching out, putting a hand on the side of his neck, staring into his eyes. "I'm okay."

He had no response, just kept his gaze locked on mine.

I reached for him, but he gave me a slight shake of his head before he reached up for the chain. "I don't want to take it off," I said, "but...."

"But it was used as a weapon against you," he said roughly, his hands moving slowly, gently, over my skin.

Once it was unlocked, he put it around his own neck and locked it, flipping the *A* to the *D* before moving his hands away.

"What do you think?" he demanded gently.

"I think I miss the feel of it for some reason, but it looks really good on you."

"The ownership thing is odd, isn't it?"

"It is," I answered, my voice low and husky.

He slumped against me, pressing his forehead to mine, and soaked in the closeness, same as I did.

"We'll be home soon," I offered by way of solace.

"Good," he said and suddenly pivoted to face the two men.

"Mr. Sutter, I—"

"No!" he said flatly, and I could hear the tremor in his voice. He was furious.

Goran sucked in a breath. "I had no earthly idea that this man belonged to you. I—"

"Yes," Aaron agreed. "You didn't know... or you did."

"I swear! I would never attack you or test you in any—"

"It's not real," Clay pleaded. "Mr. Sutter, he's done it many—"

"No!" he roared, and it was loud and I heard how incensed he was. I heard again what I had thought was anger but now knew was fear. There was nothing worse than making someone not only mad, but scared as well. People did surprising things when pushed to that extreme. Aaron Sutter was at the end of what he could take. He was tired of the uncertainty.

Gently, I reached out and put my hand on his shoulder. He covered it with his a moment later.

Clay cleared his throat. "Mr. Sutter, please—"

"Mr. Wells," he cut him off. "You will see Mr. Begović from your resort immediately, or I will simply leave here and direct my people to purchase this property by any means necessary and then raze it to the ground."

Clay Wells looked absolutely terrified, and it took him a moment to gather himself enough to speak. "Mr. Sutter, I can't simply—"

"Make your choice now," Aaron said implacably. "Me or him."

"Mr. Sutter," Goran began. "I—"

"Mr. Begović, please advise your board that Sutter will no longer be joining with your company to purchase the previously agreed-on telecommunication companies in Europe. We will not be doing any business together."

"You—no, I—this is absurd! One does not conduct affairs in this—"

"I do," he cut off the older man, who was now turning red in indignation. "If you leave now and I never, ever, see you again, perhaps I won't partner with Mihovil Cvetko and buy out your shares of your own company. But you have to go now."

"Mr. Sutter, one is business and one is—"

"My heart," he whispered, and I saw the slight shudder run through him. "You are on the receiving end of a great gift, Goran. I don't have my phone. If I leave here, I'll have it in minutes. The second I get it, your company is mine. If I were you, I'd run away."

"I—"

"Scurry home."

"I'll ruin you!" he almost-shrieked at Aaron. "Everyone will know of your—"

"Everyone knows already," he cut the older man off. "This is my partner you put your hands on, and the whole world knows who he is."

He fainted.

"Holy shit," I gasped. I had never actually seen a man faint, and it was weird. He went stiff, his eyes rolled back in his head, and then he was on the floor.

Aaron Sutter had frightened the man unconscious.

"Damn," I muttered, grabbing Aaron and easing him around to face me. "You're a scary motherfucker, Aaron Sutter."

I was hoping for a smile, but he was in too much pain. He looked broken.

"Awww, honey, I'm okay," I promised, wrapping my arms around him, pressing my face down into his shoulder.

"Do not placate me," he rasped, clutching his fingers into my hair. He massaged my scalp as his lips placed gentle butterfly kisses along my jaw.

"You fucking liars."

Both our heads snapped up, and when I saw Clay's face, I understood what had happened.

"He's not your boy or your slave or your possession," he snarled, taking a step back toward a phone on the wall. "He's something ridiculously ordinary. He's your boyfriend, and you love him."

"And if I do?"

I really needed to school Aaron Sutter in the fine art of deflection and plausible deniability.

Christ.

"Then that means you have no intention of letting me fuck him," he accused Aaron. "And he has no intention of going into business with me."

But we had been doing so well….

"Who are you?" he roared.

"He's a homicide detective from Chicago," Aaron spat. "And you killed Evan Polley, and you're not going to get away with it."

It was too bad he didn't shake his fist at Wells too. That would have just completed the ridiculousness of the scene.

Clay spun around and lunged for the phone, and thankfully, I was hurt but not dying, so I could leap off the table, grab him, and drive him face-first into the wall. He slid down it when I let him go, out cold as he puddled to the floor.

Turning, I looked at Aaron and threw up my hands.

"I don't care!" he snapped irritably, gesturing at me. "You think I'm going to let this go on?"

The scream startled us both, and poor Miranda, who had just stitched me up, spun around and pulled the fire alarm beside the door she had just walked through.

Perfect.

Aaron bolted to me, and I grabbed his arm and yanked him out the other door so we were together on the path outside the infirmary.

"I cannot believe you just completely lost it like that," I barked, tugging him after me. "What were you thinking?"

"I want you to come home with me!" he returned, agitated and annoyed.

"We're going home right after this," I volleyed, irritated at him for ruining everything. "I can't believe you just fucked the whole op by—"

"Who cares? I don't care! Fuck them! Fuck all of this!" he bellowed. "You got hurt!"

"You can't just say fuck the op when you feel like it! This is the Federal Bureau of—"

"They can send me a fuckin' bill! I will not have you hurt!"

"I always get hurt!"

"Not anymore!"

I shook my head as I led him at a brisk clip back toward the security tower.

"Don't treat me like I'm naive," he warned crossly. "I want you in one piece, and I want you living with me where I can keep an eye on you the second we get home!"

"Oh?" I huffed out, a bit more sore then I thought I was, moving us along faster and faster. "I thought you didn't move people in anymore."

His eyes were blazing, which was good because it meant he was focused on *me* and not on us getting shot, or God knew what else. We still had a chance to salvage everything if we could just get to the security room.

"I changed my mind," he fumed as he increased his speed, now jogging along beside me.

"And when did you do that, Mr. Sutter?" I asked, hearing people yelling behind us as we turned the corner and charged down another path.

"Back there," he shouted. "When I walked in and saw you hurt. Everything changed."

"How come?" I prodded, keeping him diverted, seeing the tower far to the left.

"I decided I want you in my bed and in my house and on my couch—I just fucking want you!"

It was really very sweet. It was too bad his timing was for total shit.

"Did you hear me?"

"It impossible not to hear you," I assured him, pointing. "We're going there."

We ran together and the gravel we pounded over flew up in the air, plaster from the side of the buildings exploded, and then a light fixture burst close enough we had to swerve around it as we picked up speed.

"Faster!" I roared.

"Wait." Aaron was trying to make sense of things even as he kept up with me. "What's happening?"

"People are shooting at you," I snapped, reaching the tower door a second ahead of him, slamming the key card flat against the faceplate, and hearing the buzz as the door opened.

We scrambled inside, shoved the door closed behind us, and stood there, leaning against it. I was panting, winded from the fight and the anesthetic, but Aaron was fine, just stunned.

"What?"

"People can't shoot at me. I'm Aaron Sutter!" He was so indignant, and it would have been funny if, on the other side of the solid steel door, there weren't bullets ringing off as they hit.

"I think they want to kill you." I burst his bubble. "Sorry, honey."

He studied my face.

"What?"

"I like it when you call me honey."

"Seriously, we're about to be killed here. You get that, right?"

"Not today." He smiled wide, his eyes scanning the room. "But you go upstairs, see if there's anybody up there, and I'll find something to disable the key card entry with."

It seemed reasonable, so I bolted up the short, winding staircase to the second floor.

No one was there. Since we hadn't been shot at when we came in, I was pretty confident there wouldn't be. But the wall of monitors on three sides was impressive. If, as we'd been told, there were fifty bungalows—adobe-style casitas, or whatever—then it looked as though each one had four cameras. Others monitored the grounds. Sitting down at the console, I saw digital controls for everything.

"Aaron!"

"I haven't found anything yet to disable this door with!"

"It's okay," I called to him over my shoulder. "I can do it from here."

He was up the stairs and sitting down beside me in moments.

"Where's the lock?" he asked me.

I showed him the manual override, tripped it, and then flipped on the exterior camera so I could see the door. There were easily thirty men there, guns drawn, half with rifles, and they would certainly have stormed in if there had been a way for them to do so. But the door was seamless, and once triggered, it swung in, not out. It had no handle, and when I hit the override, metal bars slid across to secure the door from the inside. The outside of the tower was steel as well. Not one window anywhere, and basically, it was like being inside a submarine. We were safe. They couldn't get in. Unfortunately, neither could we get out.

"Check and see if there's water or anything else in here," I said, feeling my head start to pound.

While he went to look, I tried to figure out where the search function was. I had to see what I could find on Evan Polley before Clay

Wells figured out a way to get in. By the time Aaron joined me, I could barely see. Even the light from the computer monitor was painful, and I had more than a headache.

"Hey," Aaron said softly, returning with two bottles of chilled water. "There's a small refrigerator downstairs, but there's only water in it. And the storage room has cables and things like that, probably for the TVs and computers at the front desk. There's also cleaning supplies and crap like that."

"Okay," I sighed, squinting at the monitor.

"What's wrong?"

"Nothing."

"Don't give me that. Your color is for shit. You're actually gray, and your pupils are just—baby, you need to lie down."

"I can't lie down," I snapped. "I have to—"

"Let's just trade places, and you can put your head down, all right? You can stay right here with me."

"I know more about this than you do."

He scoffed. "Oh, I doubt that. This is surveillance. I have corporate security, and I have spies who do some serious hacking."

I twisted around to face him. "Are you breaking the law?"

"Yes." He smiled at me. "Now move."

"That's bad," I said, sliding over into the other chair as he took my spot.

He scoffed.

I realized how lame I sounded.

"That's bad?" he repeated.

"I'm dying," I muttered. "Gimme a break."

"You're not dying," he said seriously. "But yes, it is bad. I promise to start being a much more solid citizen now that I have secured my place at Sutter, have controlling shares, and most importantly, have a hot boyfriend."

"Really?"

"What?"

"You are acting so weird."

He shrugged and then started typing seconds later. The weird B-movie villain laugh came shortly after that. "Oh, Keystone, my old friend."

"What's Keystone?"

"It's a surveillance program we used to run at Sutter, before we upgraded to Você, that monitors all our in-house cameras, as well as all the devices in Sutter Plaza."

"You mean your program basically is on everyone's computer at your company."

"Yes," he answered, not looking at me. "Except mine, Levin's, Miguel's, and Margo's."

"And do your employees know it's on there?"

"I'm sure they can guess, but you can't see it. Even if you're good, you can't."

"You can't just know all their private stuff."

"If they're doing private stuff on my time, on my computer, I have every right."

"I don't think so."

He grunted.

"Aaron, that's an invasion of privacy," I chastised him.

"They can have no expectation of privacy while they're on my clock," he replied, still typing, looking for Evan Polley in the database. "And by the way, there is no audio on this surveillance."

"Not that it really matters anymore but that's good."

He typed furiously.

"Okay, wait." My brain hurt, and I put my head down on my folded arms and closed my eyes. "You said *all* the devices at Sutter Plaza."

"I did."

"So just what's on the premises, or what comes in too?"

"You're very quick, Detective."

I growled.

"But yes, everything."

"So, cell phones too?"

"The program checks all devices for any crumb connected to Sutter. So say, while you're in my building, you even text a word about Sutter, the program is alerted and your device is scanned."

"How?"

"Wi-Fi."

"It just accesses the device without you knowing?"

"Yes."

"So my phone, because I have your number in there and I'm at Sutter, the program is basically hacking me to see what information I have about your company?"

"No."

"But you just said that all devices—"

"All phones belonging to law enforcement personnel are off limits to the program, Detective."

"I have sensitive information on my—"

"Are you listening to me? We don't scan any devices belonging to anyone in—"

"And this program just knows that, does it?"

"Don't sound so snide." He chuckled. "Of course it knows."

"How?"

"I'm sorry, Detective; I think I'll need to put you in contact with the people in my tech department if you need a full explanation of all the ins and outs of a program I did not, in fact, create."

"You know that's bad, right?" I groaned, feeling the splintering headache starting to make me nauseous. "God, I think I actually have a concussion this time."

"What can I do?" he asked sharply.

"Nothing."

He took a breath, and I felt his hand in my hair. "I have to do something."

"Just keep doing what you're doing and talk to me."

"Okay."

"So how does the program work?" I changed the subject.

"I don't—"

"Just dumb it down for me."

"I would never have to do that with anything."

"Yes, that's very nice," I placated him. "Just talk."

"Fine. It works sort of like a virus," he began. "We had a couple of really great hackers try to get in to Sutter about three years ago. They were good, but our firewall held, and we were able to track them down to this tiny little ass crack of a town in Brazil—Caetés, Pernambuco."

"And?"

"And I hired them, of course, and they made me Você, which we market a scaled-down version of called Bloodhound to the masses."

"So you have Você at Sutter, and you sell Bloodhound."

"Right."

"Okay, so Bloodhound is what Wells has?"

"No. Like I said, he has what we used to use five years ago when I took over Sutter."

"And it does what?"

"It only does surveillance, not the web. It's all internal; nothing external."

"Okay."

"But the one thing they all have in common is the program lets you monitor everything from one centralized interface."

"Which is how you're messing with it."

"Yes."

I made a noise and then just listened to him type for a while until he gently shook me.

"Head hurt?"

I made a noise of agreement.

"Maybe you should drink some water?"

"Yeah, okay."

I drank half of the twenty-ounce bottle and then put my head back down.

"If you have to pee, I'll get you another bottle."

"I'm okay," I whispered.

"Okay. Rest some more. I'm transferring different chunks into one file. If I could just get to my phone, we could have Internet."

"And, ya know, backup," I teased.

"Well, yes, there would be that."

"So you found Wells and Polley together already?"

"I did."

He didn't sound happy. "What's wrong?" I asked, rolling my head to look at him.

"There's someone else on the surveillance too."

"Oh? Who?"

"Nick McCall."

I groaned loudly. "Are you kidding?"

"No."

"I totally bought it. The whole concerned friend thing. Fuck, I'm an idiot."

"You were a horny idiot," he said playfully, kissing my right eye closed because I was turned that way. "Lucky I didn't let you fall into his clutches."

"Yeah, because hanging out with you is so much safer."

He laughed and so did I, even though it hurt.

WE COULD drink water and pee. The problem was, after three days, we would need food. I also suspected from the way I was losing time my head was in worse shape than I thought.

"You have a serious concussion," Aaron assured me. "You get beat up too often."

No argument there.

"Hey," I began, watching as he continued to type. "I wanna tell you about my juvenile records, if you still want to hear."

"Yes, please." He cupped my face, giving me all his attention.

"Check on the door real fast."

"There are only maybe five men out there now; the rest of them went with Wells to walk around the grounds. Maybe they're looking for a rocket launcher."

"What?"

"Or a bazooka."

"Really?"

"Would a flame thrower help?"

"You're not funny."

"I'm a little funny," he said, sliding his thumb over my eyebrow. "You know, if I haven't said it enough, you are just beautiful."

"You're biased. I'm yours, so you gotta think I'm pretty."

He stiffened.

"What?"

"You belong with me."

"We already settled that."

"No. I mean…." He took a breath. "When we get home, just move in."

"If we get home."

"No. When."

"Let's talk about it later," I placated him.

"I want to talk about it now."

"Aaron," I began. "You—"

He laughed. "It's going to suck for you."

"In what way?"

"In the being taken seriously way," he snorted out a laugh.

"I can shoot somebody. I bet that would let them know I mean business."

"Stop. Just think about it a second."

"Gimme an example."

"Okay, let's say you show up at a crime scene, and before you can even ask a question, the press is there and they'll yell out crap like 'Hey, we saw you on TV at the black-tie event to open the new exhibit at the Field Museum. How were the hors d'oeuvres, Detective?'"

"Yeah?"

"Yeah." He nodded. "And you'll go places with me and I'll get out and then you, and you think they went after you in Vegas? Oh, baby, when you're in your tux standing next to me, it will be insane."

I absorbed that.

"Your days of ever going undercover again are over."

But I already knew that.

"We're talking about newspapers, magazines, the web…. I mean, people will Google 'Aaron Sutter's boyfriend', and your picture will pop up."

Yes, it would.

"I mean, are you getting this? Are you truly understanding—"

"I got it," I said, reaching for him, sliding my hand inside the collar of his shirt so I could touch his warm skin.

He flinched.

"What's wrong?"

"Your hands are freezing." He sounded worried. "Why are you freezing?"

"I don't know."

"Can you hold me?"

"Sure," I grinned.

"No, idiot. I mean, will it hurt you if I get in your lap and give you some of my body heat?"

"No. C'mere. Make with the heat."

"Such a hedonist you are."

"I dunno what that means," I said, leaning back so he could get up and then sit down in my lap, straddling my thighs. "You wanna maybe—oh."

He wrapped me in his arms, and only with him against me did I realize how cold I was.

"You feel so good," I said.

"So do you, Detective. Now tell me about your juvenile record."

"Okay."

And he listened attentively, never once glancing away, as I recalled the greatest horror of my life. When I was done, I waited for his response, the outrage, the righteous anger for me and for what had happened, the yelling that was the usual reaction of everyone I ever confessed the truth to.

"He must have loved you so much," he said gruffly, tears in his voice as he leaned forward to hold me as tight as he could.

No doubt about it, Aaron Sutter knew my heart as no one ever had. I was never going to let him go.

FOURTEEN

THE following morning, Saturday, I understood the mess we were actually in when I woke up and realized the image of the outside door I was looking at had changed. "What happened to the camera angle?" I asked Aaron.

"They shot down the camera over the door last night."

I jolted. "Why didn't you wake me?"

"For you to do what?" Aaron studied me. "Yell? You needed your sleep and I can still see them, just now from a little further away."

"Aaron—"

"Lay down," he ordered me. "Everything will be fine."

He was being very optimistic but the reality was that Clay Wells could not let us out of his surveillance tower.

Wells wasn't stupid; he probably had a pretty good idea why a homicide detective would have gone in there and what I was after. He also had to have figured out that either Aaron or I could work the interface. He was probably kicking himself for not putting a passcode on it. His biggest problem, however, was time. Monday morning, Aaron Sutter was supposed to walk off the property. Miguel Romero would be waiting for him at the gate in forty-eight hours. If Aaron didn't show, Miguel would start with a call to Special Agent Summers, move on to a press conference, and end by calling the governor. It was, Aaron assured me, Miguel's SOP to basically scramble the marines. There was no way that Clay Wells had ever had such a public figure as

Aaron Sutter on his property. There just weren't a lot of billionaires wandering around, and even if he had, inviting my boyfriend had been a mistake, one I was certain he regretted. We could see him pacing the grounds close to the tower.

Even though they had shot the camera down over the door so we couldn't see, there was another higher up that no one had yet bothered with and another in a jacaranda tree across the way. Clay Wells probably didn't even know it was there. I couldn't imagine anyone could just sit down and recall how many cameras there actually were on any one property. We could see him walking up and down, flailing his arms, worrying his bottom lip, and kicking at the ground. The man was getting more and more wound up by the second.

"See," Aaron said to the man on the screen as if he were schooling him. "This is what comes of letting your little head think for your big one."

I watched from the floor, where I was sprawled out on a tarp using Aaron's suit jacket for a pillow. "What are you talking about?"

He turned in his chair and looked down at me. "If Clay Wells had been less interested in your ass and more focused on business, he would have surmised from what he knew of me that I don't share. I never share, and thus inviting you and me here was an exercise in futility."

"That's crap," I scoffed.

"What the hell do you mean by that?"

"You told me when we first met you shared your boyfriends. You used to get off watching them get fucked by other people."

"Yeah? So?"

"So you did, in fact, use to share them," I pointed out.

He scowled at me.

"Right?"

"I guess," he snapped.

"No guess, it's the truth." I pinned him down. "So what you're actually asking him to have known is that, with me, your agenda suddenly changed."

His eyes were locked on my face.

"Isn't that correct?"

He nodded.

"The man had no idea that you weren't actually going to give me to him or to anyone else for that matter."

"No one touches you but me. Ever."

I laughed softly. "Which is real nice of you to say and all, very scary alpha, but I'm the one who makes that decision Sutter, not you."

He took a quick breath.

"And since you're the only one I'll let touch me, we're on the same page."

It was endearing the way he was biting the inside of his left cheek as he quickly nodded.

"But your point, that you don't share, I mean, how the fuck was he supposed to know that?"

"I would have," he groused at me. "I make it my business to stay up to date on everything."

"That's gotta be hard to do."

"Hard yes, impossible, no. It's lazy to do anything less. I know everything about anyone I'm even thinking about going into business with."

"Oh yeah?"

"Of course."

"So that guy Goran, you know all about him?"

"Yes."

"You know who he fucks?"

"Names and dates, yes."

I was impressed, and Aaron could see it on my face. "I'm sorry you stopped a business deal because of me."

"No," he said, smiling. "I'm glad you discovered the man was a snake. Imagine if I had made the mistake of going into business with him. Then any one of his indiscretions might have tarnished my reputation. But now I'm free of him, thanks to you."

"Okay. So what do you think Clay Wells is going to do now?"

He thought a moment. "If I was him, I would try to find some leverage to get us to open the door."

"Like?"

"Like holding a gun on someone you love and threatening to shoot them if we don't open up."

"Yeah, that won't work," I replied, yawning and rubbing my eyes. "You're already in here with me." Clay Wells would be wasting valuable time looking into my background, only to find an estranged father, stepmother, and half sisters who weren't sure what city I lived in.

I was thinking I should get up and give Aaron a chance to rest. The cement floor covered by the thin tarp wasn't much, but he had to be exhausted. "Hey," I said, looking up to make the offer that we switch places only to find him sitting there, frozen, staring at me. "What's wrong?"

"Do you know your voice is different when you talk to me?"

"What do you mean?" I wasn't sure what his point was.

"I mean it changes, just the sound."

"Does it?"

"Yes. So I always know when you're speaking to me."

I watched him as he stood up and then sank to his knees beside me.

"You don't even know what you said, but even if the words had been lost on me, I would have heard the tone."

It took a second, and then it hit me.

Everything I loved was in the room with me.

Way to fuck up the declaration. "Shit, Aaron I'm sorry. I didn't mean to—"

But he cut me off when he rolled forward, took my face in his hands, and kissed me. He led with his heart, and I felt it as his mouth claimed mine, as his tongue pressed inside, as his hand cupped the back of my head to keep me still.

He made love to my mouth, coaxing, sucking, his other hand lifting to my throat, curling gently over my Adam's apple. The pressure was slight, but like his hand in my hair, immobilizing. He wanted me there, under his power, his mouth sealed to mine, making me his with every kiss, halting breath, whimper, and moan.

God, I loved him, and when I couldn't breathe, I tore free so I could. "I love you," I said, and it wasn't half as terrifying as I figured it would be.

"I know." He smiled, lips hovering over mine. "And I love you back, Duncan Stiel, and we're going to live happily ever after."

"As soon as we get out of this giant thermos," I said wryly, taking hold of his hips and easing him close.

He loved me. And I loved him back, so fiercely, so completely. I had been blindsided from the start. People would say it was too sudden, but I knew my heart just as well as I knew my mind, and it was as true for me as it was for him. I had wanted to be his from the moment the man had first taken hold of my hand to lead me toward the cab the night we'd met.

I was a sucker for hand holding—that fast, I had been a goner.

"Oh shit!" he gasped.

"What's wrong with you?"

He was staring at me with wide eyes. "I'm so stupid."

"No, you're really not."

He made a noise like the jury was still out. "Yeah, I am. I'm a huge dumbass because I just now figured out a way to get us out of here."

"Good," I grumbled. "Because I was stupidly thinking you were focused on me, you unromantic piece of crap."

He snorted out a laugh, kissed my forehead, and then got up and walked to the computer.

"What's your idea?"

"Have you ever had a subscription to an antivirus software site that runs on your computer and has live updates?"

"Sure."

He nodded. "Well, that's the same way Keystone works, with web support, so technically, if I put this interface offline, someone should check."

"But there's no Internet on the grounds. Clay explained that to us."

"No, he said there was none for guests to use. But think about it: he checks people in just like at a regular hotel, and he has to have Internet access to do that. More importantly, this system could be hacked just like any other program if he didn't have help."

"I hate to tell you this, but it's Saturday. Nobody gives a crap."

"Unless they're paid to care," he explained. "If you bought the special upgrade that included 24/7 support, like Clay Wells probably did to make sure the surveillance at this resort never goes down, then maybe someone is monitoring it as we speak."

"That's a big gamble."

"Yes, it is."

I got up and sat down beside him. "Okay, take it offline."

He turned to me. "If I take it off and no one's there, we're screwed. I won't be able to see anything at all while it's down. We'll be blind."

"It's okay," I comforted him. "Do it."

It took only minutes for him to pull the system down, and it was really strange to see the usual blue screen of death on every monitor on three walls at once.

We sat together in the darkened room with the cerulean glow, and after a minute, I felt his hand slide into mine. "I have a villa, remember? The one on the Amalfi Coast."

"Yeah."

"I really want us to go there after this. Can you do that?"

"Is it nice there now, in April?"

"It's nice all year round."

"I can ask," I promised, "though I did just get back from a different FBI task force. I bet my captain would like to actually get some use out of me."

"Sure," he agreed. "But you should see it. The ocean comes right up to the edge of the property, and then I have this infinity pool that is separated from the Jacuzzi by only a small rock wall you can just go right over. It's very decadent."

"Oh yeah? You get laid there a lot?"

"I have, yes. But I've never taken anyone I loved there, and if you let me, I'd love to give it to you so only you could say who's allowed in it from now on."

"You're just going to give me one of your homes?"

"Yes, if you'll allow it."

"How 'bout you just put my name on it, too, and I'll put your name on the greystone I own in Lincoln Park."

"You own a greystone?"

"Yeah. It's nice too. I mean, it's just a small row house, but it's really pretty."

"Why don't you live in it?"

"I need to get some more cash to finish the renovations on it."

He scowled. "How long have you been fixing it up?"

"Couple years. The thing is, the contractor keeps finding more and more things wrong with it, but I'm just not ready to give up on it yet. He even offered to take it off my hands."

"How nice of him." Aaron smiled, but it wasn't a nice one. "What's his name, baby?"

"Don't do that," I warned him. "He's Jimmy's cousin, so you know he's not screwing me. He's a really good guy. It's just trashed."

"I'm sure it is." His grin turned positively evil. "The contractor's name, please."

"Parrish Remodeling," I said, studying his face. "So you don't really want half of it, do you? Too small-time, right?"

"No," he insisted. "I would love if you'd put my name on it. Really. As I said before, your sense of quid pro quo makes me delirious. To you, it's not the amount of money, it's the thought. It's the doing things together. I've never had that before, with anyone, and to have someone finally get it, understand how I see the world… you have no idea what kind of gift that is."

"Yeah?"

"Oh yes," he said, leaning in.

I moved sideways so he missed me.

"Duncan!" He was incredulous.

"Look."

He spun around, and there, flashing in the bottom right corner of the screen, was a chat window. We couldn't get out, but they could get in. The flashing yellow box was a lifeline.

Aaron didn't take any chances and immediately asked for the supervisor. Once he had the right person, once Lisa Deems was on the line with us, he asked her to put us through to law enforcement and to ignore any other communication coming from the same server or from Buona Sera.

The typed-back "absolutely, sir" was very nice to see.

FIFTEEN

WE SAW the FBI, state police, and Sedona police come to the front gate of the resort. I had no idea before that point Clay Wells had a helicopter. But he did, and Aaron and I watched it fly away from inside the room. His men watched from the ground. They made the smart decision to open the gate, and once everyone was in, Aaron and I came out, squinting in the early morning light on a beautiful Sunday in Sedona.

Agent Summers arrived with the FBI contingent, and while Aaron went over what we had found on the tape, including Nick McCall, she explained it turned out the DEA also had Wells under surveillance, and between the two of them and what we'd found, he would certainly be going away once they caught him.

Aaron was thrilled, but getting me to the hospital and eating were on the top of his priority list. Agent Summers said she would get me there immediately and he thanked her graciously, but refused.

He got to his phone, and half an hour later Miguel was there, driving a Hummer, traveling with the same security team from Vegas. Two of the men were dispatched to our room to pack and gather bags, and two were sent to find Jaden while Aaron spoke to Miguel.

"What must that kind of money be like?" Agent Summers asked me, shaking her head.

"I think I'm gonna find out."

She chuckled. "I think you are, Detective. I will see you Tuesday morning in my office in Chicago."

"Yes, ma'am. I'll be there."

"Duncan!"

Aaron put me into the back seat of the Hummer, and said until I was checked out, I probably shouldn't eat. It was fine with me. I was freezing, light-headed, and nauseous, none of which were conducive to food.

"So is there a hospital in Sedona?" I asked as I reclined in the seat, looking over at him.

He was scowling as he brushed my hair back from my face. "Probably, but you're going to Banner Good Samaritan Medical Center in Phoenix."

"Why?"

"Because I don't have enough time to fly my own doctor out."

Which wasn't really an answer, but I took it and stopped talking. I was really sleepy, and when Aaron moved over next to me, I leaned my head on his shoulder and closed my eyes. "Thanks for worrying about me and taking care of me."

"It's my pleasure," he said, rubbing his cheek in my hair. "I can't wait to do it full-time."

I wasn't awake when Jaden Cobb was added to our party but woke up when we finally drove away. He sat quietly between the two men who had roused him from his room, looking uncomfortable as he clutched his backpack to his chest. I waited to see how Aaron was going to handle the situation.

"So let's recap. You got scared, talked to my father, decided to sell me out, let me bail you out of that mess, and finally decided cooking school was too much for you and sold your ass to Clay Wells."

"Aaron—"

"Did I miss anything?"

"Please," he snapped. "The Wells part was all for show. He didn't even fuck me; he just wanted to rattle your cage."

"And you let him?"

Jaden's eyes filled fast.

"Have you always hated me, or is it new?"

"I don't hate you," he rasped, his voice heavy with tears.

"Then I don't get it. What was your intent?"

His gaze flicked to me and then returned to Aaron. "I wanted you to see me again, but it doesn't look like that's going to happen."

"No," he agreed. "We're done, except...."

"Except what?"

"Do you want to be a sous chef at Cabo, like you professed you wanted to, or not?"

His eyes were riveted on Aaron. "You would still let me work at your restaurant in Vegas?"

"It's not mine, its Madeline's," he replied smoothly. "It's her restaurant."

"She's the head chef, Aaron, but it's yours."

He shrugged. "She liked you, saw potential. She said you were lazy, but she thought she could fix that, and being pretty, she says, never hurts a chef. It's how they get TV shows on Bravo."

He sat up and tipped his head as the tears rolled down his cheeks. "Jesus, Aaron, what's with all this white-hat bullshit? Since when are you the hero?"

"He's always been the hero," I chimed in. "You were just too busy being kept to notice."

The look he turned on me was murderous. "And you're not?"

"I'm a homicide detective," I explained. "I work for a living."

The way his mouth fell open was almost comical.

"So?" Aaron pressed until Jaden's focus shifted from me to him. "Do you want to work at Cabo or not?"

"I do."

"Good. I'll have Miguel take you to the airport."

"Aaron, I—"

"And get you a plane ticket."

"Thank you." He caught his breath. "Please come see me if you're ever in Vegas."

"If I am," Aaron said, slumping in his seat, resting his head on my shoulder, "I will."

But what were the chances when we had the whole world to see?

AS IT turned out, Aaron's insistence I go to the hospital was warranted. I was dehydrated and needed food because my body started to shut down. It was why I couldn't regulate my body temperature. What was nice was Aaron stayed with me the whole time, hovering, making the staff insane with his demands; he asked so many questions my doctor finally yelled and told Aaron yes, he could take me out for a steak when we were done.

We weren't allowed to leave until the evening. Between the endless bags of saline, and the other of glucose, it was hours before my body regulated itself. Aaron fell asleep in the recliner—what passed for one in a hospital—beside my bed. He didn't let go of my hand, though, even when he started to snore. When Miguel came in, he was stunned.

"What?"

He gestured at Aaron.

"He's tired."

He turned to me. "I know, but normally he would work through that. He tends to go until he's such a prick I want to put a bullet in his head."

"Yeah, don't do that," I said coolly. "I like him all living."

"No, of—don't you get it? That's you right there. He just wants to sit beside your bed and hold your hand. He's never done that before. He's never slowed down for anybody."

"Even for—" But I stopped myself before I got out the name. I was jealous of what he'd felt for Jory, and I needed to get over it because Sam Kage's partner was a memory, and I was Aaron's present and future.

"Yes," Miguel answered. "Even for Mr. Harcourt. There's a difference between wanting someone because you can't have them and wanting someone because you're in love. I've been with him longer than anyone; I can speak to the difference."

I squinted. "You love him."

"I do, but not how you think." He chuckled. "He's my boss. He takes care of more people than you can even imagine across entire continents. We're all very happy to work for the man. We would follow him anywhere."

I was surprised. "In the papers and stuff, all you ever read about is him being a playboy."

"Yeah, but that's the same stuff they say about Batman."

My smile was huge. "Oh yeah? Batman?"

He waggled his eyebrows at me. "He doesn't have a cool lair or gadgets, but when you see him wheel and deal and save schools and libraries and put up green factories in small towns to create jobs and not kill the environment in the process... you'll get it."

"So you're saying he's actually a good guy."

"He's the best guy, but he's also a selfish asshole."

"And possessive and smothering," Aaron added without opening his eyes. "If you guys are gonna talk about me, you should do it somewhere I can't hear."

I squeezed his hand, and he leaned forward, kissed my knuckles, and then returned to his reclining position.

"Now please shut the hell up so I can nap."

I noticed he had left his phone, turned off, beside my hip. "Don't you have people to call?"

"No. Not right now."

Miguel could not have looked any more surprised, even as he smiled and nodded. Apparently, he was enjoying seeing the billionaire at rest.

ON THE plane flying home, after wine and steaks and baked potatoes with all the fixings, Aaron passed out on the couch. I sat, leaning back, and he basically used me as a pillow, while I talked to Agent Summers.

"We picked up Mr. Wells trying to cross the border into Mexico. Mr. McCall had a one-way ticket booked for Paris, but he's in custody as well, thanks to your partner."

I had called Jimmy, and he had gotten right on top of finding McCall.

She coughed significantly. "Detective O'Meara does his police work somewhat outside the box."

"Which is a nice way of saying you liked his results," I interpreted with a laugh, "but his methods scared the crap out of you."

"Not scared," she hedged. "More, was appalled by."

"Yeah, well."

"He sort of kicks down doors and takes no prisoners," she offered.

"Yep," I agreed. "But no one will say a word about him. They wouldn't dare."

"And are you the same way, Detective?"

"Depends on the case, Agent," I answered honestly.

She didn't ask any more questions after that.

AARON wanted our cohabitation to begin immediately. When we landed in Chicago, I grumbled to him that I needed to sleep in my own bed. "But you're invited," I offered.

"That's very sweet." He smiled. "But may I simply ask you what good things have ever happened to you in that loft?"

"It's home."

He put his hand over his heart. "No, wherever I am is home."

And because that made sense, I said okay to moving in right that second.

The kiss I got sealed the deal.

SIXTEEN

ASTRID was so sorry. She kept looking at me, her eyes all soft and wounded. Max was upset, the clench of his jaw told me so even though he hadn't said a word.

"You guys shouldn't have been eavesdropping."

Astrid pursed her lips together tight.

"Yes," Max agreed tightly.

We all heard the front door open and Aaron called out to me. "I hope you're ready, because I'm just changing, and then we're picking up Max and—"

"We're here already." Max forced a smile for his brother as he charged into the room.

Aaron was always gorgeous in a suit—in anything, really—but in a three-piece, like he was wearing today, I would have bent over for him anywhere, any time. Something so hot about him all buttoned down when I knew what his body could really do.

"Hi, Aaron," Astrid Takahashi greeted him, blushing because she was still getting used to calling the real estate mogul by his first name. She and Max had been dating for six months, and in that time, she had gone from being a faceless ASA, Assistant State's Attorney, to the girlfriend of the gay billionaire's little brother. The one thing she said she missed was not being able to get Starbucks in her sweats anymore. She really hated putting on make-up to go to the gym.

"Hi," he answered, giving her a trace of a smile, not really focusing, distracted....

"Hey." I smiled, shoving one of our cook's potato pierogies into my mouth from the bowl I held in my hand. She made them for me by the ton now that she knew how much I loved them.

Aaron had instituted changes in my life, but I'd made adjustments to his as well. For one, he made me stop making my own breakfast in the morning because I didn't want to bother the cook. What I had failed to realize was I was hurting her feelings by doing it myself. Mrs. Kappel wanted to feed me; I needed to let her. So suddenly I had someone making my meals for me, and I, in turn, changed where Aaron ate.

No longer did we have breakfast on the patio or in the salon. We ate in the kitchen with Mrs. Kappel. She slid crepes off the pan right onto our plates and spooned on the butter and dusted them with powdered sugar. It was fun to watch her fuss over Aaron and tell me what a good eater I was. Sometimes Miguel would join us, and that was nice too.

"So what's your costume for the Halloween party?" Astrid queried Aaron.

"I'm a—sorry." He crossed quickly to me, peeling off his topcoat and dropping it on the back of the couch on his way. "What are you... what do you have on?"

I was wearing a ruffled shirt, a thick leather belt, and black breeches tucked into knee-length black leather boots. A real sword hung from a scabbard at my side. The answer to the question was obvious. "This is the pirate costume you got me."

His breath rushed out. "I-I don't remember it looking like that."

"I didn't put this on when it was delivered; you said it wasn't necessary because your tailor made everything with the measurements you sent him."

"I did?"

"Mmmm-hmmm," I murmured.

"I don't remember."

"Well, it was right after we went to court and testified against Mr. Wells and Nick McCall, so your mind was occupied with bigger issues."

"Uh-huh."

I grinned. "Max and Astrid are Romeo and Juliet."

"Before," Astrid added.

"That's funny."

"Thank you." She beamed at me.

"May I speak to you upstairs a second?" Aaron asked, and his voice was low and husky.

"No," I responded, licking the side of my mouth to catch a drop of filling. "We gotta hurry or we're gonna be late for the event. Alzheimer's is one of your pet projects, and since Sutter is hosting the benefit, you need to be there on time."

"There's a receiving line when you walk in," Max apprised his brother. "Mr. Levin thought since Sutter was sponsoring it, and since we just purchased Armada and some members of their senior staff would be there—"

"Sure," Aaron cut him off, his gaze sliding up and down my body.

"Aaron?"

"I," he rasped, "don't think that costume is supposed to look like that."

"Like what?" I took a step forward and bumped his nose with mine before kissing him lightly.

"Oh," Astrid whimpered and was suddenly bawling.

"For crissakes," I mumbled, shoving the bowl at Aaron before turning from him and grabbing Astrid, crushing her to me.

"What's going on?" Aaron demanded.

"Nothing," I said quickly. "Go upstairs and change."

"There's obviously something," he insisted, moving close to me, his hand on Astrid's shoulder. "Sweetheart, tell me what's wrong. Whatever it is, I can fix it."

"Duncan's father left a horrendous message on his voice mail," Max blurted shakily. "Astrid and I didn't mean to overhear it, but we came in unannounced and—"

"Wait," Aaron stopped him, his gaze moving from her to me. "She's upset for you?"

"Yes, because she has a really soft heart," I murmured, lifting her chin and cupping her cheek so her eyes met mine. "Which, as I've told her on a number of occasions, is not going to serve her well as an ASA in the great city of Chicago. You need to toughen up, girlie."

Instead of punching me or pinching me like she normally did, she threw her arms around my neck and squeezed tight. "I'm so sorry your father is a homophobic prick," she rushed out the words.

"Me too, doll." I laughed in her ear, which made her squeal and pull away from me. "Now enough, already. Just let it go."

"Okay."

"Go fix your makeup," I directed her before wheeling on Max. "And you, have a shot of something and perk up."

"Yes," he agreed.

My eyes were on Aaron next. "And you, go change. We gotta go."

Before he could respond, I grabbed the bowl out of his hand, turned, and walked into the kitchen. The pierogi stuck to the roof of my mouth; I needed something to wash it down with. Drinking orange juice from the carton was bad, but since we didn't have one—just a decanter, since Mrs. Kappel squeezed it fresh every day—I figured that was okay. When I closed the door of the Sub-Zero, Aaron was there.

"Yeah, I drank from it. So what?"

"What?"

"You know, the glass door on the thing is awesome," I said playfully.

"I don't give a fuck about the refrigerator!" he shouted. "I want to know what your fucking father had to say!"

I reached for him, but he walked backward beyond my reach.

"Now."

"It's no big deal; it's the same thing he's been saying for weeks. I just forgot to block him from my phone. I did it on my e-mail but—"

"For weeks? Why didn't you tell me?"

"Why would I?"

"Because we share things."

"Yeah." I was indignant. "Important things."

"No, all things, every little bit. I want to know it all."

We were silent, him waiting, me weighing my options.

I sighed deeply. "Okay."

"Okay, good. So can I hear the message?"

"You think I keep that shit?" I chuckled.

"Well then, what did he say?"

I made a show of closing one eye in concentration.

"Duncan!"

"It's just the same old bullshit." I shrugged. "I'm going to hell. I'm making him the laughingstock of his community, and he and my stepmother are ashamed they ever took me in."

"Oh, for—"

"He also said he wished Ian had lived instead of me, and that Ian is probably rolling over in his grave at this very moment."

Aaron lunged at me.

"This is why I didn't wanna tell ya." I grinned into his hair, hugging him back as tight and hard as he hugged me.

"I... Duncan...."

"Honey," I soothed him. "He's full of shit. I know that, and you know that. The shit with my brother is where he knows he can make me bleed. But Ian was my champion; he would've never let me down. Gay, straight, black, white, or blue, Ian would've said, 'Just be happy, Dunc'."

Aaron shivered in my embrace, his mouth opening against my throat.

"So again, it's on me for not blocking his number. I have no one to blame but myself."

"I'm so sorry."

"It's okay. I promise I'm all right. He's exactly how I knew he would be if he ever found out. I've been prepared for this since I moved out."

Aaron released a deep breath and then took a step back from me.

"Hey, come on, lighten up. I mean, imagine how weird it would have been if he was all 'live and let live' about it. I might've died of a fuckin' heart attack."

He was really attempting to look better for me, trying to perk up.

"You know," I purred, "if you play your cards right, I might let you play pirate with me later."

"I don't know if I'm in the mood to—"

"To what?" I taunted him, rubbing down over my groin, watching him follow my hand with his eyes, the progression slow until—

"Oh shit," he gasped painfully, his eyes huge. "Duncan, you're not wearing any underwear!"

I cackled. "Yeah, I didn't put the jock on yet. I wanted you to see the show."

"Are you kidding? Your dick is perfectly outlined, and you can see every… I… you can't go out like that! I forbid it!"

"I'm not going out like this; I'm putting on a jock, idiot."

"Yeah, I don't… think…."

"I'm fine about the shit with my father," I assured him. "I swear. Now come grab me like you mean it."

He was on me like prey, shoving me up against the counter, hands down on either side of me, his knee parting my legs.

"Oh man, I was kidding." I laughed into his ear. "Did you miss the part where I said we had to hurry?"

He leaned in to kiss me.

I lifted and turned my head at the same time. "Knock it off. A hard-on while I'm trying to put on that jock will not help me."

"You're the one killing me," he cried softly. "Jesus, Duncan, you might as well be naked!"

I squinted.

"The shirt is too tight, the breeches are insane, and the boots are just hot. Please take me upstairs and play marauding pirate with me."

I snickered. "So you're a captured banker, and I've taken you prisoner?"

"Yeah, okay, whatever," he moaned, hands on my hips. "Can we just go there, please?"

"No," I said, pushing him back gently but firmly. "People are counting on you showing up tonight."

"And you're gonna go out like that?" he half yelled. "Your picture will be everywhere tomorrow morning, and you'll—"

I took his face in my hands. "It'll be funny, and the guys'll give me crap... again... but I'm the same as anyone else dressed up in a costume. It's just this Halloween party is early, and instead of just friends taking pictures, everyone will be."

"Yes, but—"

"It won't turn into the white party your friend Ron had; it's a much more upscale event."

At a big blowout extravaganza Aaron had taken me to, a party he went to every year and had subsequently vowed never to go to again, some paparazzi had gotten past security and come after me. It was fine until the point one of them got too close and ended up ripping my shirt. We got tangled, I fell, and the guy crashed down on top of me. Blood was really noticeable on all white. Until the moment Aaron came around the corner, the press had no idea he could get quite that mad or move quite that fast. I did; I'd seen the man in action. I ended up having to hold him and tell the reporter to run. Now he only attended parties he himself threw or Miguel accompanied us to.

"I'll send a check with Max."

"No," I objected with a laugh. "I gotta go just to hear someone make the booty joke."

"What?"

And an hour later, when we were squinting because of the flashes, one of the reporters yelled, "Hey pirate, show us your booty!" I put out my hands like, of course.

Clapping, catcalls and whistles, and more flashing lights—enough to momentarily blind me—ensued before I turned and Max was there with one of those big foam-core-mounted checks so everyone could see the five million dollars Sutter was donating to Alzheimer's research. Unfortunately, even that did not take the interest away from my ass. It was funny, and the press was just having fun. My boyfriend, however, could not find the humor in the situation.

"That's it," Aaron said when we walked inside the gala. "We're going out the back."

I shook my head. "No. We gotta go take our place in line now, and besides, I wanna see Prentiss."

He rounded on me. "Why?"

"Because he's our step—" Max cricked his neck and made a face at Astrid like she would know what the hell he was asking. "—half brother?"

"Half, yes," she confirmed.

"I get confused with all that."

"I know, sweetie." She sounded playfully patronizing.

"Yeah. I wanna meet him," I said, taking hold of Aaron's hand and tugging him after me. "And you know you're the big draw here, Sutter. There's no way you're leaving."

We made it to the line as the first people were coming through, stopping on our way to the end to say hello to Mr. Levin and his wife. Aaron shook his hand, and then it was my turn.

"Always a pleasure, Detective," he said warmly, holding my hand in his grip longer than he had Aaron's. "You remember my wife, Sarah."

"I do." I tilted my head as I regarded her, and both Aaron and the chairman of his board were charmed when she rolled her eyes at me. "You owe me money."

She grunted. "It's only a dollar."

"It's the principle."

"Betting on college basketball is against the law, Detective," she informed me haughtily.

"Is it?" I taunted.

"Fine." She clipped the word. "When we dance later, I'll give you your money."

"I don't take quarters."

She growled under her breath, which made Mr. Levin break out in a huge grin, as Aaron and I walked around Max and Astrid to take our places.

"You look nice in that," I complimented Aaron. "What are you supposed to be?"

He was nonplussed. "I'm so obviously Phileas Fogg from *Around the World in Eighty Days*."

I coughed. "Oh, of course."

"Are you kidding? This is ninth grade reading here."

"You know what they say," Max chimed in from beside me.

"No, what do they say?"

"If you have to explain it"—he winced at his brother—"it's not good."

I coughed again.

Aaron's distaste for both of us was evident.

Most attendees who moved through the line were pleased to meet me and really could have cared less that I was a man. A couple of people were uncomfortable, and a few more were abrupt, but no one was out and out rude to me. It wasn't smart. Aaron did not take kindly to me being rebuffed. When Max jabbed me in the side with his elbow, I glanced up to see a blond man shaking Astrid's hand.

Prentiss Sutter was handsome—all the sons of Gordon were—but he had neither Aaron's charisma nor Max's style. I was a little disappointed.

"So good to finally meet you," Max lied through his teeth. "Really looking forward to working with you and Father on bringing Armada on board."

Prentiss jolted, and Max let his hand go, as the youngest son took two steps and was in front of me, white as a sheet.

I offered him my hand, and he took it, his head snapped up so our eyes met. "It's nice to finally put a face to the name. I'm Duncan Stiel, your brother's boyfriend."

He was mute as he let go of my hand, and then he was in front of Aaron.

The man I loved took his brother's hand in his and then covered it with his other. "You and my father began Armada Brokerage three months ago."

"What?" He was flustered.

"Yeah, you don't have to keep it a secret, as if I didn't know you were planning to come after Sutter and our clients and whatever else," Aaron said gently. "I know. My father—your father—what he doesn't get is that I always know."

I put a hand on both men's backs and moved them just enough out of the way so other people in line would know they were speaking privately. I motioned to Max to take over at the end of the receiving line for the next few minutes.

"Okay," Aaron continued. "So a week ago, you merged with Drazan Hess out of Hong Kong."

"Yes, we... how—"

"Drazan Hess is a subsidiary of Sutter."

It took him a second to process that.

"No."

"Yes," Aaron confirmed. "It's actually Max's holding company, so he oversees it, but it does still belong to Sutter, and therefore, to me."

"I... he doesn't know."

"No, I know," he comforted the younger man. "But we invited a lot of your board members and senior staff from Armada to this party tonight so they could meet Max and Max's team because, as of next week, you, my father, and your board will all be working with him."

Prentiss did a slow pan so he could see Max.

"So as soon as we're done with the meet and greet here, you two can talk."

His head swiveled back to Aaron.

"We changed the seating chart so you would be at our table."

Poor kid. He was just absolutely gobsmacked.

"Or, if you're uncomfortable staying, you can pull Max aside and make an appointment for you guys to meet privately."

"But the board is here, you said, and... people I know."

"Yes."

He looked like he was about to barf. "You're being really nice."

Aaron put a hand on his shoulder. "I'm not nice, but this thing our father has dragged you into, this war with me, is not fair to you."

Prentiss listened and that was good.

"What you should do and what you will do are maybe two different things."

"Such as?"

"Like, you should work with Max and figure out a way to buy the old man out. That would be the best thing for you because eventually Max wants you to run Armada on your own. He likes to invest in start-up companies but he doesn't want to be there long-term."

"Okay."

"Now, if you decide you would rather keep faith with the old man, that's okay too. But in that case, Max will never give you enough shares to threaten his controlling interest. So like I said, it's really up to you."

Prentiss's eyes, which were darker blue than either Aaron's turquoise or Max's violet, were locked on his older brother. "I really do appreciate you having this conversation with me. I was told not to expect it."

"Because he told you I was the Antichrist. I know."

"Have you changed since you—" His gaze flicked to me, sized me up, and then returned to Aaron. "—are in a relationship?"

"Yes."

"I'm glad."

"Oh, you should be," Aaron said with a thread of warning in his voice.

He took hold of Prentiss's shoulder and guided him over to Max. We retook our places in line, but Aaron put Prentiss between him and Max, with me on the very end.

I put my hand on the small of Aaron's back and leaned close to his ear. "You're a very good man."

"As long as you think so, that's all that matters."

The moment the receiving line emptied, Aaron grabbed my hand and yanked me after him, around tables, past the dance floor, and into a darkened alcove at the back, further hidden by bunched curtains hanging from the ceiling of the ballroom. It was quiet there, unused, and filled with stacked chairs and extra tables.

"What are we doing?" I questioned, rounding on him now that he wasn't dragging me around anymore.

"I know you read the article in that magazine about the heir apparent?"

"It's not funny." I had been so hurt for Aaron, about the things his father had said about his lifestyle choices, about me, and about where he was leading the company.

"You realize he can't do anything at all to me, right?"

"No, I know."

"And every antigay word he utters diminishes him in the eyes of the business community, here and everywhere."

"Sure."

"But you're still worried."

"Not after what you said to Prentiss."

"But you knew all that. I told you when Max did it."

"With your blessing," I reminded him.

"And my money." He grinned wickedly, taking a step toward me. "But tell me, can you remember the name?"

"The name of what?"

"The name of the magazine," he began, closing the distance further, "the article about my dad and his new protégé was in?"

I had to think. "I don't think so."

"Exactly, because when I'm in print, I'm in *Forbes*, *The Economist*, *Fortune*, but my father and his heir, are not."

"Sure."

He tilted his head and kissed my ear, which sent a shiver down my side. "But don't worry; I will never let my guard down where Prentiss is concerned."

"And I'm here."

"I know," he said hoarsely. "Hey, take a look out there and make sure cocktail hour is going well."

I did as I was directed, moving a few feet away from him to peer out at the room from the safety of the heavy drapes. Everyone was standing or sitting, milling around, talking, laughing, and drinking.

"Well?" he inquired, his hands on my hips undoing the belt that held the scabbard on.

"What are you doing?" I spoke to him over my shoulder.

"I just want this off for a second."

"Why?"

He didn't answer, dropping the sword on the ground before going to work on the second belt I was wearing, the one not holding an antique weapon on my hip. His nimble fingers had it unbuckled in seconds.

"Aaron?"

"You're not checking on the guests."

I went back to survey the crowd. "I think it's going okay."

"Good," he said, kissing the back of my neck quickly before he was suddenly on his knees behind me, biting my ass through the thin fabric of the breeches.

"Aaron." I bucked hard.

"So guess what got finished today?" he asked as his hands released the toggle clasp on the front of the breeches and made quick work of the trouser stays.

"I...." He wanted me to carry on a conversation? "What?"

"Your greystone," he answered, sliding the pants and the jock down together until both hit the top of the boots.

"Oh," I moaned, opening my legs as far as they would go, bending forward, hands fisted in the drapes, holding tight as I arched my back.

"So now," he said, parting my cheeks, "we can start buying things for it."

"Yeah, we—oh," I groaned softly as he slid his tongue inside me.

"That was a good, sound investment on your part," he praised, then speared his tongue in deeper and deeper before pulling out and swirling it around my hole.

"Aaron." I jerked back against him.

He pushed back in, licking and laving, stretching me slowly, relaxing the muscles, his face pushed between my cheeks, massaging as he feasted on me until I was coated with his saliva.

When he added a finger, sliding back and forth over my prostate, I started fucking myself on it, harder and harder.

"Here," he purred, and I felt the stretch in my ass as he added another finger, still moving gradually, in and out, back and forth, the rhythm slow but steady, relentless.

When he reached around and took my cock in his hand, I begged.

"Can you take me without lube?" he asked, rising behind me, stroking me from balls to head, repeatedly. "Can you?"

In answer I thrust out my ass for him.

"God, I love that you would," he purred, kissing my back as I heard the tear of foil. "But that's what lube packets are for."

"Are you kidding?" The planning was impressive. "You had the presence of mind to grab lube on the way out of the house?"

"The way you're dressed," he said, his voice dark and low, "there was no way you were making it home without getting fucked."

"That's kind of romantic."

"Only to you," he husked, hands on my hips, positioning himself behind me before sliding easily between my cheeks, the press of him at my entrance making me gasp. "Ever since I got home and saw you…. Jesus, Duncan, do you have any idea how gorgeous you are?"

His entry burned, even with the lube, and instead of the usual slide, he had to wedge himself in, grind and shove, inch by inch.

"Jerk yourself off. You're so tight and hot there's no way I can do anything but fuck you."

His words, my hand on my shaft, tugging and pulling, and his thick cock moving inside me made me jolt backward and impale myself on his length.

"Oh fuck," Aaron rasped, hands like claws on my shoulders, holding tight as he eased back. "Baby, can you feel me?"

My muscles twitched and rippled around him, clenching, wanting to keep him steady and still even as the throb that resonated through me encouraged him to move. "Aaron, please."

He pushed in deep and a shiver that was half-pain, half-pleasure rolled through me.

"I don't want—to hurt—"

"No," I said, feeling dazed and heavy with need.

"I just want to bury myself in you."

"Yes," I pleaded. "Hurry."

"You have no idea how badly I want those boots over my shoulders and you under me."

"I'll keep them on all night," I promised, my breath catching, "if you fuck me now."

"I'm taking you right here," he swore and rammed himself all the way inside me.

That fast it went from sharp and stinging to a dull, blooming ache I wanted to rub, over and over, on the end of his dick.

He stroked in and I bent forward, taking him deeper, the languid pace opening me until my body stopped fighting, stopped trying to push out and sucked in.

"Holy fuck, baby, your ass."

I needed to be on the ground and so sank to my knees. Aaron followed, connected, his thighs plastered against mine before he pistoned inside me.

Fists clenched on the carpet, I took the pounding because I wanted it, too good to stop. When I felt the sizzling heat tighten my balls, rise from the base of my spine to my stomach, I whispered I was close.

"You're not touching your cock."

"Don't—" I gasped. "—have to."

He bent over me, his fingers lacing with mine as he sucked between my shoulder blades, biting down as his driving rhythm, the forward and back, became only about being buried inside of me. He wanted to be *in*, and that was all.

I bit my lip hard so I wouldn't scream and came on the ground under me, spurting thick and messy.

Aaron hammered me through my drowning orgasm and his own release seconds later. He spilled, hot and thick, and then collapsed across my back, replete and panting. "Ohmygod, I love you," he groaned.

"That is sex talking," I said as I tried to calm my racing heart.

"No," he countered, lifting up and easing gently from my still spasming channel.

Luckily, his Phileas Fogg costume had lots of layers, so he took off his jacket, then the waist coat, followed by the fancy shirt under that, and finally the sweaty T-shirt sticking to his torso, leaving on only an off-kilter silk scarf.

"You look completely debauched," I teased.

"Oh, Mr. Pirate," he said, leaning over to kiss me, "it's all you. You, sir, look utterly ravished."

"Is that hot?"

"Oh fuck yeah," he answered as he used the T-shirt to wipe my ass, the insides of my thighs, and finally mop up, and then rub in, the come splatter on the floor.

"You ground it in," I scolded him.

"Baby, they have to clean all the carpets in here after this event—the whole place, all right? Let's not worry about some spooge on this one little area."

I laughed.

"Hey."

"What?" I couldn't stop smiling.

He cleared his throat. "Marry me, all right?"

That fast we were all serious. "You're sure?"

"I am."

"Can't get married in Chicago," I said, running my fingers over the chain at his throat.

It turned out Aaron was the one who needed grounding, especially when he had to fly away from me for business. The collar he had removed from me that night in Sedona had never come off of him and was always flipped to the *D* for Duncan. I would have been the only person who saw it, but the chain had been visible in pictures snapped at a hot springs in Landmannalaugar, Iceland.

"We'll have a civil union here and go get married in New York."

"I'm sorry, what?"

"Are you listening to me?"

"Yeah, sorry. I was admiring your collar, Mr. Sutter."

Instantly, his smile returned.

"So where are we getting married?"

"In New York."

"Well, that's kind of fitting, isn't it?"

"Yes."

I stared into his eyes and he held my gaze. "Okay, then."

His face lit up. "That's a yes?"

"It is."

He reached for me, and I met him halfway, kissing and hugging and trying to press together tighter.

Once we could both stand and get dressed, we rejoined the crowd, grabbed drinks, and found our seats at the table with Max and Astrid and Prentiss. Aaron lost no time telling them and asking Max to be his best man.

Max nodded quickly and lunged at Aaron; Astrid, seeing him, covered her mouth with her hand. I could tell she was trying really hard not to cry. It was nice to see the brothers Sutter having such an unguarded moment. I put my arm around her and tucked her against me. The way she snuggled in was nice. I had a family again, and I was so very thankful.

After dinner, while people were dancing, Aaron sat with his long muscular legs in my lap as we talked. His face was flushed, and the white cravat at his throat contrasted beautifully with his bronze skin and gold hair. His eyes were soft as he stared at me like he was drunk.

"You look wasted."

"No, just looking at you." He sighed. "I like looking at you."

"You know all this lovey-dovey crap will fade, right?"

"No, I don't think so," he said thoughtfully. "It's permanent. I'm in love."

"Me too," I said, massaging his calves, using the strength in my hands to push into the muscles and knead them.

He whimpered in the back of his throat.

"Feel good?"

"God, yes."

"Maybe I should take you home and give you a full body massage."

"Will you wear the boots?"

I couldn't stop smiling. "Sure."

"Okay, you're on."

And as usual, when we left, after saying goodnight to Max and Astrid and even Prentiss, he was holding my hand.

MARY CALMES lives in Lexington, Kentucky, with her husband and two children and loves all the seasons except summer. She graduated from the University of the Pacific in Stockton, California, with a bachelor's degree in English literature. Due to the fact that it is English lit and not English grammar, do not ask her to point out a clause for you, as it will *so* not happen. She loves writing, becoming immersed in the process, and falling into the work. She can even tell you what her characters smell like. She loves buying books and going to conventions to meet her fans.

Read more

Also from MARY CALMES

BUT FOR You

MARY CALMES

Foreign Language Romance from MARY CALMES

http://www.dreamspinnerpress.com

Romance from MARY CALMES

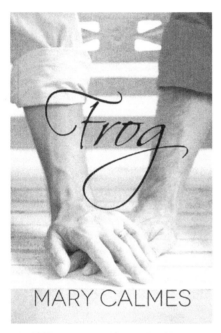

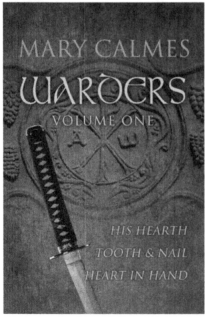

Audiobook Romance from MARY CALMES

http://www.dreamspinnerpress.com

Romance from MARY CALMES

Change of Heart from MARY CALMES

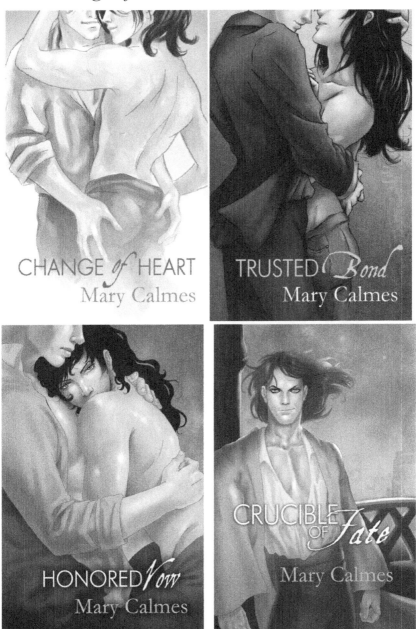

CPSIA information can be obtained at www.ICGtesting.com
Printed in the USA
BVOW11s1351221213

339795BV00007B/233/P

9 781623 808747